Naked Believer

—— *Naked Believer* ——

Douglas Alan Walrath

RESOURCE *Publications* · Eugene, Oregon

NAKED BELIEVER

Resource Publications
An Imprint of Wipf and Stock Publishers
199 W. 8th Ave., Suite 3
Eugene, OR 97401

www.wipfandstock.com

PAPERBACK ISBN: 978-1-4982-8633-6
HARDCOVER ISBN: 978-1-4982-8635-0

Manufactured in the U.S.A.

Once again
to
Sherry

A vocation is an act of love: it is not a professional career.

—GRAHAM GREENE

Schuylerkill Falls, New York

October, 1960

$$1$$

He heard her before he saw her standing on the other side of the yard at the Petersons' "Annual End-of-Summer Cookout" arguing vehemently with Jerry Ward, the high school principal. The overly tall man was barely holding his own against her.

Walter stood still and watched her. Strands of her long black hair had broken free of their clips and were blowing in the wind. She wore a varsity crew sweater over a white oxford-cloth shirt, and jeans that fit tightly to her legs and ankles. She was obviously fifteen years younger than any of the women gathered in lawn chairs on the patio between the house and the pool. About his age.

Though he couldn't understand most of the words she and Jerry exchanged, he could hear the intensity in their voices. He guessed that she was one of the teachers at the high school; though he was surprised that anyone would argue with her principal in public the way she was sparring with Jerry. When Becky Peterson brought him a glass of iced tea fixed just the way he liked it—lemon, no sugar—he asked, "Who's the young woman with black hair talking with Jerry Ward?"

"That's Mary Kerrigan, the high school English teacher."

"Looks like a pretty heated exchange. What are they arguing about?"

"Apparently a member of the school board objected to one of the poems Mary included in her poetry elective. He's concerned that the poem will cause students to question religion, and he thinks that kind of questioning is inappropriate in a high school class room. When I walked by Jerry was suggesting that Mary might want to consider substituting a different poem the next time she teaches the course. That suggestion triggered Mary's Irish temper. She objects to the idea that a school board member could dictate what she will include in her courses."

Becky noticed a concerned look on Walter's face. "Don't be worried, Walter. Jerry's known Mary since she was a little girl. He grew up and went to school with her dad. He knew she'd be a feisty addition to the faculty when he hired her. It's a familiar dance they do every so often. Now you'll have to excuse me. Erik is taking the meat off the grill and I need to get out the rest of the food. He's the doctor and I'm the nurse, so we follow his schedule." She smiled.

A sumptuous offering of food was soon laid out on the long table on the patio. As he moved through the buffet line Walter kept glancing back at Mary and Jerry. Their argument seemed to be over; they were laughing and talking now like old friends.

After Walter filled his plate he stood for a few moments and watched the guests gathering with old friends in clusters of chairs around the yard. He saw that no one was sitting at the nicely-shaded picnic table under an apple tree next to a large garden by the pasture fence. He walked over to the table and sat down.

He had just begun to eat when he raised his head and saw her walking across the yard toward him. She smiled when she saw him looking at her. His usually well-controlled heart beat quickly as he stood up and she stood across from him. "I'm Mary Kerrigan and you must be Reverend Macdonald. Looking over the clusters of happily married, middle-aged couples, I've concluded that I must be your date." As she spoke she saw the surprised and then pleased look on his face. Her smile broadened. "May I sit down?"

"I would be delighted to have you join me, Mary. Please call me 'Walter.'"

She sat down opposite him. "Please be assured, Walter, that I didn't know ahead of time that you and I would be the only under-aged and unattached people at this party."

Her easy manner relaxed him. "Probably if you had known ahead of time, you wouldn't have been excited at the prospect of eating dinner with a Presbyterian minister."

"To be perfectly honest, when I look over all of the men at this gathering you are the last one I would pick out as the minister. You don't look the part; you are too tall and—I hope I won't embarrass you if I say—too good-looking." Her eyes sparkled.

He blushed; he felt exposed, but not uncomfortable that she had looked him over. "I could say the same about you," he responded. "If someone hadn't identified you, I would never have picked you out as the schoolteacher." Her face colored.

He looked closely at her. She was definitely a colleen. Her eyes were an unusual shade of green and quite small. Her high cheekbones framed them and enhanced their appeal. Her fair skin made her black hair seem even blacker.

"I don't know very much about Presbyterians," she said as she began to eat. "Except for a brief stint in a Presbyterian Sunday school when I was in seventh grade, my exposure to clergy has been limited to Catholic priests. I've found very few of them are as interesting as the priests in Graham Greene's novels. But you may be disappointed to know that your reputation at the high school has little to do with your ministerial skills. You are better known for your ability with a baseball bat than for your eloquence in the pulpit. But that's understandable; church-going is not a popular contact sport among teen-aged boys."

He laughed. "I know it isn't; I remember what it was like to be a teenage boy. But it also sounds like you have never hit it off with clergy."

"I haven't! When I graduated from Barnard, I discovered that my favorite boyfriend at Columbia had decided to become a priest. That made him off-limits, and I had no back-up. All he left me was this too-big crew sweater. My friends all went off to get married, so I either had to go to school or to work. A degree in English literature doesn't prepare you to *do* much of anything, so I decided to pursue a master's degree in education. To be honest, I prefer books to babies anyway. And, in case you haven't already noticed, my mouth and my brains scare men off. Do I put you off?"

"Actually, you don't," he said. And it was the truth; she intrigued him.

"Well, then we're off to a good start. What do you think about besides God and baseball? Read any interesting novels with ministers in them?"

Her blunt questions caught him off guard. He *didn't* think about much besides God and baseball. He read a lot of books, but it had been years since he had read a novel. "I don't read much fiction," he admitted. Then he thought of a novel that had impressed him. "One novel that did impress me is *Light in August*."

"That's fitting. The minister at the center of the novel, the Reverend Gail Hightower, is a Presbyterian. A man with a woman's name: there's an identity crisis for you. He sits in his high tower watching life go by. He can't sort out the difference between Jesus and his Civil-War hero grandfather. His wife leaves him and he gets booted out of his church. He has more problems than your predecessor, Reverend Cook, did. I'd use the novel in my senior honors course in American literature, but I've already got a school board member upset because of one of the poems I include in my poetry course."

Walter was tempted to ask her what had happened to Nate Cook, but he thought better of pursuing that subject where someone might overhear. "Becky Peterson said that's what you and Jerry Ward were talking about earlier."

"I included an Emily Dickinson poem in my poetry unit. The first stanza ends with the phrase 'God cannot be found.' I realize that much of Dickinson is too advanced for most high school students, but with help they can access this poem. If they get a taste of her, some of them will remember and come back to her when they're older and more able to appreciate her. Anyway, a school board member whose kid was in the class objected to the poem. As you might expect he belongs to that Bible Church in Millerton Center."

"That's not surprising; they're very conservative—much more than I am."

"I'm glad to hear that. I doubt the board member has ever read the poem, but he objects to the idea that a high school teacher would let her students read a poem that implies that someone would search for God only to discover that God cannot be found.

"I tried to explain to Jerry that I think this was in fact Dickinson's experience, and that it is important for students to understand the sense of loss people like her felt in the nineteenth century when science began to undermine believing. But Jerry is more concerned about the flap I am causing than any educational rationale that explains why it might be worth causing it. I think students need to learn how to think for themselves and learning how to doubt is part of that process. What do you think, Walter?"

"The poem might be an accurate reflection of Dickinson's experience, and helping students learn to question seems important to me, but doubt is more than questioning. I'm not sure it's a good idea to push sixteen- and seventeen-year-olds to doubt."

"But Walter, don't you . . .?"

Erik Peterson cut her off. "You're missing the last volleyball game of the season."

"To be continued?" Walter asked as he stood up.

5

She looked up at him, nodded her head and said, "Yes, I want to know what you think."

He smiled. "So do I."

An apple fell on the table between them. She picked it up and looked it over; it was unblemished. She took a bite and made a face. "Sour! But still quite good." She held it out to him, "Want to try it?"

He looked carefully at her. "This reminds me of another garden from long ago."

She laughed as he took a bite of the apple.

2

It had just begun to sprinkle as Mary left the high school to walk home. When she passed the entrance to the athletic field Melanie Chase was jogging down the driveway. "Melanie!" she called out, "Looks like the rain put a stop to field hockey practice. Want to walk with me and share my umbrella?"

It immediately began to pour and Melanie stepped quickly under the umbrella. "Thanks, Miss Kerrigan. I didn't bring my slicker; I thought I'd get home before the rain came."

Mary laughed. "Well, you didn't Melanie. But that's all right; when we get to my house, I'll duck inside and you can take my umbrella home with you. You can bring it back tomorrow. I'm not going anywhere tonight and I doubt that it will be raining in the morning."

"Thanks, Miss Kerrigan. I'll put it by the side door at home so I remember to bring it back tomorrow."

The rain continued to pour down on them; they walked along rapidly struggling to stay under the umbrella while they dodged puddles. When they neared the walkway that led up to Mary's front door the rain let up and they could finally talk without shouting to be heard.

"I've been hoping to find a time to talk with you, Melanie. I noticed a look on your face when we discussed Emily Dickinson's poems last week that suggested one of them really spoke to you. Am I right?"

Melanie stopped walking and turned toward Mary; she looked uneasy. "You mean the one that says 'God cannot be found?' "

Mary saw the concern in her eyes and nodded. "Yes, that one."

"It did."

"Is what you felt sharable?"

"Miss Kerrigan, do you think Emily Dickinson believed in God?"

"Probably not—at least not in the way most people seem to. Why do you ask?"

"Wasn't that a problem? I mean, what did her husband think about that?"

"She didn't have a husband."

"Did she live alone?"

"No, she had a sister and a brother and her father at home."

"What about them? Did her father and brother believe in God? And if they did, and she didn't, didn't they give her a hard time?"

"Sometimes, but mostly she kept what she believed to herself. That's what women had to do then. In that time, if a woman thought differently from the men around her, the only way she could be her own person was to keep her thoughts to herself."

"I have to do that. I could never talk with my parents the way I'm talking with you. If I told them I wasn't sure I believe in God, they would be angry."

"You may be right. If what you believe is different from what most people believe, even if you talk about it carefully, sometimes it frightens them." They had reached the walkway that led up to the house where Mary had a second-floor apartment.

"Does what Emily Dickinson says in that poem frighten you, Miss Kerrigan?"

Mary smiled gently. "No, Melanie, it doesn't frighten me."

"I can't find God, Miss Kerrigan. Everybody around me acts like they have. I know I'm supposed to, but I can't. I'm nearly eighteen now and I don't want to pretend anymore."

Mary measured her words carefully. "I can understand why you don't want to pretend, Melanie, but sometimes you have to wait for the right time to say things that are hard for people to hear."

Melanie smiled and nodded. "Okay, I get it. I have to wait for the right time to tell them." She looked puzzled. "But how will I know when it's the right time?"

"Probably when it feels like they might get it."

She laughed. "I guess I'll just have to trust my instincts—and hope I don't get in trouble!" She hesitated. "There's something else I wanted to ask you about that has nothing to do with literature. It has to do with what I'm going to do next year after high school. But maybe there's not enough time today to talk about it."

"Are you expected home soon?"

"Not really. My father is out of town somewhere at a sales meeting and my mother is working three to eleven at the hospital. My sister said she would probably go to a movie with friends when she got out of work. So, there's nobody waiting there for me to come home."

"Well then, I suggest we stop standing here in the rain and go inside! If you don't mind leftover stew, you're welcome to come in and have some with me. We could eat and talk for a while—but not for too long; I have papers to grade and I suspect (she grinned) you have homework."

"If you're sure it's not a bother, I would like that. I can call home and leave a message on the answering machine, in case someone comes home and wonders where I am. I won't stay too long."

"Well, then let's go in out of the rain."

In less than half an hour they were sitting at the dining room table in Mary's apartment finishing warmed-up stew. As Melanie ate her last spoonful she looked through the archway into the large front living room. She saw Mary watching her. "I like your apartment, Miss Kerrigan. It looks like you—lots of books, a beautiful desk, comfortable chairs, lots of color on the walls, the drapes, the pillows—even a chess game set up on that small table by the window."

"Thank you for noticing." She picked up the empty plates. "I have some cheesecake. Would you like a piece?"

"Oh, yes. I would. I love cheesecake."

Mary returned with two pieces of cheesecake. "Now, before we run out of time and you have to go, what is the something else you want to talk about?"

Melanie sat back in her chair. "You probably know that Eri Peterson, Dr. Peterson's son, is my boyfriend. (Mary smiled and nodded.) He wants to be a doctor like his father is. He'll make a great doctor. He's kind and very smart. Since I've hung around their house and gotten to know Eri's dad and listened to him talk about what he does, I've started thinking about being a doctor, too."

"That's wonderful, Melanie; you are kind and smart like Eri. I think you would make an excellent doctor."

"Thank you, the problem is that's not what my parents want me to do. Last month I told my mother and father what I've been thinking about doing after I graduate from high school. They were kind; they listened to me, but when I finished my father said I'm setting my sights too high. He thinks I would do better to become a nurse like my mother is." She sighed. "So, I've been looking at nursing schools. I know nurses do important work, that they really help people. But being a nurse is not enough for me; I want to be a doctor. I want to go to Cornell for pre-med, like Eri is. But I'm not sure I can do it, especially if my father doesn't want me to. What do you think, Miss Kerrigan?"

For a while Mary didn't say anything; then she spoke carefully. "Well, he is your father—and you do need to respect him. But you are also almost eighteen and a woman. In the end, you have the right to decide about your life. I can tell you what I think, but then you will still have to decide what to do."

Melanie watched closely as Mary sat back in her chair. "When I was in eleventh grade, during the Christmas vacation, my college professor father suggested one day that I consider taking shop in the spring term. I was startled. 'Why?' I asked him. 'Because it would be good for you to learn how to work with your hands. Your head will work better if you know how to work with your hands—besides it's a man's world and you're a woman; you won't get anywhere unless you know how to do everything that matters better than the men.' So I took wood-working shop in the spring term."

Melanie laughed. "With all the boys?"

"Yes, with all the boys; I was the only girl in the class." She smiled. "But the boys didn't complain; they were happy to spend time with me."

Melanie nodded. "I bet they were, Miss Kerrigan."

"About the middle of the term the teacher said we all needed to choose a project—something special to make. The boys all decided to make something practical: chairs, tables, stools, cutting boards—things like that. I wasn't sure what I wanted to make. So, that night I asked my dad at supper if he had any suggestions. 'Why don't you make a chessboard?' he said. I was surprised, 'But I don't know how to play chess.' He looked straight at me—like he always did when he had something important to say, 'You make a chess board and I will show you how to play the game.' And so I did."

"Is that it on the table over there in the corner by the window?"

Mary nodded. "That's it. Why don't you come over there and look at it with me." She stood up and walked over to the small table. Melanie followed her. "The summer between my junior and senior years he taught me how to play chess. I took to the game; actually I play quite well.

"One hot evening we sat late at the chessboard and finally I beat him. I hardly ever did; but I did that night. He sat back in his chair and said, 'Mary, you're good. You outplayed me.' I was startled. My dad is brilliant and very proud. All I could say was, 'Thanks.' Then he went on, 'Life is like a chessboard, Mary. It's full of knights and bishops and castles and kings and lots of pawns. There's only one woman on the board: the queen. But she is more flexible and can move with more agility than any of the men. She's smarter and cleverer than any of them. You need to be that queen, Mary, or you won't beat me—or any of the other smart guys who come into your life."

She looked down at the chessboard set with a game in progress. "Do you know how to play chess, Melanie?"

"Eri plays against his dad. I watch them sometimes. I know enough about the game to follow when someone else plays."

"What do you see?"

She studied the board for a while. Finally she said, "This queen has the opposite king checked; she controls the game."

Mary nodded and said in a steady voice, "You're right, Melanie. When I was your age I decided to be that queen. I hope you decide to be that queen. Go to Cornell. Become a doctor."

She stood at the front window and in the light of the streetlight watched Melanie walk across the street holding her umbrella. Maybe she had overstepped with her? If she had, it would make today a day like every other day. She rarely contained herself when it mattered.

—————————— 3 ——————————

SUNDAY EVENING IT WAS nearly nine when Walter reheated three pieces of leftover pizza and settled into the comfortable chair across from his television set to watch the weekly episode of "Bonanza." The program's new Sunday night time slot was just right for him; at the end of the longest day of his work week he needed an hourlong escape into the world of the Ponderosa ranch. Just after the second commercial break, the telephone rang. He walked out across the hall through the door into his study and answered it.

"Reverend Macdonald?" a man's voice asked.

"Yes, this is Reverend Macdonald."

"This is Burton Brundidge, the funeral director. I have one of yours here."

The statement puzzled him. "One of mine?"

"Yes, one of yours: Melchior Rivenburg. Locals know him as 'Mac.' Lived in Schuylerkill Falls his entire life, except when he went to Europe during the War. When he worked, he worked on the town crew. He died at the VA hospital in Albany last night."

While Mr. Brundidge talked Walter paged through the "R's" in the stack of 3 x 5 cards on which he had listed the church membership by households. He had just finished counting them the previous week; there were 134. He said, "I don't see any Rivenburgs listed as church members."

"That may be so," Mr. Brundidge said. "But if the family says he's one of yours, then so far as I'm concerned he's one of yours—no matter what the official membership list says. They want the service Thursday afternoon at two o'clock. Can you do it then?"

Walter looked at his calendar. "I can do a service at two on Thursday."

"This one'll be a military service with all the fixin's," Mr. Brundidge went on, "guns and taps at the cemetery. Bring earplugs. Why don't you try to arrive at the funeral home by one-thirty? I get nervous when I think I might have to do a service at the last minute because some preacher didn't write the right date and time in his calendar. Just to be sure, it's this Thursday at two o'clock."

"I'll be there Thursday at one-thirty. Do you have a telephone number where I could reach someone from the family—like a wife or, perhaps, a son or daughter?"

"He had a wife years ago, but she's long gone. His son, Jack, is the one that's making the arrangements. He married Linda Stevens a couple of months ago. Her husband up and left her last fall with a couple of kids. She cooks in the cafeteria at Schuylerkill Falls Central School. They live in a mobile home just beyond Millerton Center. You been down to Millerton Center yet?"

"No, I haven't. I've seen the sign for it at the end of River Street just before the railroad tracks, but I haven't been there yet."

"That's where River Street becomes Millerton Road, just follow the road and you'll come to Millerton Center. But stay alert or you'll whiz right through and miss it. There's less to Millerton Center than meets the eye. Jack Rivenburg drives a semi for Price Cutter Supermarkets. He's gone home to catch a couple of hours of sleep. He said he has to leave at three in the morning to pick up a load of produce in the City, but he expects to be back home by late tomorrow afternoon."

Walter took down the telephone number Mr. Brundidge gave him. After he hung up the telephone he went back to his chair in the living room. His pizza was cold and the episode of "Bonanza" was nearly over. He shut off the TV, put the leftover pizza back into the refrigerator and went to bed.

The next afternoon he telephoned the Rivenburgs. A woman answered. He identified himself as Reverend Macdonald, and asked when he might stop by to speak with Mr. Rivenburg about his father's funeral service. "Late this afternoon is as good a time as any," she said. "If you start out at five, he'll be home by the time you get here."

"That will be fine, but I'll need directions to your house."

"Just drive through Millerton Center and after about a half mile look for a mailbox marked 'RD 3, Box 687.' That's us."

After he hung up the telephone he decided it would be smart to have an early supper before he drove to the Rivenburgs. He reheated the leftover pizza for a second time. As he sat and ate the last piece he promised himself that he would do better with meal preparation the rest of the week.

The road to Millerton Center followed the Schuylerkill Creek and passed through lush farmland. The only two farmers who belonged to the Presbyterian Church in Schuylerkill Falls had built large farming operations by buying up small family farms along the creek. The old farmhouses scattered along the road remained as residences, but the two successful farmers now owned all the farmland.

So far as he knew he didn't have any church members who lived in the hamlet. As he drove slowly through he could see that Millerton Center had known better times. What had once been a creamery was now a building in disrepair. Several of the houses had been grand in their day, but it was obvious that the present owners could not afford to maintain them. Morton's Market seemed to be the only operating store. A church stood across from the market—probably a Methodist or even a Presbyterian Church in better times. A large wooden cross had been imposed on top of the bell tower. The sign in front of the church boasted that it was now "An Independent, Bible-Believing Church." He drove through the village and, about a half mile beyond it, turned into the driveway next to a mailbox that was hand-lettered "RD 3, Box 687."

As he approached the mobile home at the end of the driveway a large German shepherd charged his Volkswagen. When he stopped the car the dog stood next to his door and barked. Walter made no effort to get out of the car. There didn't seem to be anyone around. A couple of well-used, unlicensed cars sat between a shed and a small chicken barn. Except for well-worn paths between the mobile home and the buildings, the area surrounding the trailer was overgrown with brush and weeds. Weeds gone to seed covered what had likely been a small garden plot during the summer. There was a small mown grassy area in front of the trailer; earlier in the season there had obviously been flower gardens on either side of the front steps.

Finally a man emerged from the barn and in a loud voice said, "Prince! It's all right!" The dog stopped barking immediately, wagged his tail and ran over to the man. The man and the tail-wagging dog walked toward Walter's car. When they were a few feet away the man stood and patted the dog. He spoke in a loud voice. "He won't bite you; he was just doing his job. It's okay to get out of your car; just let him check you out when he walks over to you. His name is 'Prince.'"

Walter opened the car door and stepped out onto the dirt driveway. The dog walked over to him. He held out his hand and the dog sniffed it; when the dog seemed comfortable he patted him and ruffled up the fur on his back. "Hi, Prince," he said. "My name is 'Walter.'" The man smiled slightly and said, "He likes you. I'm Jack Rivenburg; you must be Reverend Macdonald."

"I am," Walter said, "I'm happy to meet you, Mr. Rivenburg." He extended his hand and they shook hands. "I called earlier and asked if I could stop by to find out what you might like to have included in the service for your father. I am so sorry to hear about his passing."

Jack Rivenburg showed no emotion. "I know this may sound crass, but actually it's just as well. There wasn't much left of him. The doc at the VA hospital said he died from liver disease brought on by years of drinking. To be honest I can't remember when he didn't drink. After my mother died it just got worse. He'd spent all the money he had on her care. I was twelve when she died. We got evicted from the house he rented and I went to live with my Aunt Margaret.

"Dad took a room in town with the Brights—I think they go to your church." Walter nodded. "Weekdays he didn't spend much time in the room except to sleep. He ate supper every night at the Schuylerkill Grill. He spent Saturdays at the Legion and Sundays in his room with a six-pack, playing solitaire and listening to the Yankees on the radio. He worked for the town, but he never was able to be more than a road worker. Even though he didn't drink in the morning before he went to work they wouldn't let him drive truck because everybody knew he drank.

"As I think about it, the only thing dad had to be proud of was his military service. He tied his Purple Heart to a ribbon and hung it across the corner of an old framed photo of my mother. He kept them on the table next to his bed in his room. He must have taken them with him when he went to the VA hospital. It was with the stuff they gave me when I stopped there today. I said to Linda—that's my wife—when I got home and showed them to her just a little bit ago, 'Dad won the war against Hitler, but he lost the war against booze.'"

Walter could see that he was not going to be invited inside. "I stopped by to see if there is anything particular you would like me to include in the service on Thursday, like a special Scripture or hymn that your father liked?"

"I can't think of anything. Dad never went to church. I doubt that he ever read the Bible. We're not much for church ourselves. Linda sometimes takes the kids to the Bible Church Sunday school, but that's about as close to church as we get. The minister at the Bible Church has come to call several times, but I don't like him. He's too pushy."

Walter nodded. "That's okay; I understand." His response seemed to relax Jack.

"We're really grateful that you are willing to do the service, Reverend Macdonald. Just do the standard service, nothing fancy. You do know that there will be military honors at the grave?" Walter nodded. "That's the only thing special I can think of. Now, I'm sorry to have to ask you to excuse me. I've been up since three this morning and I have to leave at three tomorrow morning to pick up a load for Price Cutter. Linda and I still have to get our supper and grade and pack the day's eggs for the wholesaler to pick up in the morning before we can turn in."

"I need to go along anyway," Walter said. "Thanks for your suggestions about the funeral. Your father had his struggles, but I'm sure you also have some good memories of him." He noticed Jack's eyes were moist as he turned away. He paused by his car and watched the lonely figure and his dog walking past the shed to the chicken barn.

The town crew, Chief Haines, and a few others gathered with Jack and Linda on Thursday afternoon for Melchior Rivenburg's funeral service at the Brundidge Funeral Home. The service was brief, as Walter had promised. He couldn't add much to the Scripture readings and prayers provided in the Presbyterian Book of Worship; he knew very little about Melchior Rivenburg. By two-thirty he and Burton Brundidge were seated in the front seat of the hearse taking Melchior Rivenburg's remains for the short drive to the village cemetery.

"Good service, Reverend," Burt said as they drove along, "nothing maudlin and it didn't go over fifteen minutes. Nice to have a warm fall day; won't be many more like this one before it turns cold. Glad we can get Mac into the ground before freeze-up. People don't like having to keep someone in cold storage at the funeral home like they do in the winter when you can't dig a grave—they need a sense of closure." Walter nodded, but Burt didn't seem to notice.

"Did you meet my son-in-law, Jeremy? He's driving the limo with the family in it. Should say, 'Brundidge & Son-in-Law' on the side windows of this wagon, but it doesn't. I'm 'the son.' My dad's been gone for ten years. But Jeremy's become a son to me. All I had were daughters and none of them wanted to walk in my shoes. Jeremy was my last hope—became attached to the youngest. One day he said he'd like to marry her and join the business. I said he'd have to pass a test. I'd let him know when the opportunity came.

"It did about ten days later. Some kid on a motorcycle missed that curve just beyond Doc Peterson's on the North Battenville Road. When the call for the ambulance came in I called Jeremy and said, 'I'll pick you up in two minutes; your test is today.' The kid that had been thrown off the bike was a real mess, barely alive. We put him on a stretcher and into the back of this hearse. It doubles as the village ambulance, you know. Pretty efficient. If the patient dies en route—which this one did—you just wait for the coroner to say 'dead' at the ER and then you turn around and bring him back to the funeral home. Saves a trip.

"Anyway, when we got back to the funeral home Jeremy helped me clean the poor kid up and get him respectable looking. 'You pass,' I told him when we finished. I gave him my daughter and sent him to funeral director school. I was relieved to have somebody who'd give me grandchil-dren and who would run this business when I retire. I've already got the grandchildren."

The sentence ended as they stopped in the lane several yards from a freshly dug grave. He turned to Walter and said, "You can stay here in the hearse until we get things arranged. I'll look over at you and nod when everything is ready and it's time for you to bring the family to the grave." He stepped out and shut the door. It was quiet. After the long soliloquy it was a relief to have quiet. Walter sat and listened to the quiet.

After Burt placed a spray of flowers bound with a ribbon that said "Father" on top of Mac Rivenburg's casket, he and Jeremy lowered the cas-ket part way down into the grave. In front of it they arranged the two other bouquets of flowers that had been given in Mac's memory. Burt stepped back, looked toward the hearse and nodded to Walter.

Walter stepped out of the hearse, walked over to the limousine and escorted Jack and Linda to the graveside. He walked to the head of the casket and read the words of committal. When he finished there was total silence. He watched the white-gloved military honor guard lift and fold the American flag that had been draped over Melchior Rivenburg's casket. The young sergeant carried the folded flag and gave it to Jack. He stepped back and saluted. He turned right-face toward the casket and stood at attention. He and the Marine standing at the head of the casket saluted slowly and precisely together.

As he watched the scene unfold Walter's mind rolled back to another funeral: he was standing between his brother, Eddie, and his mother, listening to a minister read the exact same words of committal over his brother William's casket. He could hear his mother sobbing. Only his father's strong arms prevented her from collapsing as a young lieutenant presented her with the flag that had been draped over William's casket.

The honor guard for Mac Rivenburg raised their rifles and fired a salute. The sound of the shots echoed across the hills. It was both then and now. Tears welled up in Walter's eyes. When the bugler played taps the tears ran down his cheeks. He made no effort to wipe them away. He was now the minister reading from the Book of Revelation the promise that "God shall wipe away all tears." God had not wiped away his tears.

4

SATURDAY JUST BEFORE TWO o'clock Walter finally finished typing the preaching notes for Sunday's sermon. He fixed himself a sandwich, placed it on a plate and walked into the parlor and switched on his TV. He had just settled down to watch a football game when the telephone rang. He recognized the caller's voice before she said her name.

"Hi, Walter, this is Mary Kerrigan. I don't have a date for Halloween the day after tomorrow. Would you like to come over and bob for apples and have dinner with me?"

For a moment he was speechless. When he found his voice he said, "That would be wonderful, Mary. Can I bring something?"

"Don't be so hesitant, Walter, I do know how to cook. And don't worry about bringing anything. Don't worry at all. My landlady has gone to visit her daughter in Poughkeepsie for a week. Will seven-thirty be all right? I like to eat late, and the assault of trick or treaters should be over by that time."

"Seven-thirty is a good time; I like to eat late, too."

"Do you know where I live?

"Actually I do—upstairs in the yellow house on School Street right around the corner from Church Street. One of your student admirers pointed it out when I was driving home from the high school ball field with him last summer."

"I hope the poetry I taught him was what he had on his mind."

"I'm not very good at poetry," Walter said with a chuckle, "but I do enjoy eating."

"So do I and I will be happy to see you again and continue the conversation we began at the Petersons."

"Thanks very much for inviting me. It will be wonderful to see you again." After he hung up the telephone he sat back in his desk chair and looked out the window. He nodded his head and grinned broadly as he said to himself, "I really am looking forward to spending an entire evening with you, Mary Kerrigan. Alone."

He was glad Mary mentioned trick or treaters. He had completely forgotten to put in a stash of candy. When he made his weekly Monday shopping trip to Jim's Market, he added several bags of candy to the usual hamburger, chops, potatoes, frozen vegetables, sliced pastrami, bread, rolls and ice cream in his shopping basket.

Local people wondered whether Jim's would survive when the new Grand Union opened on the edge of town. But Jim offered the best custom-cut meat in the area, and he willingly took orders for groceries from elderly residents and delivered them to their homes Monday and Thursday evenings after he closed his store.

The "assault" of trick or treaters, as Mary so aptly termed it, began about three-thirty in the afternoon. By quarter of seven Walter realized it was over. He was relieved; he was nearly out of candy. He turned off his side porch light and went upstairs to change his clothes.

He looked at three different shirts before he decided to wear a blue oxford-cloth shirt with a button-down collar. He wondered whether he should wear Levi's or corduroys or dress slacks. Somehow Levi's didn't seem appropriate for a dinner date. Dress slacks seemed too formal. He settled on a pair of dark brown corduroys. When he laid them on his bed next to the blue shirt he realized he would need to change out of his black socks.

As he changed his clothes he caught a glimpse of himself in the mirror over his dresser. He stood still and looked at himself; the concern he felt about his appearance surprised him. When he shut off the light he happened to look out the bedroom window that faced the back of Miss Simpson's house. There were no lights on in his elderly neighbor's house. That was strange. Probably she had gone somewhere with her friend, Gert McCain.

He put on his jacket and was ready to leave by five minutes after seven. As he walked out of the kitchen door and stepped on to the side porch next to the driveway, he paused and looked at his black Volkswagen with its distinctive roof rack. "It's a nice evening and I'm early," he thought. "Maybe I'll walk." He opened the doors to the old carriage house that served as his garage and drove the VW inside. His car looked ridiculously small sitting in the middle of the wooden plank floor of the huge two-story carriage house. He smiled and shut the doors and locked them, checking first to be sure that one of the keys on his key ring unlocked the padlock to the doors. He had never locked the doors to the carriage house before, but locking them seemed the prudent thing to do on Halloween.

He walked along Church Street toward School Street. A cold wind had come up and the last of the trick or treaters had gone home to count their booty. He was relieved that he didn't meet anyone as he walked along. It was only twenty after seven when he walked on to Mary Kerrigan's front porch. He knew it was gauche to be early, but he pushed the top doorbell button anyway. She bounded down the stairs and opened the door. "You're early," she said, "but I knew you would be. Please come in." She held out her hand and he took it in his. It was warm.

He let go of her hand and shut the door behind him and watched her go up the stairs ahead of him. Her black ponytail flashed back and forth across her white oxford-cloth shirt. She had on the same tight-fitting jeans she had worn to the barbecue at the Petersons. When he followed her through the door that led from the landing into her living room, she turned and smiled. "I am delighted that you were free tonight. I am very happy to see you again."

"Me, too," he said. Immediately he corrected himself. "What I meant to say is, I'm happy to see you again." There was an awkward pause. "Well, you can tell that I'm nervous."

"So am I," she said. "Maybe a glass of wine will help us. I cooked a pot roast. I never cook one just for myself. I bought a nice bottle of red wine when I visited my parents in Saratoga last weekend. It will go well with the roast. Would you like some now?"

"I would," Walter said. "Pot roast is one of my favorites; I could smell the wonderful smell of it cooking as soon as we started up the stairs to your apartment." She smiled. He took off his jacket.

She gestured toward a loveseat. "Please make yourself comfortable while I check on the roast. I'll bring the wine back with me." She took his jacket and carried it through the door in the far corner of the dining area. He assumed that this door led to her bedroom and that she was going to lay his jacket on her bed. He stood and watched her go into the dark room. She smiled at him when she came back out into the dining room; he felt embarrassed to be caught staring at her bedroom door. She walked through another door that led out of the dining room; he could see through this door into her kitchen.

He turned and saw a large floor-to-ceiling bookcase along the wall that backed on the stairwell. A long library table stretched between the two windows that fronted on the street; it was strewn with books and magazines. A finely made open mahogany pull-down desk with a tall stack of what he assumed were students' compositions stood in the middle of the far wall. A large overstuffed chair sat to the right of the desk. He decided to sit in this chair rather than the loveseat.

The dining room was barely large enough to accommodate an expandable mahogany dining table, four chairs and a sideboard. Matching wine glasses and water goblets stood at the heads of two place settings set around the corner from each other on the table. He suspected the plates were bone china. The folded linen napkins and china looked similar to the Irish linen napkins and bone china he had seen at his grandmother's house. He knew he could tell if the plates were authentic by placing his fingers behind them and holding them up to a light like he had done once as a child (and earned a reprimand from his father), but today he let manners overcome curiosity and resisted the temptation to conduct a test. He was surprised and intrigued by what he saw in Mary's apartment; everything was far more elegant than one would expect to find in the apartment of a beginning schoolteacher.

He stood up when Mary walked out of the kitchen door carrying a tray. It held a bottle of wine, a corkscrew, two wine glasses, small slices of cheese and some crackers. She set the tray on the coffee table in front of the love seat and handed the wine and the corkscrew to him. "The gentleman does the honors," she said. He picked up the wine bottle and looked at the label. "I grew up in a family of Scots," he said, "but we enjoyed good French wine. This is a very good, full-bodied French wine. Exactly what is called for with pot roast."

She was surprised at how deftly he opened the wine bottle. He picked up one of the glasses. He poured a little wine into it and handed it to her. "The mistress of the house gets the first sip," he said. "That is the custom in my family." She tasted the wine and pronounced it fit. He filled both glasses half full. He held his glass toward her. "To friendship," he said.

"To our friendship," she responded. They touched their glasses together. The ringing of crystal resonated throughout the room.

With the first sip of wine he felt himself relaxing. He settled back in his chair. "I like your apartment; it matches you very well."

"Thank you for noticing."

He looked at the large bookcase. "You have almost as many books as I do. I don't mean this to be insulting in any way, but I'm curious. How did someone with such a large library end up teaching here in Schuylerkill Falls? It looks like the kind of library a college professor would have."

"Actually, both of my parents are professors at Skidmore. My father teaches literature and my mother teaches religion. As you know from our conversation at the barbecue, I have two degrees. I did a BA in English at Barnard, with a concentration in nineteenth-century American lit. The program was excellent, and my mother went there, too, so Barnard was really attractive to me. But as I said when we were out at the Petersons, what does a BA in English equip you to *do*? After I recovered from shock when my boyfriend dumped me for God I decided to do a master's in education. Then at least I could be a teacher. Even before I completed the master's I realized that I wanted to teach at the college level, but I needed a break; I was worn out with going to school. So I decided to do some teaching before going on for my doctorate."

"Sounds like a good idea."

"It actually turned out quite well. The bachelor's in English/master's in education combination made me quite employable. Jerry Ward our principal—I think he's on your church board—what do you call it?—("the session," he responded)—recruited me here. Miss Simpson retired unexpectedly after she fell that spring. Jerry and my father are old friends; they grew up together in Glens Falls and went all through school there. They keep in touch—like former high school basketball teammates do, so Jerry knew I was going to finish my master's in May.

"At first I wasn't keen on coming back upstate—I loved living in New York City, but Jerry was convincing. He said I could teach college prep students, offer a poetry elective at least every other year, and, if I decided I wanted to stay, he said he would see that I got tenure after three years. The package was much more than I had the right to expect in a first teaching job. So I signed on, and I've been here ever since."

He watched her closely as she talked about herself. She was delightfully self-assured. Her voice was strong, and the well-measured phrases she used to express herself testified to an informed and disciplined mind. She was a potent woman—so unlike the compliant women most of his seminary classmates had hurried to marry. But she didn't seem harsh. Quite the opposite: she was someone who was strong enough to be tender—even vulnerable. He liked her. He liked her a lot.

She got up and refilled their wine glasses as she continued. "I assumed that this apartment would be temporary quarters when I rented it four years ago. I thought I would either be back in the City by now or would have found someone who would be just right for me. I've never lived in a village this small, and I didn't realize that the only single men of marriageable age would be truckers or millworkers—that is, aside from you." She paused and looked directly at him and smiled. "I've got nothing against truckers and millworkers," she went on, "but if I have to spend every workday with adolescents, I want someone at home whose intellectual life consists of more than what he saw on television last night."

He laughed, "Thanks for the compliment."

"Okay, that's enough about me. What drew you from metropolitan New Jersey to Schuylerkill Falls?"

"To be honest, what is drawing me right now is the aroma coming from your kitchen."

"Well, then let's eat while we talk."

"Can I help you bring the food to the table?"

"If you want to help, I'll fill a pitcher and you can pour the water. There's only one pot to carry in; I cooked the potatoes and vegetables in with the roast."

He followed her into her kitchen. It was quite small. He guessed that one door at the back of it led to a bathroom and that the other was a rear entrance. She handed him a pitcher filled with cold water. He went back to the dining table and filled the stemmed goblets that sat on the edges of each placemat. She appeared carrying a steaming pot that she set on a trivet. She motioned that he should sit in the chair nearest the pot. He held the other chair for her and then sat in his own chair.

"Would you like to ask a blessing?" she asked. "Probably the food will taste better, if you pray over it." She grinned.

He grinned back. "It smells so good that I doubt prayer will improve it, but I will pray anyway." He bowed his head and offered a prayer of thanks. He felt very comfortable.

She gestured toward the pot roast. "I cooked it so you have to serve it." The meat was so tender he was able to break it apart with the large serving spoon. He filled her plate and then his own. The food was delicious.

As they ate dinner they shared their feelings about living and working in Schuylerkill Falls. She told him about the difficulties she had convincing the high school faculty that the English curriculum should include more than drilling students in grammar and composition, and exposing them to a few tame English and American novelists and poets. She described the controversy she caused the second year she taught when she asked students to read *The Scarlet Letter*.

He talked about how difficult it was to follow in the footsteps of a heroic minister like long-serving Dr. Morton. It seemed that every older person he visited—and there were lots of them in his congregation—compared his preaching and his prayers to Dr. Morton's. She laughed out loud when he told her about a parishioner's images of Dr. Morton as President Eisenhower and of him as the soon-to-be President Nixon. They agreed that John Kennedy had out-thought and out-talked Richard Nixon handily in the televised debates—though Walter wasn't entirely convinced he would win the election. Even after they had viewed the debates most of the middle-aged and older members of his congregation were still very much for Nixon.

"Okay," she said when he had eaten a second helping of her excellent chocolate cake, "you've put me off long enough. I want to know about you. How did a kid from a Schenectady hardware store family find his way into the ministry? The two don't seem to me to be connected at all."

"In my growing-up experience they were," he said. "The order that rules William Macdonald Hardware molded my believing. Like John Calvin's theology, everything in the family store has its proper place; every nut and bolt and screw goes into an assigned bin. I started restocking bins at the store after school when I was still a boy. On one of the first days I worked I put some three-eighth inch cap screws into a bin with three-eighth inch carriage bolts. The next day when I reported for work my grandfather made me remove the errant cap screws and put them in their proper bin. He was gentle, but firm, and I knew the mistake was serious. I never made that kind of error again. I was careful to put every piece of hardware exactly where it belonged. I learned that there is an overarching order that rules a hardware store."

She shook her head, "That does sound like church."

He laughed. "That's why I said they were connected. The ruling order in the hardware store is symbolized by the mechanical gadget that Grandfather Macdonald invented to collect customers' money and return their change. That gadget provided my childhood image of the way God keeps order in the world. It's an ingenious mechanism and they still use it at the store. When clerks make a sale, they list the items a customer wishes to purchase on a sales ticket, then they take the customer's money and the sales ticket and place them in a tube-like receptacle. They attach the receptacle with a clip to one of the thin moving overhead cables that hang in a loop behind the counters that line one side of the store. The mechanism is set up much the same as clotheslines that are sometimes stretched between pulleys mounted on the back porch of a house and a pole at the back of the yard."

As his story unfolded Mary began to shake her head back and forth. Then she started to laugh. "Walter," she said, "That thing sounds like something Rube Goldberg invented!"

"No, it's not," he insisted, "just hang in there with me another minute and you'll see why it's so important to me." He continued. "When the clerk has attached the receptacle containing the sales ticket and the customer's money to the cable, he pushes a button that rings a bell in the office upstairs at the back of the store. The cashier upstairs turns on the motor that sets the cable in motion. The container jerks along the cable that takes it back toward the office where it enters through a small open window. The cashier stops the machinery, unhooks the container, opens it, rings up the sale and places the receipt and any change into the container. He rings the bell and clips the container to the outgoing cable and starts the machinery again. When the container reaches the clerk, he stops the machinery, unhooks the container, opens it and gives the customer his receipt and any change." He grinned. "Isn't that wonderful?!!"

She burst out laughing. "It is," she struggled to say, "but what's the point?"

"Well, here's the point."

"Finally!" she said.

"I know it may be hard for you to believe, but for a long time I thought God operates his creation like the cable system in our store. God is as reliable as the trolley. You send up prayers to God and you get back what you're entitled to: an acknowledgement of your prayer and whatever change you deserve. Prayers go up and grace comes back. It's absolutely orderly. God is dependable and absolutely just."

"You said, 'For a long time I *thought*'; your use of the past tense implies that something happened that challenged your neat picture of God. What happened? Did the trolley break down?"

He wasn't sure he wanted to say. It was not something he had planned to tell her about when he began talking about the hardware store's trolley. But he didn't know how to turn back graciously, so he went on. "For a while it seemed like it did. When I was fourteen my brother, Bill, was killed. It was terrible. He enlisted in the Marines; he'd turned eighteen and he was going to be drafted anyway. He was in a training accident; he fell off the back of a fast-moving truck. It was such a waste. Our family has never really recovered. It was especially hard on my father. Once we got through the terrible days right after it happened, we rarely talked about him. We're Scots Presbyterians so we're reserved; we trust God and suffer inside ourselves."

"How awful, Walter. To be hurt and not be able to share it."

"It was. My father talked openly about the way Bill's death affected him only once. The second summer after Bill was killed he invited me to go up to our family's cottage on Sacandaga Reservoir for two days of fishing. Just the two of us. We didn't catch anything, but during those days I felt closer to him than I had ever felt before in my life. At the end of the second day of not catching any fish we went into town and bought T-bone steaks. We cooked them over a charcoal fire and afterwards sat around and talked. I was amazed when he began to talk about Bill. He said Bill's death had made him angry at God. He said he was still angry at God. 'Walter,' he said, 'when I married your mother and you boys came along, I began to pray every night that God would take care of my family.' He stopped and looked at me and tears ran down his cheeks. 'But you know, Walter, it doesn't work.'"

He paused and looked at Mary. "I have never seen anyone look so bleak." His voice quavered as he spoke; tears threated to spill out of his eyes. He wiped away the few that managed to escape with the back of his hand. He watched her look at him. He felt naked, but not ashamed. Finally he spoke, "I'm sorry," he said with a deep sigh. "I shouldn't have gotten into all of this with you."

She reached out and touched his hand. "It's all right, Walter," she said; "you don't have to know how it works. Maybe no one knows how it works? Maybe no one can know how it works?" He saw the longing in her eyes. "I wish things like that didn't happen, but sometimes the trolley just breaks down." They sat quietly. She withdrew her hand slowly. "Perhaps, I shouldn't have done that."

"I liked it; thank you for caring." He was drawn to talk more about his feelings, but he didn't. He was stuck on her "maybe no one can know how it works" statement.

When he continued his voice was stronger. She noticed his eyes seem to be looking both at her and beyond her as he spoke. "I know the trolley memory is one of those childish imaginings that stays with you even after you grow up. I don't have the same naïve faith I had when I was a child; in seminary I grew up theologically.

"I can't explain how God works as simply as I did when I believed grace comes into our lives like the overhead trolley—it's much more complex than that, but I know that when we trust God absolutely, God works in our lives so that whatever happens to us happens for our good. I am certain that God is in charge even when it appears he is not in charge. I'm sure that God has some purpose in permitting things to happen like what happened to Bill . . . but it still hurts."

He paused; when he continued he spoke softly, reflectively, but also urgently like he might be preaching to himself. "No matter what happens I will keep on believing God cares. I have to." When he stopped speaking he looked expectantly at her face.

After a pause she said softly, "You still have the same tears."

He nodded and watched her look at him, then he took a deep breath and sat back in his chair. "Well, probably that's enough religion talk for one night. Now that we are having a moment of truth I want to ask you about something that's bothered me ever since I came to Schuylerkill Falls. What happened to the Reverend Nathaniel Cook? A painting or photo of every one of my predecessors hangs in the church parlor, but not one of Nate. I suspect I know what he did to lose his pulpit, but no one ever talks about him, and everyone seems to imply that I shouldn't ask them about him. You were here in 1958. Do you know what happened to Nate Cook?"

"He had an affair with a parishioner. Apparently it went on for some time. One afternoon her husband came home unexpectedly and found them together. That was the end of him as pastor. The church tried to keep it quiet, but everyone knows what happened."

"I suspected something like that, but when I actually hear you say what happened it seems surprising to me. Why would he take that kind of risk when he was married and had a couple of kids?"

"People said it was a terrible marriage. You know what they say about unhappily married middle-aged men, 'Deprivation leads to depravity.' As a Calvinist, probably you were already familiar with that."

"Not firsthand," he said.

She smiled. "Don't look so concerned, Walter. They won't fire you for having dinner with a single non-Presbyterian schoolteacher."

He grinned at her, "With you I'll take the risk." Her eyes sparkled. The mantel clock struck the half hour. "It's ten-thirty! I've been enjoying myself so much that I lost track of time. It's late and we both have to work tomorrow. I should be going."

She sighed. "I hate to agree, but you're right. I have to be at school for a meeting at 7:15 in the morning. I'll get your jacket." She switched on a lamp next to her bed when she went into her bedroom. Walter watched as she took his jacket off her bed and brought it to him. She handed him the jacket. As he put it on he noticed that it smelled like her. They walked down the stairs to the front door. At the bottom landing he turned toward her, "Thank you for a wonderful evening."

"My pleasure," she said. "Thank you." He turned toward the door and placed his hand on the door knob. "Wait!" she said. He turned around. She had stepped up on to the bottom step of the stairs. Her face was directly opposite his. He looked into her green eyes. She shut them and kissed him on the cheek. She whispered into his ear. "You're lovely."

"Thank you," he said. He stood and looked at her. He felt lovely. "I want to see you again—soon," he said.

She smiled. "I would like that."

He turned, opened the door and stepped out on to the porch.

She closed the door behind him and stood watching him through the door window as he walked away. "He's smart and strong, but he's so cautious," she thought. "I think there's much more inside of him than he can let out; he's seems so earnest all the time. It would be so much better if he could just let himself go, but maybe there's some reason he can't that I don't understand?" She shrugged her shoulders and walked up the stairs.

———— 5 ————

WHEN WALTER STEPPED OFF Mary's porch he was glad he had worn a jacket. A brisk, cold wind was blowing. Fortunately, it was at his back as he walked home. When he stepped onto his back porch, he found a note tacked to the screen door. It was written on a prescription blank that had "Erik Peterson, MD" printed across the top. He took it inside and read: "Adele Simpson had a stroke. If you get in before 11, call me at home. Erik." He looked at his kitchen clock; it was almost eleven. He went into his study and dialed Erik's number. Erik answered. "Hi, Erik, this is Walter. I am so sorry to hear about Miss Simpson's stroke. When did it happen?"

"I'm not exactly sure," Erik said. "Jim of Jim's market found her lying on the floor in her kitchen about seven-thirty when he delivered her groceries after he closed his store. He called me from her phone and I went right over. I suspect she'd lain there quite a while—maybe more than an hour."

"That's terrible. What a shame no one knew sooner."

"I tried to find out if she knew how long she had been on the floor, but she wasn't able to tell me. When I talked to her, she seemed to understand me, but other than squeezing my hand with her left hand when I asked her yes and no questions, she wasn't able to respond. Going down hard and then lying there for so long could have crushed some of her muscles and could lead to a kidney-clogging condition called rhabdomyolysis. That possibility plus the apparent stroke suggested that it was essential to get her to the hospital as quickly as possible.

"I called Burt Brundidge and he and Jeremy took her to the hospital in Saratoga in their ambulance. I followed them in. Luckily, Pete Shapiro—he's an internist—was in the hospital. He went right to work with aggressive hydration to flush out her kidneys. I hung around for a little while, but there

30

wasn't much for me to do. Pete's more experienced in dealing with stroke patients than I am so I left her in his care and came home. She does seem to have some paralysis on her right side, and she doesn't seem to be able to talk. So, it looks like a stroke to me. I don't think there's any sense going over there tonight. I'll call you in the morning after I talk with Dr. Shapiro and let you know what he thinks."

"I'm just so surprised, Erik. I visited her at home on Friday, and Sunday at the church service she seemed to be fine."

"Well, for a long time she's had more issues than people know about. She's had very high blood pressure and we just haven't been able to get it down. She's been unsteady ever since she fell when she broke her leg. That's why I insisted that she use a cane. She hit her head pretty hard that day. We knew she had a slight concussion, but maybe she suffered damage inside her skull that wasn't apparent.

"We should try to reach Adele's nephew in Albany first thing in the morning. He's the only close relative I know about. It's too late to contact him tonight. But we can talk more tomorrow about getting in touch with him. Get some sleep and I'll call you about seven in the morning and let you know what's happening with Adele."

"Thanks for leaving me a note, Erik. I'll be sure to be here when you call in the morning." He switched off the light on his desk after he hung up the telephone. He sat in the quiet. Then he broke his own silence. "I should have checked on her. I'm her pastor."

It was precisely two o'clock (the agreed-upon time) on an August afternoon when he walked up the steps onto her front porch for the first time and faced two weathered isinglass-paneled doors. Below the isinglass panel on the right-hand door was the ringer handle of a twisting door bell. He turned the handle and the bell rang very loudly. Miss Simpson opened the door immediately. She had been standing inside the door waiting for him to ring. "Welcome to my home, Mr. Macdonald. Please come in."

She ushered him quickly through the dim entrance hall into a small sun-lit parlor. A matched pair of upholstered chairs stood in the corners of the room nearest the porch. A large cat was curled up in the closest one. He took no notice of Walter. Miss Simpson gestured Walter toward the upholstered chair in the far right corner. "That's the largest chair in this room," she said, "please take it; I think you will find it comfortable. I will sit in this straight chair. Since my fall I find it is not so easy for me to extricate myself from overstuffed furniture."

He was careful not to bump the Duncan Phyfe table covered with knickknacks as he sat down in his assigned seat. "I was sorry to hear about your fall, Miss Simpson. But you seem to have recovered quite well. Even when I see you at church services, I never see you use your cane. You always just carry it."

"I carry it to please Dr. Peterson. He insists that I need to use a cane, but I have not leaned on it even once since I was released from the rehabilitation center. That fall in 1956 changed my life, Mr. Macdonald. I had expected to teach several more years, but after the fall I discovered that I can't stand on my feet all day anymore. I didn't want to give up teaching. But I heard my father's voice in my head—he was a Presbyterian pastor, in case no one has told you, 'God often sends some adversity when our lives need to change direction.' So, I changed direction. I understand the new English teacher, Miss Kerrigan, is very well qualified. Though I hear she spends more time on literature and less time on grammar in her classes than I did when I taught. But that's change, and we have to accept it."

Walter nodded. "Yes, we do," he said in a measured voice.

His agreement encouraged her. "Things were certainly different when I began to teach English at the old high school that was located down the street from the Presbyterian Church. World War I had just ended. Mr. Wilson was President. He was a Presbyterian, just like Mr. Eisenhower. Did you know that, Mr. Macdonald?"

"Yes, actually, I did. He was president of Princeton University before he became President of the United States."

"It's nice to have a church-going President. When the session voted to call you as pastor my dear friend, Virginia Gillespie, said, 'Isn't it symbolic? Just as this November our country I am sure will elect Mr. Nixon to succeed our dear Mr. Eisenhower as President, our church has elected Mr. Macdonald to succeed our dear Dr. Morton as pastor.'" She paused and looked a little embarrassed. "Now, where was I?"

"You were saying that life was different when you began to teach here."

"Oh, yes. For the first twelve years I taught I boarded in the home of Mr. Gillespie, Virginia's father. Virginia taught history and I taught English so I saw her at home as well as at the school. That's how Virginia and I became such good friends. Her mother was an invalid and her sister, Beatrice, gave up her teaching career to return home to care for her. After their mother died Beatrice married Jackson Smith who is our church organist.

"Everyone calls Jackson 'Smitty,' but I prefer his proper name. Mr. Gillespie owned Gillespie's Department Store on Main Street.

When Beatrice married Jackson her father invited him to become a partner in the business. He is the sole owner of the business now. Beatrice lived only ten years after they were married; she died of cancer on Christmas Eve. Such a terrible disease. Poor Jackson; he never got over her loss."

Walter looked appropriately concerned. His look encouraged her to continue.

"Sadly, Jackson developed a drinking problem after Beatrice died—though only after work, and, of course, never on Sunday. Gillespie's was a much smaller store in those early days. It was called 'Gillespie's Haberdashery.' 'Haberdashery.' That word has such an engaging sound. When I taught composition I encouraged my students to choose words that have an engaging sound." A troubled look came over her face and she stopped speaking. "Oh dear," she said, "I've lost my place."

"You were talking about how much closer everyone lived when you first moved to Schuylerkill Falls."

"Oh, yes, thank you. In those days a single-woman schoolteacher would not have been permitted to have her own apartment like Miss Kerrigan does. There were clear expectations of schoolteachers. We were expected to remain single. We were expected to be of good moral character. Our presence at weekly worship was required. We did what we were expected to do. There were consequences if we didn't. "

Walter looked down and realized he was fidgeting with his fingers. He stopped immediately. He hoped Miss Simpson hadn't noticed. "When did you move to this house?" he asked.

"It was in 1937. My poor father—he was a Presbyterian minister, in case you didn't know—had a heart attack and died. It was such a shock to lose him; he was such an inspiration. He was everything people think a minister should be. His moral character and his believing were above reproach. I never saw him touch strong drink, and I never heard him question or contradict anything in the Holy Scripture. Don't you agree that all ministers should exhibit such fortitude, Mr. Macdonald?"

Her manner of believing seemed too rigid and confined to him, but he didn't challenge her. It would be neither kind nor prudent to argue about believing with an elderly parishioner. "Yes," he said, "I do agree that sound theology and morality are essential in a minister." He could tell by the expression on her face that she was not quite satisfied with his calculated response. He was glad she didn't ask him to expand on it.

"Now that you have lived here for nearly three weeks, do you think you will like being the minister of the leading church in Schuylerkill Falls?"

"I already know that I will like it very much!" The Seth Thomas mantel clock struck three.

"I am so pleased to hear that. I would be interested to know more about your life before you came here: about your family and your experiences as an assistant pastor in New Jersey."

He told her what it was like to grow up working in the family hardware store in Schenectady, and then went on to describe some of the difficulties he faced as an assistant minister in the Presbyterian Church in Rahway.

When the clock struck three-thirty, she glanced at it and interrupted him. *"Oh, my goodness it's getting late. I hope you will have some time for some refreshments."*

"I certainly would," he said enthusiastically. *"I've been smelling something I know will be delicious since I first arrived."*

The coffee was delicious, and the pie even more so. *"Yours is the best apple pie I have eaten since my Grandmother Richards died, Miss Simpson."*

She smiled diffidently in response to the compliment. *"I never had the good fortune to have a husband, but in anticipation that I someday would be able to attract one, my mother taught me how to make a good pie. I have made many excellent pies during my life, but none of them produced the desired result, Mr. Macdonald."*

He smiled and thought to himself, *"If pie were all that mattered in attracting a husband, Miss Simpson, you would have been married long ago."*

At four-fifteen, as he walked away from Miss Simpson's house carrying a plastic container with more than half a pie in it, Walter was weary, but also content. His visit had been successful: Miss Simpson was a parishioner whose opinion mattered and she had accepted him as her pastor. They were family.

The telephone rang the next morning just after seven o'clock. Walter had already showered and had his breakfast. He'd been restless and awake on and off most of the night.

"I just talked with Dr. Shapiro," Erik said. "His diagnosis is what I suspected: right hemi-paresis with aphasia. In layman's terms that means Adele's stroke was on the left side of her brain so she has lost at least some use of her right arm and leg and has some paralysis on the right side of her face. 'Aphasia' means that she has difficulty with language. While she seems alert, she hasn't talked at all to anyone caring for her at the hospital. She may be having difficulty with receptive language as well. We probably won't know the extent of the aphasia or what the long-term picture is for several days. Pete has decided to keep her in the ICU for the time being.

"If you want to visit her, I think she will know you are there even if she doesn't respond by talking when you speak to her. I know it will give her some comfort just to see you. She has great regard for you."

"I'm pleased to hear that, Erik."

"Before I head off to the office and forget to mention it, Adele has a cat she loves dearly. His name is 'Willie.' She'll be worried about him. He ran out the door when I was at her house yesterday. Maybe you could stop over there and let him back in and be sure he has some food and water?"

"I can do that; I'll stop by this morning and feed him."

After he hung up the telephone he left the manse by the side door, walked past the carriage house, across his back yard into Miss Simpson's back yard, past her garage and up on to her side porch. As soon as he opened the kitchen door Willie came out from under the porch and ran through the door into the kitchen.

He looked in the refrigerator and found an open can of cat food, almost stepping on Willie as he carried the can over to the counter. He found a spoon in one of the drawers under the linoleum-topped counter and spooned some cat food into Willie's dish and placed it on the floor. Willie quickly ate all of it.

While Willie sat cleaning his paws, he walked through the house and made sure all the windows and the front door to the house were locked. When he walked into the front parlor Willie was curled up in his chair by the front window. Walter stopped and talked directly to the cat. "Miss Simpson is sick and had to go to the hospital, Willie. She'll be gone for a few days. But I will see that you have plenty to eat and a clean litter box. Try not to worry. I'm sure she will be better soon and be able to come home." He felt strange talking to a cat, but the encouraging words he spoke to Willie somehow comforted him as well.

By ten o'clock he was on his way to the hospital in Saratoga Springs. When he arrived he took the elevator to the third-floor intensive care unit and told the nurse on duty that he was Miss Simpson's pastor. She said he could visit Miss Simpson but asked him to limit his visit to five minutes. The doors to the ICU swung open automatically when he walked toward them, and closed automatically after he had walked through.

Only two of the four beds in the unit were occupied. The person in the middle bed on the left was receiving oxygen. He decided that Miss Simpson must be in the corner bed on the right. He walked quietly up to the side of her bed. He looked at her face; the right side of it sagged slightly. Her left eye was fully open, but her right eye was only partly open. "Miss Simpson," he said quietly, "it's Mr. Macdonald. I've come to see how you are." He reached between the raised bars on the side of the bed and gently took hold of Miss Simpson's left hand. "I thought you might be concerned about Willie. I went over to your house this morning and let him inside. He ate almost two cans of cat food. I talked to him for a little while. I told him you would be here for a few days, but that you would soon be back home. He seemed to understand. I left him with fresh water. Is there anything special I should know about taking care of him? If I feed him twice a day is that enough?"

He felt a slight squeeze.

"Does that mean 'yes?'"

He felt another slight squeeze.

"These accommodations are not quite as nice as your parlor. I bet the food is not as good as you make either. I miss the aroma of your delicious pies. But there will be other times for us to share some pie and conversation at your house, won't there?"

He felt another squeeze.

For a minute or so he stood quietly and looked at Miss Simpson. "The nurse said I can stay only for five minutes, so I will have to leave soon. I want to pray with you before I go. Would you like me to pray with you?"

He felt another squeeze.

He closed his eyes and bowed his head. "Dear God, Adele and I feel very close to you. We feel your grace surrounding us and upholding us in this hospital room. We pray that you will touch Adele with healing and restore strength to her body. We admit that we are frightened because we don't know exactly what the days ahead will bring. But we do know that wherever the journey leads, you will be there. We know that whatever happens to us will not and cannot separate us from your love and care. So we walk on boldly in faith, trusting in you and our dear Lord and Savior, Jesus Christ. Amen."

After he lifted his head and opened his eyes he squeezed Miss Simpson's hand gently. Though he couldn't be completely certain, he was sure he felt a slight squeeze in return. As he withdrew his hand from hers he said, "You're going to be all right, Miss Simpson."

As he left the hospital parking lot and drove toward Schuylerkill Falls, he felt tired. Several times along the way home he had to fight to stay awake. He was relieved when he pulled into the manse driveway. It was after two. He had thought of stopping for lunch in one of the restaurants he passed on the way home, but he hadn't. As he walked up the porch steps he glanced at the screen door and was thankful no note was tacked to it.

When he went inside into the kitchen he took some sliced ham from the refrigerator and made himself a sandwich. He carried the sandwich and a cup of reheated coffee to his desk. He sat and read the prescribed Scripture lessons for the coming Sunday. None of them inspired him—which gave him a moment's panic because he knew that by Sunday he would have to produce a sermon based on one of them. He sat back in his chair. Yes, he really was very tired. He finished the sandwich, moved over to his reading chair and sat down.

He let his head fall back and closed his eyes. He thought of Miss Simpson lying for hours on the floor in her kitchen. If only he had gone over to check on her last night when he first noticed her lights were not on. He tried to push the feelings of guilt away.

He thought about the delightful dinner and evening with Mary. When he was with her he felt completely relaxed and free. He recalled what she said when he was telling her about Bill's death and tears welled up in his eyes. It was a vulnerable moment, uncomfortably revealing. She was kind; her comment, "you don't have to know how it works," was comforting, but the added "maybe no one knows how it works," and especially the added "maybe no one *can* know how it works," were troubling.

Suddenly he sat up straight and opened his eyes. "I wonder if she believes God's in charge? Now that I think about it she didn't agree with any of my statements about God the whole evening." He touched his cheek where she had kissed him. "I hope I'm not tasting forbidden fruit." He took a deep breath, let it out through pursed lips, smiled and relaxed against the back of his chair. "Well, there's no reason we can't be friends. I really like her."

When he awoke it was dark.

6

MISS SIMPSON FULFILLED WALTER'S prediction: after several days some sensation returned to her right arm and leg, and she began to try to speak. Her utterances were sometimes difficult to understand—which obviously frustrated her. Walter could see that the prospect of limited speech was as frightening to her as the prospect of limited mobility. Language had been her life. She faced a long recovery, but within three weeks it seemed likely that she would regain most of her speech and mobility. She could speak in two- and three-word sentences, and she could move her right leg and arm, though not very much.

The next few weeks were uneventful. During the week following Thanksgiving Christmas cards began to appear in each day's mail. Walter was delighted to receive one from the Petersons that included an invitation to their annual "Sunday-before-Christmas Open House." As the advent season progressed he began to make notes for his Christmas Eve and Christmas Day sermons. Over the years he had listened to a host of Christmas sermons; this year he would enjoy preaching his own.

The weather was unusually mild for December. The middle Wednesday of the month had a frosty beginning, but by noon the temperature was forty degrees. He decided he would eat an early lunch and take advantage of the nice weather and drive to the rehab facility in Saratoga to visit Miss Simpson. He made himself a grilled ham and cheese sandwich.

He had eaten only half of the sandwich when he noticed a New York state trooper's car drive into his driveway. Schuylerkill Falls Police Chief Pete Haines and a very tall state trooper got out of the car and walked up the steps on to the side porch. He met them at the door.

"Hi, Reverend Macdonald," Pete said. "This is Trooper Jerry Randall."

He shook the officer's hand. "I'm pleased to meet you," he said. The trooper nodded.

"Sorry to bother you in the middle of lunch, but Jerry and I wonder if you could spare an hour or so to help us. We've just come in from Millerton Center. Jack Rivenburg is holed up in the shed between his trailer and his chicken barn and refuses to come out. Linda is inside their trailer. She called the state police dispatcher and told her that Jack is very upset and made some threatening statements to her.

"We've had the trailer and shed surrounded for over an hour. We've tried to get Jack to come out of the shed, but we can't get any response out of him. We wonder if you might be able to talk him out of the shed. If you could, it could prevent someone from getting hurt. If you're willing to try, we can fill you in on the details as we drive out to Millerton Center."

Walter shook his head back and forth in disbelief as Pete talked. "I met Jack when I did his father's funeral at the beginning of the summer. He impressed me then as a hard-working, level-headed guy; I can't imagine him threatening anybody. But it sounds like he's very upset. If you think I might be able to help by talking with him, I'll come with you."

"Thanks, pastor," Pete said. "Bring your sandwich along, if you want to; you can eat it on the way."

Walter picked up his sandwich and followed the two officers out to the police car. The trooper opened the right rear door and Walter got in. "I'll ride in the back with the pastor so we can talk on the way," Pete said as he opened the other rear door of the cruiser. The trooper got into the driver's side of the front seat and backed the cruiser out of the driveway. As he headed down Church Street he turned on the flashing red lights and siren. He drove quickly through Schuylerkill Falls. When they were out of the village and on the Millerton Road Walter saw the speedometer hovering near seventy.

Pete turned to him and said, "Here's what the state police investigation has turned up so far. They checked with Price Cutter, and the transport manager there told us Jack arrived at their terminal about four-thirty this morning. He checked out his tractor-trailer and headed for the City to pick up a load of produce. The truck broke down just south of Albany. He was still in range of the company base station so he called in on his CB and told the transport manager he suspected the truck had blown a head gasket. Price Cutter sent a replacement truck and driver to New York to pick up Jack's load.

"They hooked the trailer on to the new tractor and towed Jack's broken-down tractor to the Price Cutter garage. He had no work there for the rest of the day so he came home. When he got there he probably saw a car in his drive and recognized that it was Randy Hatch's, a guy Linda works with. We didn't want to get close enough to the trailer to read the plate on the car, but it matches a car registered to Randy. I checked with the school and they said that both Randy and Linda called in sick today. So, they probably had a date!"

"I'm amazed. When I met Linda she didn't seem like the type that would do something like that."

Pete shrugged his shoulders. "Well, you never know. Anyway, Linda probably heard Jack drive up and we suspect when he went in one door of the trailer Randy must have run out the other door and into the woods. Randy's car is still parked in the driveway, so he must be out there somewhere hiding in the brush. Jack may have thought that Linda and Randy had been in bed together—knowing Linda's past history, that could be."

"But I can't believe Jack has any history of violence."

"Not that we know of. Apparently he didn't harm her physically, but she told the dispatcher he was really out of control and has gone out into the shed where he keeps his gun. She said that when he walked out the front door of the trailer he yelled, 'I'll fix that bastard—and you, too.' He slammed the storm door so hard he broke the glass in it. Linda told the dispatcher she suspects he's out there in the shed with his gun waiting for Randy to come back for his car. She's afraid he'll shoot Randy and that he might shoot her if she tries to leave—and anybody that tries to come in there to help her."

"What do you want me to do?" Walter asked.

"Maybe you could try to get close enough to talk to Jack and convince him to come out of the shed without his gun."

"But Linda thinks he might shoot anybody that tries to get close to the shed."

"That's what Linda believes, but I don't think he would shoot you."

"Why not?"

"Because you're a minister. I don't think he'd shoot a minister, particularly not the one that buried his father." He grinned.

Walter shook his head. "I wish I could be as sure about that as you are!"

The trooper slowed down a bit as they passed through Millerton Center. As they approached the Rivenburgs' driveway, Walter saw several police and sheriff's deputies' cars parked along the road. When they got out of the car Trooper Randall beckoned to him to follow. He guided him through the group of policemen to a trooper who seemed to be in charge. His name tag said "Lt. Hargreaves." "Sir, this is Reverend Macdonald. Chief Haines says Jack Rivenburg knows him and might respond to a request from him to give himself up."

Lt. Hargreaves cast a skeptical gaze in Walter's direction. "I'm not keen on the idea of a civilian getting involved"—he paused and reflected for a moment—"but nothing else is working. If he stays down and out of sight and talks on the bull horn, I don't think he'll be in any real danger." He turned to Trooper Randall, "Take Polanski and Davis with you and work your way up the driveway to that cruiser parked across it. Stay low and stay behind the cruiser when you get there. Take that bull horn, and one of these walkie-talkie handsets." He looked directly at Walter. "You be very careful, pastor. Do exactly what my officers tell you." He turned to the troopers, "Keep him under cover so that he doesn't get hurt. I'll hold you personally responsible if anything happens to him. Understand?"

"Yes, sir," they said.

"I'm going. too," Pete said, as they started to walk up the driveway. "He's my civilian."

"Suit yourself, Pete," the lieutenant responded. "Just don't get yourself shot."

Walter didn't say anything. His heart began to beat rapidly as he crouched down and followed the police officers up the driveway. When they were safely behind the parked patrol car Trooper Polanski handed him the bull horn. He aimed it toward the shed and pressed the button that said, "Talk." "Jack, this is Reverend Macdonald. I'm over here behind the police car. Please come out of the shed without your gun. Nobody will hurt you." His words reverberated several times. The only response came from Jack's dog, Prince, who stood in front of the shed door and barked.

He pressed the button and tried again. "Jack, this is Reverend Macdonald. Please come out of the shed without your gun. Nobody will hurt you."

Again no answer.

"This will never work," he said to the officers. "I'm sure he's scared to death. The bull horn just makes it worse. I know it sounds crazy and too risky, but I need to go in there and talk with him. If I can get five minutes alone with him, I'm sure everything will be fine." Slowly he began to stand up.

The officers grabbed him and pulled him down. "Are you crazy?"

Walter gently pushed them away from him. "I know the idea may seem foolish to you, but I know Jack. He may be upset, but he's a gentle man. Your way isn't working. I think my way will. As you said, Pete, 'He won't shoot a minister.'" He looked straight at them and said slowly, "I'm a minister." He sounded more confident than he felt.

The troopers looked at one another and then at him. "What about the dog?" Trooper Randall asked. "Do you want us to take him out, if he goes after you?"

"You won't have to," Walter said. "The dog and I know each other."

"Okay," Trooper Randall said, "but I don't like it."

Walter stood up slowly. He walked gingerly out from behind the cruiser. The dog barked and ran toward him. "Hi, Prince," he said, "it's all right; it's Walter." The dog stopped barking and wagged his tail. He patted the dog and asked, "Where's Jack?" The dog seemed to understand; he turned and walked toward the shed. Walter followed slowly, his heart pounding. Out here by himself he didn't feel as brave and confident as he had when he was sheltered behind the police car. He could hear the lieutenant's voice on the walkie-talkie, "Polanski, what the hell's going on back there?"

He shouted toward the shed, "Jack, this is Reverend Macdonald." He sounded composed but he could feel his legs shaking inside his pants. "If you look out the window, you can see me. Please throw your gun out the door. I'm alone. ('That's for sure,' he thought.) No one will hurt you."

No response.

"Jack, I know you're upset. I understand why. I want to come in there so you can tell me about it. Is that all right?"

No response.

"Oh, God," he prayed softly, "why did I agree to this? I wish I was John Wayne in a movie, but I'm not and I can't turn around now. Please don't let me down." He walked up to the door of the shed, took hold of the latch, opened the door slowly and stepped inside. The dog followed him. He pulled the door shut.

The officers behind the cruiser and in the woods waited two minutes. With guns drawn they rushed the shed and threw open the door. They found Walter inside holding Jack who was shaking and sobbing. The dog lay on the floor beside them. There wasn't a gun anywhere in sight.

"I think you can all leave now," Walter said quietly. "It's really all right. He told me he doesn't keep his shotgun in here anymore. Linda must have panicked when she called you. I doubt that you can arrest a man for being distraught. In a little while I'll go inside the trailer with him and see if I can help him and Linda work things out. I'll get him to give me a ride back to Schuylerkill Falls when we're done. Maybe you can get Butch Chichester to tow Randy's car?"

It was late afternoon when he arrived back at the manse. He walked into his study and called the rehab care center in Saratoga and told the receptionist he would need to postpone his visit to Miss Simpson. When he hung up the phone he collapsed into his reading chair. "Whew!" he said aloud, "that was very scary. I hope I never have to do that again."

The following morning after he ate breakfast he drove to Saratoga Springs. When he arrived at the center the receptionist greeted him with, "You're a brave man, pastor." He looked puzzled. She handed him the front page of the *Saratogian*. There was a picture of him taken from behind as he and Prince walked from the state police cruiser to the shed across the drive-way from Jack Rivenburg's trailer. In the foreground three police officers crouched behind the cruiser. The headline said, "Pastor Ends Stand-Off."

"Thank you," he said. "I had no idea it would be in the paper. I'm embarrassed. To be honest I was very relieved when everything came out all right. I sure didn't feel brave; I was scared to death."

When he entered Miss Simpson's room he found her sitting up in a chair. She smiled broadly. If he hadn't known about her stroke, he wouldn't have noticed the slight droop on the right side of her mouth. Very distinctly she said, "You're a holy fool!" Obviously she had seen the newspaper.

He blushed. "Thank you," he said. "I'm relieved that it ended well."

She wanted to say more, but didn't. There was an awkward silence. "Want to see me walk?" she asked.

"I sure do." he said.

"I'll need that contraption," she said, pointing to the walker. She had difficulty pronouncing "contraption," but he understood her. "You'll have to help me up." He noticed that she was speaking in contractions. Before her stroke she never used contractions. Now every phrase was a struggle; but she was determined. She would use whatever assistance she might need to talk and to walk.

He placed the walker in front of her and helped her stand. Together they walked slowly into the hall. As they made their way down the hall, Miss Simpson struggled some to bring her right leg along. He could see that she did not want sympathy. They walked side by side to the end of the hall and back to her room. She leaned on the walker and turned around in front of her chair. She looked at him standing in front of her. "Please go around and push the chair under me when I let go." He did and she collapsed into it. After she caught her breath they talked for a while. He could tell that the walk had tired her. Before he left he offered prayer and congratulated her on her graduation from a wheelchair to a walker.

Though he didn't mention the incident at the Rivenburgs during the worship service on Sunday, nearly everyone that he greeted as he stood at the door after the service did. Many of them paused and shook his hand more warmly that usual.

At three o'clock the high school young people met at the manse to go caroling. With the help of several parents who volunteered to be drivers, they visited all the old and shut-in church members and sang Christmas carols to them. By quarter of five the young people were sitting on the furniture and floor in the big manse parlor eating pizza. Now that they were alone with Walter, all they wanted to talk about was the incident at Jack Rivenburg's on Wednesday. What was going through his head as he walked toward that shed? Was he scared? Did he pray? Did he think God protected him because he is a believer? How did he convince the police officers to let him go to the shed on his own? Did Mr. Rivenburg really not have a gun, or was it hidden somewhere in the shed? He was very uncomfortable being the object of attention, but he responded honestly to their questions.

He had expected to be on his way to Petersons' Sunday before Christmas Christmas Open House by six, but it was nearly quarter to seven when he arrived at their farm bringing Eri and Melanie Chase in his VW. He had to leave his car along the road; the yard was parked full. The party had begun more than two hours before.

Eri led Walter and Melanie into the house through the back door. Becky hugged Walter warmly.

"I'm so glad you finally were able to get here. Please come inside and relax. The buffet is in the dining room. I just put out a stack of clean plates." She leaned toward him and whispered, "To help you relax I'll get you a cup of Erik's special recipe eggnog. Nobody will know which bowl I took it from, but when you taste it you'll know that it's high test. It's really good—and it's very potent!"

"Thanks," he said. "I do need some help to relax. Even my doctor tells me that!"

He made his way past groups of laughing, talking people. A ham stood at one end of the dining room table and a standing rib roast at the other. The buffet in between was sumptuous. Half-dozen different wines were available on a side table. In anticipation of this buffet he had eaten only one piece of pizza with the young people. Now he was sorry that he had eaten any. The sight and aromas from the food on Becky Peterson's buffet quickly restored his appetite; he filled his plate. Becky appeared with a cup of egg-nog. When he lifted it to his lips he could smell the rum before he tasted it.

As he moved from group to group throughout the large, crowded living room, everyone wanted to talk with him about the stand-off. He tried to shift the conversations to other subjects, but had little success. Each time he left a group he scanned the room; he didn't see Mary anywhere. He began to wonder if she hadn't been able to come to the party, or if she had already left and he had missed her.

He walked from the living room across the large center hall into the library. He was relieved to see her standing in the far corner of the room, next to Erik's desk talking with Jerry and Ellen Ward. For an instant he hadn't been sure it was her. Her black hair was pulled up, held in place by a sparkling rhinestone comb. She wore a white, long sleeved satin blouse, a black flared skirt, a wide shiny black belt and matching black satin heels. She looked at him and smiled as soon as she saw him walking toward her. When he was close to her she said, "I thought you weren't coming. I'm really happy to see you."

"So are we all, Walter," Jerry said. "Given what we saw on the front page of Thursday's paper, we're all grateful to see you. What you did took guts."

Walter felt his face coloring up. "Actually, I was scared. But I've come to know Jack pretty well and I honestly didn't think he would hurt anybody. I figured he was only upset, and fortunately it turned out that I was right. I hope I just did what any of you would have done in similar circumstances." He watched Mary smile and shake her head "no." He quickly shifted the focus of the conversation away from himself. "I didn't mean to interrupt, but it looks like you are having a friendly conversation, may I join?"

"It is friendly," Jerry said. "Mary and I never argue during the holidays. We always have a Christmas truce. Besides, Walter, you shouldn't take our occasional debates too seriously. Mary came about as close to being a daughter-in-law as she could get. She and our son, Jeff, were like brother and sister when they were growing up. We thought that for sure she would someday marry him. But it didn't happen. She went off to Barnard and Jeff went to Cornell, where he met his wife, Cindy. She was a student at Ithaca College."

"They have words to describe sisters that marry their brothers," Mary said under her breath.

Jerry shook his head in feigned disgust. "We were just talking about some good news we received last night: Jeff and Cindy are expecting our third grandchild."

"Maybe this one will be a girl!" Ellen said.

"That's wonderful news!" Walter said. "And don't worry if she has another boy; I had two brothers when I was growing up. It was great. Speaking of kids," he turned toward Jerry, "I've been trying to catch you for a moment to ask you for a principal's ruling. You probably know that Eri Peterson and I have been working on his pitching at the gym once or twice a week after school."

"I did know that," Jerry said. "It's good of you to help him. If you're concerned about jeopardizing his eligibility to play interscholastic baseball in the spring, just don't make your sessions a formal arrangement."

"I'll be careful to keep the arrangement informal," he responded. "But it's Melanie Chase, his girlfriend, that I'm concerned about. One day, a couple of weeks ago I was late arriving for our practice session, and there was Melanie complete with glove and face mask catching his pitches. I think he was trying to outdo her catching with his fast balls. But even when he threw as hard as he could, it didn't faze her. She caught them all. When I told her I was concerned, she said, 'I can catch anything he can pitch.'"

"My kind of girl!" Mary interjected.

"Right," Walter said. He looked back toward Jerry. "Anyway, it's easier to watch what he's doing if I don't have to worry about her catching his pitches. As I watched those fast balls streaking at Melanie, I got to thinking what one of them might do to her if it hit her in the chest. Do you think it would be all right to ask the baseball coach if we could use a chest protector? I'm really concerned about what would happen if one of his pitches hit one of her . . ." He looked at Mary.

"... chests," she said.

Jerry shook his head again. "She's been like that since she learned to talk, Walter. I'll speak to Coach Perelli. I'm sure he can find a padded protector for Melanie to use to protect her 'chests.'" He glanced out toward the hall. "There's Bob and Molly Hutchins; we haven't shared the good news about out grandchild-to-be with them. Would you please us excuse while we do?"

Walter nodded, "Please go right ahead. I'm sure they'll be delighted to hear it."

They walked away leaving Mary and Walter alone in the room. They were quiet for a moment. Then Mary said, "I was scared for you when I read the paper. You mean a lot to me."

He looked into her eyes; they were moist. So were his own. "You mean a lot to me, too." He paused, then said quietly, "I wish we were alone."

She smiled. "So do I." Her eyes were filled with longing.

"I've wanted to call you; I've missed you a lot. I think about you every day. Sometimes when I'm working on a sermon or driving to the hospital you're so much in my head that I can't concentrate on what I'm supposed to do. I promise myself I will call you, but every day there's so much more to do than I seem able to get done. And then another day is gone and I didn't get to calling you. The weeks have just flown by."

"For you, maybe, but not if you're the one waiting to hear!" She saw him flinch at her words; she smiled and tried to soften the impact. "You sound like a first-year teacher. It takes a while to sort out the difference between what is really your job and what everyone else wants to make your job. You'll figure it out."

"I hope so," he said, but he didn't sound convinced. He paused and became very sober, "I know this is the wrong place to talk about it"—he looked at the people talking and laughing out in the hall—"sometime we need to have a longer conversation. But right now it's important to me that you know there's more involved than learning how to manage the demands and the work load. Learning how to manage is only part of the problem.

"The way I *feel* is a bigger issue: I feel like I have to get *everything* done before I can take any time off. I have to figure out why I feel so driven, Mary. I can't let *anything* go. I didn't call you because by Thanksgiving week I was so worn down that I came down with a strep infection, and had to go see Erik and get some medication. He said I probably got sick because I was exhausted from working all the time. He even preached me a sermon on the hazards of overworking!" He watched her look at him sympathetically.

"So, pastor, did you take the doctor's sermon to heart?"

He smiled. "Nice imagery, English teacher." She laughed. "Seriously," he went on, "when I was home sick during Thanksgiving I had lots of time to think. I realized there's a voice inside of me that makes me finish all the work I see even when I'm exhausted. Even when I want to, I can't ignore it. I can't do what I want to do until I've done everything I ought to do. It's the same as it was when I was in high school and I'd come home from basketball practice and we'd have supper and I'd want to go out after supper and hang out with the guys for a little while and my mother would say, 'Finish all your homework first, Walter, then you can go out with your friends.'" He sighed and looked at her.

She waited to respond, then spoke quietly. "And you never did get to go out with your friends, did you?"

"No," he said, "I never did. I still don't." He paused and looked at her. "I need to do something about that."

She let him hear his own words before she responded. "Well, Walter, I have a suggestion that might help you get started. Want to hear it?" There was a twinkle in her eye.

"I do!"

"Next Sunday is Christmas; you could give yourself a Christmas present: you could go dancing with me sometime between Christmas and New Year's. You won't be finished with all your homework, but you could still do it; it would be a gift to both of us."

"I'll do it!" he said enthusiastically. He looked at her and smiled warmly. "You look like you're ready to go dancing right now."

"All I need is a partner. Do you know how to dance?"

"I did, once; it's been a while, but with a little coaching I'm sure I will remember."

She gave him a quizzical look. "When was the last time you asked someone out on a date, Walter? You were at the church in Rahway for almost three years. Didn't you go out with anyone during those years?"

"I tried it a couple of times, but when the news got around that I had gone out with someone, the young single women in the congregation and their mothers descended on me. Every unmarried woman between 20 and 40 thought she was just right for me. Sometimes it was frightening. Some of them would even have—well, you know what I mean—if I had been willing."

"Well, did you?"

"Did I what?"

"Did you 'you-know-what-I-mean' with any of them?"

"No!" he said emphatically. "That would have been unethical. Doing it with a woman you are not married to is considered immoral, but doing it with a woman who is a member of your congregation and, therefore, under your care is unethical."

She sighed. "That gives me some comfort. At least I won't ever tempt you to do something unethical."

He shook his head. "I can't believe we are having this conversation in a public place."

She gave him a sly grin. "You worry too much, Walter. There's nobody else in the room. Anyone that may be looking at us from the hallway is probably thinking we're talking about poetry or theology, or that you're counseling me about my difficulties with my principal." She noticed some guests going through the hall toward the front door with their coats on. "Well, it's after eight, and people are starting to leave. Are you going to call me?"

"Yes," he said emphatically, "I am."

"I'll keep my date book right by the telephone."

He looked into the hallway. "Have you noticed how people leave us alone when we're together somewhere? But I have a feeling that they watch us. I'm sure I've seen Bob Hutchins looking at us several times in the last half hour."

"Tell you what, Walter; I'll come to one of your services. Then they'll think you're gaining a convert. That will squelch any gossip for a while."

They both laughed.

"You're something else," he said. "Would you like me to walk you to your car?"

"I would!" she said.

After Bob and Molly Hutchins said good night to Jerry and Ellen Ward they paused as they passed the door leading from the hall into library. "That Mary Kerrigan has some nerve toying with our minister," Bob said quietly.

Molly looked at Mary and Walter talking and laughing together. "Bob," she said, "they're not just toying with each other."

$$7$$

Fortunately, the big, all-day snow storm arrived on December 23. Actually, Walter was glad for the storm; the "snow day" on Friday gave him an opportunity to polish his Christmas Eve and Christmas Day sermons. With Christmas Eve on Saturday and Christmas on Sunday he would have to produce two excellent sermons. He worried all week that some pastoral emergency would take him away from his desk before they were finished.

By early in the day on December 24 the state and town trucks had cleared the snow from all the highways and village streets, and by late afternoon Butch Chichester had plowed out the manse driveway and the church parking lot. Walter ate an early supper Christmas Eve and took a brief nap. He walked over to the church at quarter past ten. When he opened the front door he was surprised to hear Smitty playing the fugue from Bach's Little Prelude and Fugue in G Major with great animation. He entered quietly and sat in a back pew to listen. The neo-classical E. M. Skinner organ reverberated throughout the sanctuary. He listened with delight. When Smitty finished the fugue he stood up and applauded.

Smitty slid off the organ bench and stood up next to the console. "Thank God for you," he said. "You're the only one here who knows enough about music to appreciate any of the Bach I play. But what can I expect in an out-of-the-way place like this? The truth is—and don't you tell the session—I'd play for nothing just to hear the gorgeous sound of those Skinner pipes."

"I love that little G major; it's the same piece you played the day I preached my candidating sermon," Walter said as he walked toward the front of the sanctuary, "and you play it so well. Are you going to play it before the service tonight?"

"I am," Smitty said. He almost stumbled as he stepped down from the choir loft. When Walter was close enough to him to catch the smell of Smitty's breath, he understood why. He had been drinking.

"Are you all right, Smitty?" he asked.

"Oh, yeah," Smitty said, "just feeling the effects of my usual end-of-the-day cheer. But I guarantee it won't interfere with my playing." He paused and grinned. "In fact, I'm so sure that it won't that I'll make you a little wager. When I play the Bach piece tonight I will add something Christmassy. I'll sneak in four measures of 'Mary Had a Little Lamb.' Seems an appropriate addition for Christmas Eve, don't you think? And to prove my point that you are the only one with enough sophistication to listen perceptively to my playing, I'll bet you a steak dinner that no one besides you notices the insertion. You watch and if you catch anybody smiling, you win! Are you in?"

Walter laughed. "You're really sure nobody will catch you, aren't you?"

"Sure enough to bet a steak dinner!"

"Well, I bet somebody will. I'm in!" Smitty grinned.

Two older women opened the door leading in from the vestibule at the back of the sanctuary. Walter looked at his watch; it was ten-thirty. "People are arriving; I need to get ready for the service."

"Me, too," Smitty said. "Just remember when you shake hands at the door afterward: if anyone mentions the inserted four bars from the ditty, you win. If no one mentions them, you owe me a steak dinner. It'll be a true test; the place will be mobbed tonight." Then he whispered, "Now I gotta visit the little boys' room or I'll never make it through the service."

At ten minutes before eleven Walter put on his robe, walked into the sanctuary through the door opposite the parlor, up the chancel stairs to his chair behind the pulpit and sat down. Smitty was right; the sanctuary was nearly full. As he looked up and down the rows he recognized most of the faces, but there were a lot of people he had never seen before at a worship service. One of them was a very familiar face: half-way back on the pulpit side Mary Kerrigan sat next to Ellen and Jerry Ward.

The opening notes of Bach's Little G Major Prelude interrupted his reverie. As he listened he had to agree that Smitty was right: the Christmas cheer he had consumed did not compromise his playing. He had never heard the piece played with more vitality. He had almost forgotten about the bet when he heard the unmistakable opening phrases of "Mary Had a Little Lamb" added into the fuguetta on the pedals. The addition was so

Bach-like that he almost missed it. He scanned the congregation. No one was smiling. He realized he was going to have to buy a steak dinner.

After the congregation sang "O Little Town of Bethlehem" he stood behind the pulpit. He read the King James Version of the first eighteen verses of chapter one of John's gospel from the hundred-year-old pulpit Bible. He closed the Bible and looked out at the congregation. He spoke slowly and deliberately.

> No doubt some of you are thinking, "That was a strange Scripture passage to read on Christmas Eve." But I chose it purposefully as the basis for my Christmas Eve meditation. A meditation which, by the way, can be very brief because this night is itself a sermon— and also because I know that some of you still have lots to do before tomorrow morning. There are times when being a bachelor has its advantages.
>
> (Laughter rippled through the sanctuary.)
>
> My meditation is entitled "Christmas for Adults." I think we can have some adult reflections on Christmas because at this hour most of our children are snug in their beds, or curled up asleep next to you.
>
> The text for my meditation is John 1:14: "And the Word was made flesh, and dwelt among us, and we beheld his glory, the glory as of the only begotten of the Father, full of grace and truth." The message in this text is the foundation of our faith. In Jesus, whose birth we recall this night, God speaks definitively. What distinguishes us as Christians is a fact: We have found what everyone is looking for. We have no need to search for God. We have found God. Or, to be more precise, God has found us. We have something startling to report: Jesus. As Philip said when Nathaniel asked him, "Can anything good come out of Nazareth?" We say to each other and to the world, "Come and see!"
>
> We recall an event tonight, not simply a message. God's word became flesh in Jesus. John recalls God's power of creation in the opening lines of his gospel. One could translate the first verse, "In the beginning God was speaking" and the fourteenth verse "the speaking was made flesh." Or, to modernize it, "God's speaking is embodied in Jesus."
>
> That incarnation, the speaking made flesh, is an astounding fact! We can actually see God in Jesus. If God could be personified, Jesus is God personified. In Jesus God humbles himself and becomes accessible to us. The Greek word for "revelation" means that something is conveyed so intimately to us that we can touch it. *God* is conveyed to us in Jesus. This baby that Mary holds in her

hands is God embodied. We no longer have to wonder what God is like. Now we know.

So, we sing with the angels; we stand amazed with the shepherds; we are humbled like the Wise Men. We testify to a cosmic event. From beyond the reality we know, God has come to us. Not that a long search has led us to God, but that God has arrived to us—and to the world. Come and see! Amen.

When he finished speaking he stood quietly with his head bowed. For at least a minute there was no sound in the sanctuary. He called the congregation to prayer and offered a prayer of thanksgiving. The congregation sang "Silent Night." He offered the benediction and walked to the back of the sanctuary into the vestibule where he greeted worshippers at the outside door.

When he had greeted everyone, he glanced through the door that led from the vestibule into the sanctuary. Smitty had just finished the postlude. Mary was the only worshipper who had remained in her seat and listened to it. She stood up and walked to the organ console. When he stepped out from behind the organ console and turned around she said, "That was lovely, Mr. Smith. Thank you." Smitty walked with her down the aisle to the outside door in the vestibule. She smiled as they approached Walter. She reached out to him and placed her hand in his. It felt warm. "And the meditation was profound, Reverend Macdonald." She squeezed his hand slightly and said, "Merry Christmas."

Smitty and Walter watched Mary walk down the walkway to the street. "She's beautiful, *your* Mary," Smitty said. Walter looked straight at him, trying not to appear surprised by his statement. He shut the door to the outside and Smitty went on: "My Mary died twenty-five years ago tonight. Mary Beatrice Gillespie Smith. What's left of her lies in the cemetery. Second turn off the main road that goes down the center of the cemetery, the fourth gravestone on the right.

" 'Prayer changes things,' so they claim. Old Archie Morton! Everybody still calls him Dr. Morton—how he loved that DD the college gave him—but I worked with him long before he got it, so he'll always be just plain 'Archie' to me. He really believed that prayer can change things. Over and over in his sermons he'd say 'Prayer changes things, prayer changes things.' Of course he could believe it did; he still had Eileen—that was his wife's name. She outlived him."

He paused and sighed. "Nobody noticed 'Mary Had a Little Lamb,' did they?" Walter shook his head. "You owe me a steak dinner, Walter! If my Mary had been here to hear the little lamb I put into Bach, we would have laughed all the way home. But she's not. My God, how I miss her!"

He leaned against the door into the sanctuary. "I get through the days; I'm busy at the store—and here on Sunday mornings. But the nights are terrible. I don't sleep. I tried following Archie Morton's advice. He just kept saying, 'Prayer changes things'—like a broken record. But, Walter, it doesn't—not the things that matter. The real hurts hang on—no matter what you do."

"I know," Walter said quietly. "I know they do."

"I tried some of Dr. Peterson's pills. I even tried a shrink. Nothing worked. The pain didn't go away. So, I took to dulling it." He reached into his inside jacket pocket and took out a silver flask. He gestured with it toward Walter. "This is my companion. I fill it with Black Velvet." He shook it. Walter could hear the liquid sloshing back and forth inside it. "No matter how much I prayed, prayer never gave me solace. I know now that it never will." He raised the flask up toward the ceiling and for a moment fixed his eyes on it reverently. "So, I get by with this. It keeps me warm." He lowered the flask, unscrewed the top, raised it to his lips and took a swallow. He replaced the cap and put the flask back into his pocket. "Amen," he said. He opened the door and stepped out into the cold night. He paused on the landing and looked back. "You're lucky, Walter. You still have a chance to have a Mary in your life. Don't let it go by." He looked at Walter intently.

For a moment Walter couldn't decide what to say. Then he nodded and said, "Thanks, Smitty." The two of them stood and looked at each other. "Smitty, I think there's much more to be had from prayer than you've found. Sometimes it takes a while for God to get through."

Smitty tilted his head and eyed him. "Right! I'll call you sometime."

The wind whistled outside the door. "Do you want me to give you a ride home?"

Smitty hesitated for a moment like he wasn't sure. "Nah," he said finally, "I'll be all right. It's only a short walk. And, as you can see, I need the air." He turned up his collar, tucked his hands into his coat pocket and shuffled down the walkway toward the street.

Walter stood and watched him walk to the end of the sidewalk and along Church Street until he disappeared behind a snow bank. His heart hurt for him. He closed the outside door, walked back into the sanctuary, reached out to the switches on the inside wall, and switched out the lights. He turned and looked at the outside door on the far side of the vestibule. "I'll call her."

Monday after lunch he drove east to Albany. Though he was very tired after doing two Christmas services and deserved the day as a day off, he decided he would make a brief visit to Miss Simpson. When they heard she could leave the nursing home if someone could be with her at home, her nephew Jim Simpson and his wife, Ellen, had insisted that she stay with them until she was able to go to her own home. He easily located their spacious home on South Manning Boulevard. He found Miss Simpson in good spirits. He apologized for visiting only briefly, "Willie will be getting hungry and thirsty by now so I need to go along," he explained. Miss Simpson was obviously grateful that he was caring for Willie at the manse. The cold December wind blew hard against him as he walked to his car. He arrived home just after one o'clock.

After he finished feeding Willie, he walked deliberately into his study, sat down at his desk and dialed Mary Kerrigan's telephone number. He was delighted and somewhat anxious when she answered.

"This is Walter," he said. "Did you have a nice Christmas Day?"

"I did," she said. "I drove to Saratoga and spent it with my folks. We had lots of fun conversation. And I ate too much! You? Did you go to Schenectady?"

"I did," he said. "My brother, Eddie, and his family were there. My mother overfed us, as usual, but it was delicious." He paused. She didn't say anything. "The reason I'm calling is I wonder if you're busy Friday night?"

"No, I'm not."

"Would you like to go out with me?"

"I would love to go out with you, Walter. What do you have in mind?"

"Well, you looked like someone who wanted to go dancing when I saw you at Erik and Becky's Christmas party. I would like to take you dancing, but I don't know of any place that offers the kind of ballroom dancing I know how to do."

"I do."

"Where?"

"The Gideon in Saratoga. They have dinner and dancing and a great house orchestra that plays from six-thirty to ten-thirty every Friday and Saturday night."

"The *Gideon*! I'd love to go dancing with you at the Gideon. But dinner and dancing at the Gideon is pretty steep. I hear the cover is ten dollars a person and the dinners are at least that, if not more."

"I didn't say 'dinner' and dancing at the Gideon, I just said 'dancing.' Can you afford two dollars to go dancing at the Gideon?"

"Of course, but how can we go dancing at the Gideon for two dollars?"

"Walter, I lived with poor students in New York City for almost six years. They showed me how to go dancing in the best places for two dollars. Have faith in me. I know how to do it. And afterward there's a neighborhood Italian restaurant in Saratoga where we can both eat dinner and even have a glass of wine for less than ten dollars. Is that within your budget?" She paused when he didn't respond quickly. "I will even buy my own dinner, if you need me to."

"Oh no, that won't be necessary," he answered hurriedly. "All of that is well within my budget. I just can't believe we can go dancing at the Gideon for two dollars."

"Walter, have faith in me. Can you have faith in me? Blind faith?"

He sighed. "Mary, you challenge my believability. But I trust you."

"Good," she said. "I love the suit you wore when you preached on Christmas Eve but maybe you could wear a livelier tie? In addition to your top coat, bring the heavy wool jacket you wear when you go walking in the winter. Be sure that you have a dollar bill and four quarters. Pick me up at twenty past five. We need to be sure we can arrive at the Gideon by six-fifteen."

"I'll dress appropriately, bring the prescribed money and be in front of your house at five-twenty sharp. But why do I need the extra jacket?"

"So you can dress appropriately for dinner."

"Okay, Mary," he said. "No more questions. I'll just have faith."

"Good. I'll look forward to seeing you at five-twenty on Friday."

During the rest of this week between the Christmas and New Year's holidays his workload was light. He wrote his sermon and made some visits to sick parishioners. But more than the usual thoughts of Mary Kerrigan distracted him as he worked. Though he had promised to "have faith," he kept wondering how he and she were going to go dancing in a top-of-the-line restaurant for two dollars. What if her plan didn't work? It would be embarrassing not to be able to pay the cover and have to leave the restaurant.

He was excited and relieved when Friday afternoon finally arrived. The weather was clear and cold—there would be no snow to make their drive to Saratoga Springs difficult. He arrived in front of Mary's house at exactly five-twenty. When he walked up onto the porch and rang her bell, she was already coming down the inside stairs. He was startled when she opened the door; she was wearing a fur coat and boots and carrying a pair of shoes and a well-worn everyday winter jacket with a hood. She saw the puzzled look on his face as she stepped out onto the porch. "The jacket is for later; the fur coat is my mother's. She let me borrow it for tonight. Seems appropriate for a dancing date at the Gideon, don't you think?"

"Definitely," he said. "You're beautiful; both you and the coat. I love how sophisticated you look with your hair up."

"Thank you. Now can we go get in the car? Standing here on the porch in the cold wind, even with this fur coat on, I'm freezing." She took his arm, and he walked with her to his VW, and held the door while she got in. She placed her shoes on the floor in front of her seat. He took her extra coat from her.

As he turned to walk around the car he noticed a drape in one of the first floor windows had been drawn aside. When he looked at the window, it was quickly released. He walked around the car, opened the door, pushed the seatback forward, and laid her jacket on top of his. He pushed the seat-back upright, got in, shut the door and started the car. As they pulled away from the curb Mary said, "Did you notice the drawn drape?"

"I did."

"That's my landlady and self-appointed chaperone, Mrs. Wiley. She'll spend the entire evening wondering where we are going, what we are doing, and waiting to see what time you bring me home. She'll be disappointed when we return at a reasonable hour, and you don't stay over."

"I'd never even considered that you would ask me to stay over."

"I know, Walter; you're so proper. But I wouldn't have anyway—not on our first date."

He smiled, and shook his head.

"The fact that you have a Volkswagen is the other reason I asked to borrow this fur coat. I've ridden in VWs in the winter before. They don't have a heater. What the company calls a heater is a poor excuse for the real thing!"

"Good planning."

They had light and fun conversation all the way to Saratoga Springs. The time passed quickly. It was exactly six-fifteen as they drove up the long drive leading to the Gideon Hotel. Mary pointed to the little sticker pasted on the small window on the right-hand door of his car. "That's the sticker that entitles you to park in the doctor's lot at the hospital, isn't it?"

"Yes, it is."

"Good. Just drive right up under the portico, so the doorman can open the door for me."

"Really? Drive right up to the front door?"

"Yes!"

"You're really sure this will work?"

"Walter! I know how to do it!"

He stopped the car under the portico. The doorman opened her door. "Good evening, madam, and whom do I have the pleasure of welcoming?" She gestured toward Walter who was walking around the front of the car. "Doctor Macdonald," she said. "He has just come from work so we brought the small car. It is so much easier for him to use when he is making calls. He's on call tonight so please keep the car accessible."

"Of course," the doorman said. He assisted Mary out of the car. She handed her shoes to Walter. Turning to face Walter, the doorman said, "I will have the boy place your car where we can retrieve it quickly, in the unfortunate event that you have to leave."

"Thank you," Walter said. "And you are?"

"Peter," the doorman replied.

"Thank you, Peter."

"Thank *you*, Doctor Macdonald. We will take good care of your ve-hicle." He opened the hotel door and gestured them inside. "The coat check room is down the hall, to the left."

"Thank you, Peter. That's good of you." Mary squeezed his arm. As they walked through the entrance door she looked at him and smiled. "You're getting it," she whispered.

When he helped her off with her coat he noticed that she was dressed in the same black skirt and white blouse she had worn to the Petersons Christmas open house. She sat on a bench near the coat check room window and changed from her boots into her shoes. He stared at her feet as she slipped them into her shoes. After they checked their coats and Mary's boots, he stood back and looked at her. "You are incredibly beautiful," he said.

"Why, thank you, Doctor," she replied.

"Now what do we do?" he whispered as they walked away from the check room.

"You go to the men's room and I go to the ladies' room. You will finish before I do. You can sit on the bench over there and wait for me. I will come out at exactly six-thirty when the music starts."

"And then?"

"We dance!"

He was in and out of the men's room very quickly. He sat on the bench and waited. Promptly at 6:30 the music began and Mary appeared. "Shall we dance?"

"I would love to dance with you."

"Walk straight into the dining room with me and straight on to the dance floor. Smile when you pass the maître d'. Don't say anything to him, just keep walking."

He followed her directions as they entered the dining room. The maître d' started to speak to them and then simply bowed when Walter smiled at him as they walked to the dance floor. They danced like they had danced together for years. She was amazing. She followed his every move. People gave them space. The orchestra played to them—the tall man in the black suit and his beautiful partner dressed in black and white. Every dance he had learned years ago came back to him—the two-step, the Lindy, even the samba and the Viennese Waltz. "You're the king of the dance," she whispered as he whirled her around to the music of Johann Strauss.

After playing continuously for an hour the orchestra stopped to take a break. "We have to leave now," Mary whispered. She took his arm and guided him from the dance floor. She said, "They will think I need to use the ladies' room," and smiled as they walked past the maître d' and out of the dining room. As they approached the coat check window she whispered, "Here's where you spend fifty cents." He retrieved the coat check ticket from his pocket and handed it to the young woman behind the counter.

"You have to leave so soon?" she asked.

"Oh, we do!" Mary sighed. "The doctor has a call."

"I'm so sorry," the young woman replied as he handed her the claim ticket and dropped two quarters into a bowl labeled "Thank you."

As they walked to the front door he whispered, "The dollar goes to Peter, the doorman, and fifty cents goes to the boy that parks cars, right?"

"Right," Mary said as they approached Peter. "Unfortunately, we do have to go, Peter. Please ask the young man to bring our car to the door."

"Of course," Peter said, "I'm so sorry you have to leave early." He chose a set of keys hanging on one of the hooks in a small cupboard and gave them to a young man sitting on a bench near the door. "Charles, please bring Dr. Macdonald's black Volkswagen to the door."

In less than a minute his car was under the portico outside the front door. The young man got out and closed the door on the driver's side as Peter opened the door for Mary on the passenger's side. As the young man walked past him Walter gave him two quarters.

"Thank you, Doctor," the young man said.

When Peter closed Mary's door he turned to Walter and Walter gave him a dollar. "Thank you, Doctor," he said as he saluted. "Please come again when you can stay to enjoy the entire evening."

"Thank you, Peter," he said. "I shall look forward to the opportunity." He walked around the car. Peter followed him and opened the door for him. He got into the car and Peter closed the door. They drove out from under the portico and down the long driveway. When they were almost to the pillars that marked the entrance Mary shouted, "Stop the car!"

He did. "What's wrong?" he asked looking alarmed.

She turned toward him, threw her arms around his neck and kissed him exuberantly. "You were wonderful!" she said. "You couldn't have done it better, if we had rehearsed it!"

He looked across at her and grinned and nodded his head. "You're the one who pulled it off, Mary Kerrigan; if I had known ahead of time what we were going to do, I couldn't have let myself do it. But I did do it, didn't I?" His grin broadened into a big smile. "We really wowed them; we really did. It was a little sinful, but it was such fun!" He began to laugh. He leaned back in his seat and abandoned himself to laughing.

She watched him laugh. When his laughter subsided she said, "I bring out the best in you, don't I, Doctor Macdonald?"

"Yes, you do, Miss Kerrigan, you really do." His face took on a sober look. "But I'll still have to do penance." She looked puzzled. "You'll like my penance. I'll save up my money and bring you back here another night so we can have dinner and dance the entire evening, and I'll leave them an extra-large tip to make up for what we did tonight." He grinned for a moment, then sat quietly and looked at her. She looked at him and waited. He leaned across his seat toward her and placed his hand behind her head and drew her to him and kissed her gently. When their lips separated he looked into her eyes. "You're the one who's wonderful."

For a moment neither of them spoke. Headlights from an approaching car flashed through the rear window of the Volkswagen. "I hate to break the mood," she said, "but there's a car coming up behind us. Besides, after all the dancing I bet you're hungry; I know I'm starved. Let's go to Leonardo's."

"Just show me the way!"

She gave him step-by-step directions through several side streets until they were opposite a small restaurant the sign identified as Leonardo's. It was almost eight o'clock when they arrived. When they parked across from the restaurant light from a street lamp shined on his face. "Before we go in I'll need your handkerchief to wipe the lipstick off your face," Mary said. He reached into his pocket and took out a clean handkerchief and handed it to her.

As she wiped his face he looked at her lovingly, "You take good care of me." She smiled.

When he had passed her inspection satisfactorily she said, "Now we change costumes; we don't want to appear uppity here. When we get out, I'll swap my fur coat for my jacket; and you can take off your top coat and suit coat and put on your walking jacket. We need to do it fast because it's very cold and windy out there. And please lock the car so no one steals my mother's fur coat."

They changed clothes quickly, walked across the street and entered Leonardo's. A distinguished-looking man with black hair and a black mustache greeted them. "Ah, Miss Mary Kerrigan, so nice to see you again!"

"Thank you, Leonardo," she said as she turned toward Walter. "This is Mr. Macdonald."

"I am pleased to meet you, Mr. Macdonald," Leonardo said. He looked toward Mary. "I have saved your favorite table in the alcove."

"Thank you, Leonardo. You are always so considerate." He smiled as he led them to their table and handed them two menus. "Angela will have the pleasure of serving you this evening."

After Leonardo walked away, Walter said, "You made a reservation, didn't you?"

"Yes, I did. They know me here. I have come here with my parents since I was a little girl. The food is wonderful and the prices are very reasonable."

She was right. He ordered spaghetti with homemade Italian meatballs; she ordered fettuccini Alfredo. They each had a glass of wine—and the bill was only $10.40. They lingered and talked over coffee until nine-thirty. He placed a ten dollar bill and forty cents in change on the little tray Angela brought when she refilled their coffee cups. He left a two dollar tip on the table for Angela. When Leonardo held the door for them he said, "Thank you for a wonderful dinner, Leonardo."

"Grazie, Signor Macdonald! I am so pleased to make your acquaintance. Please bring your lovely lady back to my *ristorante* soon."

Mary smiled, "He shall, Leonardo—very soon!"

When they stepped outside a brisk northwest wind blew light falling snow into their faces. They crossed quickly and got into his car. Mary directed him through several side streets and on to Route 29.

As they drove out of the city toward Schuylerkill Falls, she said, "Interesting little addition Smitty put into the Bach piece on Christmas Eve." She sang: " 'Mary had a little lamb, little lamb, little lamb . . . .' He wove it in amazingly well. Did anyone say anything?"

"No, and the fact that no one did is going to cost me a steak dinner." He told her about the bet.

"Such a sensitive and sad man. He gave his whole heart to Bea Gillespie and she took it to the grave with her. She was the love of his life. He's never recovered from losing her. Everyone knows he drinks, but he manages to get along nonetheless. I watched him look at us together Christmas Eve. I think he knows we like each other."

"He does," Walter said. "And he's more than okay with it. He wants us to be together."

Nearly twenty minutes passed before the engine produced enough heat to make it comfortable inside the Volkswagen. Mary took off her gloves. "Where did you learn to dance?" she asked. "You are an amazingly good dancer."

"In Mrs. Flint's dancing class at the Van Curler Hotel in Schenectady. When I was in eighth grade my mother made me go every Saturday morning. It was embarrassing. I had to wear a suit and white gloves, and like all the other boys I was shorter than most of the girls. But I did learn to dance. And for me it's like a sport: once my body learns the moves it never forgets them. How about you? You follow me like we have danced together for years. You obviously have danced a lot. Who did you go dancing with in New York?"

"Mostly with the boyfriend that dumped me for God." She reached up and took the combs out of her hair. As it fell down on her shoulders she shook her head.

Walter took his eyes off the road and looked at her. "I like that," he said. When he looked back to the road, he had to yank the steering wheel to bring the car back into the lane.

"That I got dumped for God?"

"No," he laughed. "I like how you look when your hair is free like that."

"Thank you. I'll wear it that way when I'm alone with you."

They were quiet for a few minutes. "If you don't think I'm out of line to ask, was your relationship with the pre-priest serious?"

She sighed. "Yes, it was. But it's been six years. I'm over him."

"No lingering tears?"

She laughed. "You really are being bold! You cried the first time we had dinner together—this time you expect me to cry. But I won't; I've shed all the tears I'm going to over the dear departed Darryl."

He persisted. "The fact that you shed tears suggests that you really liked him."

"Enough to go dancing with him."

"Lots of times?"

"Yes, lots of times. He was a good dancer."

"As good as I am?"

"No. You're better."

He paused to muster up some courage. Then he said, "Remember the conversation we had at Erik and Becky's Christmas party?"

"Yes, I remember."

"Do you remember what you asked me about the women I dated when I was in Rahway?"

"I remember."

"Well, did you ever do 'you know what' with Darryl?"

"Yes, lots of times."

He wrinkled his forehead. "Lots of times?"

"Yes, lots of times. After twenty I quit counting."

They drove along not saying anything for a while. As they entered Schuylerkill Falls he said, "Somehow, I don't believe you."

"Then, why did you ask?"

"I'm not sure," he said. "For some reason, it matters to me."

"I'm glad," she said. After a pause she added, "I was lying. We came as close as you can get, but we never actually did it."

The lights of an on-coming car lit up their faces, but he was afraid to look at her. He twitched in his seat. For several minutes neither of them said anything. As they turned on to her street, he said, "Mary, before we go any further we have to have a serious conversation."

"I agree. Your place or mine?"

He shut off the engine. They noticed the downstairs drape being pulled aside. "Mine," he said. "But we better take a bit of a break, or the whole village will think I'm putting the rush on you. In between I'll call you." He reached for the handle to open his door.

"Does it matter what they think?" Her question stopped him. He turned and saw her face lit by the streetlight in front of the house next door to hers. Her eyes were searching him.

"If you're their minister, it does."

"I see." She didn't seem convinced.

He knew she didn't understand why, but he didn't say anything more. He got out and walked around the car and opened her door. He walked with her up the walkway and on to the porch. She opened the door that led to her upstairs apartment and beckoned to him to step inside on to the landing. She closed the door.

"I've never had more fun dancing than I did tonight with you. Never."

"We really wowed them, didn't we? And you really wowed me. You're lovely."

She laid her mother's fur coat on the stairs, stepped up on to the first step and turned toward him. She placed her hands on either side of his head, opened her mouth slightly and drew his mouth to hers. He wrapped his arms around her tightly. They held each other for a long time. When their lips separated she said softly, "Next time I would like more of that."

"So would I," he whispered, "so would I." They slowly let go of each other. He stood for a while and looked at her. Finally he said, "I guess I have to go. This is our first date." She smiled. He turned and opened the door and stepped outside and walked to his car.

As he drove home the sweet taste of her lingered in his mouth and images of their evening together strolled across his mind. He was different with Mary than he was with anyone else—very different. He smiled as he watched himself whirling her around the dance floor at the Gideon. He nodded and spoke softly. "I envy the man I am when I'm with her—and I'm a little frightened of him. Of what might happen when I'm him."

He drove into the manse driveway, shut off the car's engine and sat in the quiet. He could feel the looming presence of the church next door. "She and I do need to have a serious conversation." He stepped out and walked around the back of the car. He stood in the driveway and gazed for a while at the moonlight shining on the church steeple, and then looked down at the street that led back to Mary's house. He took a deep breath and let it out slowly, "I want her in my life, but she," he looked up at the church, "and you are so far apart."

Mary hung her mother's fur coat on a wooden hanger in her bedroom closet. She sat on the edge of her bed and recalled the fun evening—and then the long conversation with Walter on Halloween. She looked at her face reflected in the mirror over her dresser and sighed. "What he believes controls him; it's taken over his life." She gazed at the two pillows on her bed and recalled the look in his eyes when they danced. "I think there are moments when he really wishes he could be free. But maybe wishing is as far as he can go?"

———————— 8 ————————

JANUARY BROUGHT RELENTLESS COLD: the temperature fell to between ten and twenty below zero night after night. Though the image seemed contradictory (because he was usually associated with heat), Walter decided that the devil must be managing the weather. The oil burner ran around the clock and still the temperature inside the manse failed to rise above sixty degrees.

On one particularly bitter night a gusty northwest wind rattled the corner windows in Walter's bedroom so loudly that he couldn't sleep. At six o'clock he gave up the attempt and got up. Even when he ran the portable electric heater in the bathroom for fifteen minutes he still wasn't able to warm the room enough to make his shower comfortable. After he dressed and went downstairs he could see why: the temperature on the thermometer outside his kitchen window read minus twenty-three. "Twenty-three below zero!" he said out loud. "No wonder it feels cold in here." He walked into the parlor and checked the thermometer on the furnace thermostat. It read fifty-eight—and the furnace was running full speed. He went back upstairs and closed the heat registers and doors to all the bedrooms he didn't use. When he passed the door to the attic he decided to see how much insulation was in the attic floor. He opened the attic door and stepped up into the cold far enough to see the open floor joists. There wasn't any insulation. He quickly stepped back down into the hall and shut the attic door. He walked downstairs and into his study and wrote: "Call Joe Pritchard before session meeting; suggest work party to insulate manse attic, add storm windows next summer" on the to-do list clipped to the calendar on his desk.

The cold brought colds. Older church members were particularly hard hit by the flu; several had to be hospitalized—which meant extra trips to the hospital in Saratoga Springs. January was also annual meeting month.

There also were extra committee meetings to attend to prepare for the congregation's annual business meeting held each year on the last Sunday in January.

In between all the pastoral calls and extra meetings he tried to reach Mary on the telephone. He was finally able to catch her late in the afternoon on the third Friday of the month. When she answered he said, "This is 'Doctor' Macdonald."

"I'm so happy to hear your voice, 'Doctor' Macdonald. Didn't we have wonderful fun dancing at the Gideon!"

"We did," he said. "We really did."

"Have you been frustrated trying to reach me?" she asked.

"A little," he admitted.

"I'm sorry," she said. "I haven't been home much. The senior class play this year is 'Our Town' and I'm directing it. So I'm at rehearsals every weekday evening."

"That explains why I haven't been able to get you on the phone. I've been trying to get you so we can schedule dinner because the last time we were together we said we would have dinner and a serious conversation 'soon.'"

"I'd love to do that soon. But with all those rehearsals plus classes to prepare for and papers to read I'm swamped with work. That's going to be true right through the week of February fifth. The performances are Thursday, Friday, and Saturday nights of that week. I hope you can come to one of them. Several young people from your church are in the play."

"I definitely will come to a performance," Walter said, "provided you agree to come to another one of my performances some time."

She laughed. "I do want to do that, but it can't be right away. The other reason you haven't been able to get hold of me is that my father has been quite sick. I've been in Saratoga on the weekends. He caught the flu that's going around and developed bronchitis, then pneumonia. Actually he was in the hospital for several days. Fortunately, he's on sabbatical this term, so he doesn't have to worry about getting back into the classroom at the college. But he's a bear to take care of. So, I've been going home on the weekends to give my mother some relief."

"If I had known your father was in the hospital, I would have visited him; I'm there two or three times a week."

"That's a kind thought, but you need to know that my father is as openly irreverent in conversation as his favorite Victorian author, Thomas

Hardy, was in his poetry. Just one comment about trusting in God and he would have gone into a coughing fit arguing with you about how you can trust something that doesn't exist! But no matter; he's getting better now."

"It sounds like the first time you and I can get together is the end of the week after the play. That would be Friday, February seventeenth. Would you like to come here for dinner that evening?"

"That would be wonderful! The next week is a school vacation week, so I'll be out from under the pressure of work and ready for a fling!"

"Great!" Walter said. "We'll fling together. I'll make you a great Italian dinner and we can mix fun with that serious conversation we said we would have the next time we got together. I have to go to Albany on Tuesday the fourteenth for a Presbytery committee meeting. I can pick up everything for the dinner then."

"I can hardly wait to fling with you!" She paused. "I really wish I could talk more, but I need to get off the phone now. I have to head to Saratoga. My mother is expecting me there for supper."

"I really was hoping to see you sooner," Walter said. "I miss you."

"I miss you, too. Thanks for calling back until you reached me. I just drew a big heart around February seventeen on my wall calendar. I'm sure we can find something appropriate to do to celebrate Valentine's Day that night." He could hear her laughing. When she stopped laughing an apologetic tone came into her voice. "I'm sorry but I really have to run now. I have to say good-bye."

"Take care of yourself, Mary," he said as he hung up the telephone. He sat back in his chair and looked out the window, and said, "Take care of yourself, my Mary." February seventeenth seemed far away.

The weeks actually passed faster than he had anticipated. The first week in February he attended the opening Thursday night performance of "Our Town." Eri Peterson was so soft-spoken whenever Walter talked with him that he wondered how well he would do playing the role of Dr. Gibbs. But during most of the performance he remembered to speak up. And even when the audience couldn't quite hear what he was saying his tall stature gave him convincing presence on stage.

The following Tuesday he drove to Albany for a presbytery committee meeting at First Presbyterian Church. After the meeting he drove down Madison Avenue to Pellegrino's market, bought some homemade pasta, two jars of homemade marinara sauce, some fresh ground Parmesan cheese, a loaf of Italian bread, and the makings of an antipasto. He even bought some bisque tortoni to serve for dessert. Farther out Madison Avenue he stopped at a small liquor store, dug deeply into his wallet, and bought two bottles of Ruffino Chianti Classico.

Before he started up the Northway he stopped at an Ames discount store in a small shopping center and bought curtains and a curtain rod for the window by his kitchen table. In the deli section of the Price Cutter supermarket next to Ames he bought several different cheeses and an assortment of crackers. It was after six o'clock when he arrived home. He put the groceries away, fed Willie, made himself a salami and cheese sandwich, and poured a glass of milk. He carried the sandwich and milk into the parlor, switched on the TV, sat down on his sofa, and watched the network news while he ate his sandwich.

There was nothing interesting on the news, so he turned off the TV. He remembered the sack of baked goods a kind parishioner had sent home with him when he visited her the day before. He walked back to the kitchen, picked it up from the counter and opened it. Six chocolate chip cookies and four brownies! Somehow she must have discovered how much he liked chocolate. He ate two cookies and a brownie. He looked at the kitchen clock: seven-fifteen. Time to call Mary. She answered on the first ring.

"Hi, Mary. It's Walter. You are still planning on Friday night dinner, aren't you?"

"Definitely!" she said. "I'll be done at school right on time and home by four-thirty. No one hangs around very long after school dismisses on Fridays—especially on the Friday before a break week."

"I just realized we never set a time for dinner Friday night. Suppose I pick you up at six o'clock. Will that you give you enough time?"

"Thank you, it will. But you don't have to pick me up; I can drive myself."

"No, I'd rather pick you up. It will feel more like a date and you won't have to drive home later by yourself."

"Oh, Walter, are you concerned about my car sitting in your driveway? There must be a million Nash Ramblers in the Northeast."

"Not a million 1958 yellow station wagons."

"You worry too much. People will think I've come to the manse for counseling."

"Not for four hours. Among preachers the nickname for the minister's house is 'the fishbowl.' People watch and gossip about everything they see or imagine happens here."

"All right," she sighed, "if you'll be more comfortable, you can pick me up. I'll be ready at six sharp."

"I'll be on time. See you soon."

Walter got up early Friday morning, completed the final rewrite on his sermon, made a quick home visit to an ailing parishioner and was back home before noon. When he sat down at the table to eat his lunch he looked out the window at the thermometer; it read thirty-five degrees above. It was nice to have a day with a touch of warmth after the bitter cold of the past month.

At five past twelve Avis, the cleaning woman, appeared at his side door. Earlier in the week he had convinced Avis to adjust her schedule so she could return on Friday to give the manse a quick once-over. Avis was the ideal cleaning woman for a minister; she pursued dirt like an evangelist on the prowl for sinners. None escaped her grasp. She was also a member of the small Holiness congregation that gathered twice on Sunday in a modest church building on Mill Street. She was the only person who had ever asked Walter directly whether he was "saved." He was a bit taken aback when she confronted him: it was not the kind of question a Presbyterian who was supposed to believe in predestination could answer easily. One's eternal destiny was a matter God determined. Walter finally managed a careful "Yes, I am sure I am" in response to Avis's direct question. He wanted to satisfy her; she was an excellent cleaning woman.

When Avis left, even though he knew it wasn't necessary, he inspected the downstairs front rooms of the house. To save oil during the winter he didn't use the front stairwell, but he knew it would be clean—Avis dusted corners where no one ventured. He decided to open the registers in the front hall and leave the doors open that led into the hall from the kitchen, the study, and the parlor. The wood in the front stairwell was gorgeous; he wanted Mary to see it. With the temperature likely to stay in the upper twenties tonight the furnace would be able to produce enough heat to keep the entire downstairs comfortable even with all the doors open.

He set up his ironing board, heated the iron, and pressed the tweedy curtains he had bought for the window by his kitchen table. When they were pressed he threaded them on to an expansion rod, hung them in the window, and tacked matching tie-backs to the frame on each side of the window. The nearly opaque curtains could be pulled back during the day to let in the sunlight and released at night so they hung straight down and covered the window.

He placed the small linen tablecloth and napkins his mother had given him ("in case you have company some time") and two place settings on the kitchen table. In the center of the table he placed two candlesticks he had borrowed from the sideboard in the church parlor. They were a bit large, but he thought they still looked nice. At four-thirty he assembled the antipasto on a platter and covered it with plastic wrap and placed it in the refrigerator. Even though he had showered in the morning, he went upstairs and showered again. He put on the new shirt and slacks his parents had given him for Christmas and a pair of loafers. When he looked at himself in the mirror, the shirt seemed too colorful, but he decided he would wear it anyway.

He came back downstairs to the kitchen and put on his white chef's jacket to protect his shirt. He poured the contents of two jars of marinara sauce he bought at Pellegrino's into a pan and placed the pan on a burner set on "low," filled a large kettle with water, added a little olive oil, and placed the kettle on a burner set on "high." He felt very comfortable making this dinner; he might not know how to make fancy dishes, but he was an experienced pasta cooker. When the water boiled vigorously and the sauce was warmed through he shut off the burners. It was time to pick up Mary.

He loosened the kitchen curtains from the tie-backs so they hung straight down and covered the window by the table, put on his boots and a jacket, and drove to Mary's house. She was coming down the stairs when he walked up onto the porch and stood in front of her door. When she opened the door she threw her arms around his neck and kissed him enthusiastically. "I am so glad to see you!" she said. "I've missed you terribly."

"Not any more than I've missed you," he said emphatically. She picked up a small cloth bag, stepped outside and closed the door. As he took her hand and they began to walk toward his car, he noticed the drape being drawn aside in a downstairs front window facing the porch. "The Wiley chaperone is on duty tonight, isn't she?" he said as they walked down the steps.

Mary laughed. "She never takes a day off; she guards my virtue relentlessly."

They drove to the manse and he brought her inside through the kitchen door. "Welcome, to my home—at last," he said.

"I am so happy to be here with you," she said. "Your table is beautiful!"

"Thank you," he said. "It's the only one I have. I haven't been able to afford dining room furniture yet—but I do have a comfortably furnished parlor."

"Walter, it's intimate and it's lovely."

He smiled his gratitude. When he helped her take off her coat he was stunned. She had on a long-sleeved black velvet jumpsuit that zipped up the front; he noticed it was not quite zipped up to the top. She wore a sterling silver choker, matching silver earrings on her ears, and several bangles on her right wrist. Her hair was up, held in place by a pair of sterling silver combs. She caught him staring at her. He felt awkward.

"You like my jumpsuit, don't you?"

"I like it a lot," he said. He kept looking at her.

"You can take off your coat now," she said, "and I'll need a chair to sit on so I can change into my shoes."

He laughed and turned a chair around so she could sit down and take off her boots. He hung her coat on one of the hooks next to the kitchen door and hung his jacket on another hook. He learned against the wall and took off his boots and put on his loafers.

"I like your shirt," she said.

"Thank you; my parents gave it to me for Christmas. My mother probably picked it out. When I saw myself in it for the first time, I wondered whether I should wear it; I usually don't wear anything this colorful."

She smiled and took a pair of silver ballerina shoes out of the bag she had brought with her. He noticed how lovely her feet looked as she slipped them into the shoes.

"We can begin the evening with hors d'oeuvres in the parlor," he said.

"Lead the way."

He took her hand and led her through the hall into the parlor.

When they entered the parlor she exclaimed, "What a beautiful room! And that has to be the biggest couch I have ever seen!"

"Please feel free to sit on it. There's a story behind it; I'll tell it to you when I return with our wine and cheese." He went back to the kitchen, turned the burner on under the kettle filled with water, and came back carrying a tray that held a cheese platter he had prepared earlier, a bottle of Ruffino Chianti and two wine glasses. He placed the tray on the long coffee table in front of the couch, retrieved a corkscrew from his pocket, deftly opened the Ruffino, poured some into each glass and handed one glass to her. He picked up the other glass and held it out toward her: "This is the best for the best," he said.

"From the best," she responded.

They each took a sip of wine.

He sat down next to her. "Well, I'm sure not as nervous as I was when we had dinner that first night at your house,"

"Then tell me about this huge couch."

He had fun telling her about finding the couch and buying it at a very good price because it was so long, and that it was his favorite napping place.

"And the long coffee table?" she asked. "Where did you find that?"

"Actually, it was a library table when I found it. One of the pedestal legs was broken off and the other had come loose when I saw it in a second-hand furniture store in Schenectady. I bought it for five dollars. After I paid for it I tied the table top with its one intact leg to the roof rack on my VW. I threw the broken leg and the support brace that goes between the legs into the back seat of the car and drove to my parents' house. My father has a well-outfitted shop. I removed the good leg from the table, stood the legs together, measured, and cut them off so that the table would be coffee-table height. When I finished shortening the legs I put them inside the VW and strapped the table top on to the roof rack. I put the table together here and refinished it. It works well with the couch, don't you think?"

"It does. You are very clever. I'm impressed."

He smiled and refilled their wine glasses.

She looked toward the back of the room: "Those big pocket doors are gorgeous. Actually, all the woodwork in this house is gorgeous."

"They are beautiful doors. They lead into the dining room, but because I don't have any dining room furniture to save oil I keep them closed except when the youth group is here for pizza. Of course, the kids don't care; there's an old rug on the floor in the room and they would rather hang all over each other anyway than sit in chairs." She smiled. "Now, you continue to enjoy cheese and wine while I check on the pasta water and put a little heat under the marinara a la Pellegrino."

"Albany Pellegrino's?"

"Yes," he said, "I think it's the best. Would you like some music? I have two Mantovani records loaded on the changer."

"I do like Mantovani, but can't I help?"

"No," he said firmly. "This is my night to cook; you can't come to the kitchen until the meal is on the table." He switched on the hi-fi and pushed the small lever on the changer: the strings of Mantovani filled the room. "If you want to, you can look at the books in my library. It's through the door and across the hall." He gestured toward the open door from the parlor to the hallway. "The light is always on in my study." He picked up his wine glass and started toward the kitchen. "How do you like your pasta—well-cooked or al dente?"

"Well-cooked; I don't like crunchy pasta."

"Good; I don't either."

"Take your time. I will have fun discovering what kind of books you read."

He returned to the kitchen and put on his chef's jacket. He set the oven to warm, the burner under the kettle to high, and the burner under the marinara sauce to low. Willie scratched at the door and he let him out; evidently the cat didn't like Mantovani any more than he liked Bach. When the oven was up to temperature he placed the bread inside it. The water in the kettle was soon boiling vigorously and he stirred in three-quarters of a pound of pasta. He took the antipasto out of the refrigerator, unwrapped it and placed it on the table. When pasta kettle settled down into a slow rolling boil he set the timer and walked back to the parlor. Mary was stretched out on the couch with her head against a pillow sipping wine. "You look like a Roman goddess at a banquet!"

"You look like the chef at Keeler's Restaurant! Where did you get the jacket?"

"My roommates at seminary gave it to me for a graduation present because I did most of the cooking on weekends when the cooks at the commons were off."

"Good thing you wore it or you would have ruined your new shirt; there's a little blob of marinara sauce on it just below the pocket."

He made a face and nodded in agreement. The bell on the timer rang. "I have to go back to the kitchen." He walked back through the hall and into the kitchen, turned off the burner under the linguini, poured the water and pasta through a colander, returned the linguini to the kettle, removed the bread from the oven, wrapped it in a napkin and placed it in a bread basket on the table. He lit the candles on the table, took off his chef's jacket and hung it on one of the hooks by the door.

She smiled as he entered the parlor; he bowed to her, then extended his arm and said, "Dinner is served, Madam." She grasped his arm with her hand and they walked through the hall and into the kitchen.

When she saw the table she said, "This is beautiful, Walter; you make me feel like a princess."

He smiled, "I want you to feel like a princess. He pulled out a chair and held it while she sat down, then sat down in the other chair at the table. He reached across the table with upturned open hands. She understood the gesture. She placed her hands in his and bowed her head. He prayed, "I thank you, dear Lord, that I am privileged to enjoy the evening with this beautiful woman. I thank you for bringing us together. We thank you for this food we are about to eat; may it nourish us to live gratefully and faithfully. We pray in the name of Jesus. Amen."

He let go of her hands slowly. "I should have warned you before I did that. We always hold hands at home when my father prays at the table."

"I liked it; it makes me feel like I belong here."

"I want you to belong here."

"Then do I get to eat?"

He laughed. "Of course!" He passed her the antipasto, the oil and vinegar, then the warm bread and the butter. He refilled both of their wine glasses. "So," he said, "tell me what it was like to grow up in a home where both parents are college professors."

"It was a challenge!" She took a bite of bread and began to eat her antipasto. "My father teaches English literature and my mother teaches religion. I am an only child, which is an anomaly in a Catholic family, but our Catholicism was more ethnic than religious. Actually my Irish father is the Catholic one—I should say 'was' because, except for weddings and funerals, he hasn't been near a Catholic Church since I was very young. My mother was raised as a Universalist. She has sort of held on to her believing, though she is much more liberal in her beliefs than her Universalist forebears were. My father is an out-and-out atheist on most days; he can be pretty caustic when he talks about Christians, especially the Catholic variety."

"I'll make sure to be on my best liberal Protestant behavior when I get to meet him. That's as close to atheist as I can get."

She laughed, "Then it will have to do! My mother thought it important for me to have at least some religious foundation so she raised me Catholic and saw me through my first communion as a child. But, if she had not insisted that he go, my formerly Catholic father would have not even have attended the mass when I received communion for the first time."

"That sounds really ironic!"

"It's very ironic; my mother has to sign an agreement to bring up any children as Catholics so they can be married by a priest—and then my father who is the Catholic parent drops out of church! As I told you at the Petersons the first time we met, I also did a stint in a Presbyterian Sunday School when I was a pre-teen—but that was my last formal contact with the church. So, to answer your question, at home I grew up in the midst of heated discussions between a committed doubter and a sort-of believer. This antipasto, by the way, is absolutely delicious."

"Thank you." He stood up. "I'm a fast eater—especially when it comes to salad, but you keep enjoying your antipasto and I'll finish getting the pasta ready."

He carefully poured the pan full of marinara sauce into one of the bowls he had warmed in the oven, slipped the pasta out of its kettle into the other heated bowl and placed pasta tongs on top of it. Glancing at the table he saw that she was finished eating antipasto and removed their small antipasto plates. He put on clean dinner plates, placed the bowl of marinara sauce in the center of the table and set a dipper alongside it. He caught her eyeing him and she smiled; she was enjoying watching him. He removed a small bowl of grated Parmesan from the refrigerator, placed it on the table and sat back down. "May I serve you?"

"I would be honored."

He dipped some linguini on to her plate and then dipped some on to his own plate. He held the marinara sauce while she dipped some on top of her linguini and then served himself. He passed her the parmesan cheese; she sprinkled some on to her pasta and passed it back to him.

"So, with that kind of beginning where did you end up so far as believing goes?"

She put down her fork and looked at him. "Are you sure you want to go down this road tonight? I want us to have a fun evening and I'm afraid you may not be comfortable with what you find if we talk about my believing."

He smiled. "I'll take the risk. Besides, it I am going to make you into a convert, like everybody thinks I am supposed to, then I need to know what kind of challenge I am faced with."

She sighed. "All right, I'll defer; you're the host." She paused and took another bite of linguini. "I'm not sure where to begin—but there's one thing

I am sure about, this sauce is delicious! I love pasta with a garlic and mushroom marinara sauce."

"You have to thank Pellegrino's. All I did was transport it and reheat it to thicken it a little."

They talked for a while about Pellegrino's and eating in the dining room with the tile floor at Lombardo's Restaurant just down the hill from Pellegrino's. They reminisced about trips to Keeler's Restaurant on special occasions as teenagers with their parents.

"Do you think we were ever in Keeler's at the same time back then?" she wondered.

"I don't think so."

She looked surprised. "You seem so sure. Why are you so sure?"

"Because I would have noticed you and remembered you."

She smiled.

"Now I have a suggestion about where you could begin to talk about what you believe. When you shook my hand on Christmas Eve you said you were 'moved' by what I said in my sermon."

His segue seemed to make her comfortable. "I was moved; you are moving when you preach. I've done enough work in drama to recognize excellent presentation when I watch it."

"Thank you for the compliment, but that's not what I mean. What did you think of what I said? Were you moved by *what* I said?"

"I was. The fact that God would take the trouble to come into human history and knowing the cost of that venture is moving. I really do think that Jesus might offer us a glimpse of what God could be like."

"So there are at least some remnants of Christian faith left in you, right?"

"Yes, but don't get your hopes up; in the end I may not turn out to be the kind of believer you are hoping for."

"I already said I'd take the risk, so keep talking."

"I *was* moved by what you said Christmas Eve. But there's a qualifying 'but' assuming there is a God, why should I believe that what he did in Jesus is the only time he ever spoke definitively, to use your metaphor—or will speak definitively? You obviously think that Jesus and the religious tradition that he represents offers definitive information about God. I'm not sure that's so. So far as believing goes, I am my mother's daughter. What I know about what Christians believe does not lead me to think that what you believe about God is definitive—or even completely accurate." She paused and looked at him: "The expression on your face suggests that you are going to be—as I suspected—uncomfortable with my believing, Walter."

"Maybe." He managed a slight smile. "You may turn out to be more of a challenge than I anticipated!"

"Much more, Walter," she said nodding her head, "much more. Are you still sure you want to keep going?" She looked at him across the table; other than slight concern his face didn't reveal what he was feeling.

"I am. It's important to me to know what you believe. Would you like more pasta?"

"Oh no, I couldn't eat another spoonful—though it was cooked to perfection."

"How about more wine? I have another bottle I could open."
"Not if I am going to stay lucid enough to continue this conversation!"

"Then are you ready for dessert and coffee?"

"Dessert! I love dessert, but can I let my pasta settle for a little while longer before we have it?"

"Of course; I'll make some coffee."

"And I will clear the table."

"All right, but dishes into the sink is the limit; I will wash everything after you leave. I don't want to waste a minute doing chores while you are here." He filled a teakettle and placed it on a burner to heat. "Now, maybe it would help me to understand why you believe as you do if you could recall some memorable incident or experience that shaped your believing. You know what shaped my early believing; do you know what happened along the way that shaped yours?"

"I do. My early believing was shaped more than anything else by a mural I saw when I was a teen-ager. My mother took me on a vacation trip to northern Maine when I was fourteen—just the two of us. On the way home we stopped at a Universalist Church. I can't remember where it is; it's somewhere west of Bangor. She wanted to photograph the mural on the ceiling so she could use the slides in her comparative religion course. A local person unlocked the church building for us. I really wasn't looking forward to the detour—I expected to be bored."

"That's not surprising; I remember how easily I was bored by what my parents thought was cultural enrichment when I was a teenager."

"But this time I wasn't bored; I was totally enthralled by what I saw. The mural covers the entire domed ceiling of the sanctuary. Moses, Isaiah and Socrates are on one end; Jesus is on the other end. In the middle the artist painted a factory and a school—probably a local factory and the University of Maine, our guide suggested. What has stayed with me is that image of a celestial conversation among Moses, Isaiah, Socrates, and Jesus. Ever since I saw the mural I have envisioned these figures as representatives of different ways of believing.

"That mural is my model of believing. I think that whatever truth we may discover about God and what God wants humans to do will emerge in that kind of dialogue. So, my basic approach to believing is quite different from yours."

"Yes, it is," he said quietly. "It's . . . it's not at all like mine."

"To be fair, I have to tell you that the mural is actually divided into three sections labeled 'Past,' 'Present,' and 'Future.' Moses, Isaiah, and Socrates are in the section labeled 'Past,' the factory and the school are in the section labeled 'Present,' and Jesus is being carried on the shoulders of some men in the section labeled 'Future.' The artist was obviously a Universalist Christian and imaged the future as a time when all people will recognize Jesus as the Savior."

"That's encouraging; it makes the mural seem more accurate to me."

"Unfortunately, that's not the way I see it in my mind. The notion that Jesus is unique among all the great teachers in the world's religions seems arrogant to me. When I was a college student I discounted the 'triumphalist' . . . (Is that the right term?" He nodded.) . . . "representation of Jesus in the mural and assigned him an equal seat at the celestial round table. I also added chairs for Buddha and Mohammed. I know these changes alter what the original artist had in mind, but they seem to me to make the mural more accurate."

"How so?"

"I am enough of a postmodernist to think that what matters most when we look at art is not what the original artist intended, but what the work of art stimulates in us. The mural supports my belief that there is something deep within humans that pushes us to believe there is Something or Someone out there beyond what we can clearly perceive. The urge to believe is persistent. It appears throughout human history and takes many different forms—like the mural suggests. Each teacher tries to conceptualize what he or she imagines. I don't think anyone knows for sure exactly what is out there—even for sure *if* there's Anything or Anyone out there."

She realized he was staring at her. "Are you upset by what I'm saying? Maybe I shouldn't keep going?"

He seemed hesitant. "I do want you to keep going. It's just . . . you need to know that no one has ever talked to me about believing like you are." He was sitting up straight in his chair with his hands folded in front of him. "But," he insisted, "I still want you to keep going."

She took a deep breath. "Well, I'm not sure it's a good idea, but I will." She waited for him to say something more, but he didn't.

"I think we insist on believing whatever we believe because it gives us comfort, because it meets some deep need within us. I know you think you know exactly what God is like—that Jesus answers all the big questions about God. While I'm most comfortable with Christian perceptions of God, I don't think they're uniquely accurate. I think Christian views of God are our cultural inventions that have become our cultural conventions."

"So, when you think about beliefs, even my beliefs, you see them as mostly a cultural product?"

"I do. I sometimes wish I could be as sure as you are that they are completely accurate perceptions of the Divine, but I'm not. Most of the time I think all religious perceptions are metaphors we invent in an attempt to describe a mysterious power that is beyond our grasp, and that may or may not actually exist. I don't think we can know for sure."

For a moment she seemed far off, but she came back quickly. "Well, that's a rough summary of my sort-of believing, and how I got there. While you were acquiring your faith by watching the trolley go back and forth to the office in your grandfather's store, I was shaping my approach to believing by contemplating the mural on the ceiling in that Universalist Church in Maine." She noticed he was fidgeting with his fingers. She wondered if she had revealed too much. She looked toward the stove. "The teakettle is whistling."

He stood up quickly, shut off the burner, lifted the teakettle, and poured boiling water into the top of the coffee pot. He opened the refrigerator, took out two bisque tortoni, placed them on plates, and carried the plates to the table.

"I love bisque tortoni!" she exclaimed.

"I'm glad," he said as he walked back to the stove and waited for the coffee to finish. He stepped back to the table and filled their coffee cups. "I forgot to ask whether you use cream or sugar."

"Real women drink black coffee!"

"So do real men!"

"Well, there's something we agree on."

"Hopefully there's something in your believing we can agree on, too. Does that image of a celestial round table still dominate your believing? Or, have you moved on to something else?"

"Yes and no. My early image of the celestial conversation was full of adolescent naïveté. The 'all-religions-are-the-same, we're-traveling-different-roads-that-lead-to-the-same-destination' is a simplistic view of religion. When I studied religion in college I discovered that there are *fundamental* differences between religions, not just surface differences. I now believe that all religions have insights to contribute and that they all have blind spots. The image of the table conversation is still central to my believing. I think we are most likely to appreciate our own and others' insights, and recognize their and our blind spots when we engage in real dialogue. By 'real' dialogue I mean dialogue that is based on mutual respect. 'Respect' is a wonderful word; it means that you believe the other is worth a second look."

"Like the dialogue we're having right now?"

She smiled and spoke gently. "Yes, like the kind of dialogue we're having right now. Have you ever participated in this kind of dialogue before with someone who is not a Christian?"

He thought for a moment before he responded. "To be honest, I haven't." He set his spoon down next to his dessert and sat back from the table. "But several years ago I did have some long conversations with someone who has. During my first summer on the staff of the church in Rahway the church sent me to a weeklong missions conference. Missions education was one of my responsibilities. At the conference I met a missionary from Cairo, Egypt. He teaches at a university there. He was about forty at the time and single like I am, so, of course, they made us roommates and over the course of a week we had lots of opportunities to talk. We developed a good bit of trust and were able to do some honest sharing."

"Was that helpful to you?"

"It was, now that I think about it. Towards the middle of the week he told me that he and a Muslim colleague had been meeting once a week for nearly ten years to talk with each other about their believing. During years of conversations with his colleague he had grown to appreciate some of the similarities between Christian and Muslim beliefs. He had come to respect the profound spirituality of his Muslim friend.

"The two of them were surprised to find so many commonalities in their believing. They could see how conversations like theirs could build bridges between Christians and Muslims. But they had a problem: according to each of their faiths they were supposed to be converting each other. As a missionary my newfound friend was supposed to be converting Muslims, not listening to them appreciatively. He said he didn't dare tell his supporting churches what he was really doing, because if he did, they would stop supporting him. I think he was doing what you're talking about."

"But it sounds like you've never been able to take it any farther."

"I haven't. I still have deep respect for this man, but I've never found a way to duplicate what he is doing. If I followed my feelings, I would reach out and embrace those who are different believers and respect their believing. But my theological convictions tell me I should be careful when it comes to feelings. If there's a conflict between my heart and my head, my theology tells me to honor my head. And my head tells me that Jesus provides *the* definitive picture of God—and godliness."

"Ah, I see your stumbling block; it's your head!"

He laughed. "Well, I'm a Calvinist; we believe with our heads!"

She'd wondered if her outburst meant to be a joke might have been too blunt, perhaps, even hurtful. But his laughter suggested it wasn't, so she went on. "The deep feeling I sense in you when you tell that story gives me hope, Walter. Maybe there are times you should follow your heart and give your head a chance to catch up? If I may be so bold as to make a theological observation, I believe God made us to feel as well as to think. Don't you think God feels as well as thinks?" She waited and watched him.

Finally he said, "I do."

"Then it seems to me that, at least sometimes, you could follow your feelings and let your head catch up. I don't know the Bible as well as you do, but I do know that in the Bible God seems to inspire some very unlikely characters. Maybe that's still true?"

"Yes, I think it is."

"Then maybe you should follow your former roommate's lead and provide some opportunities to talk and listen to unlikely characters—even people like me?" She grinned and held out her empty coffee cup. "And maybe we could have a second cup of coffee before we go on?"

"Of course, I've gotten so involved in our conversation that I've neglected my duties as a host. The coffee is cold; I'll have to reheat it." He walked over to the stove and turned on the burner under the coffee pot.

When he sat back down she said, "What's true between Christians and Muslims is even truer between Christians and people like me—whatever I am."

"You do defy definition, Miss Kerrigan."

She smiled again and continued. "People like me talk with each other, not with people like you—because most of the time you don't provide us with opportunities for conversation. Think about the Sunday service. It's all scripted; it's rote, except for the sermon, and that's one-way, top-down communication. You're up there in that pulpit, above all of us, clothed in that formidable black robe. Suppose someone stood up in the middle of your sermon next Sunday, and said, 'Wait a minute! I don't agree with that! Let me tell you about *my* inspiration.' How would people respond? How would you respond?"

"It would be unsettling, that's for sure—especially if you were my wife!"

She opened her eyes very wide. "Was that a veiled proposal?"

"No," he said with a grin, "it was just a fleeting thought."

"I'm relieved. This is only our third date!" She looked toward the stove. "The coffee's boiling."

He jumped up and turned off the burner. He refilled their cups. "If that's too strong," he said, "I'll make a fresh pot."

"Real women can handle strong coffee."

"Would you like me to boil it down some more?"

She laughed, "No, it's sufficiently strong. But I want to go back to what we were talking about—you really have me going now. Most of us who grew up as Christians were not prepared to participate in a dialogue with those who believe differently. We were taught to believe inside a box. As a former Catholic, I know how that works. As a child I didn't go to parochial school, but one afternoon a week I went to religious instruction. They used the Baltimore Catechism; it was designed to indoctrinate me. Fortunately, it didn't take."

He grinned. "That's obvious."

"I'm glad it didn't. If my mother had been the Catholic parent, probably I would have grown up to be a nice Catholic girl and would by now be a mommy having lots of babies. But my formerly Catholic father was the irreverent parent who challenged everything and everyone. You can see what happened. I picked up my mother's interest in religion and my father's way of challenging everything."

"You are definitely your father's daughter!"

"Walter, I'm mild, compared to him. I'll never forget the time he became so frustrated with the Pope's unwillingness to give any credence to modernism that he sent him a telegram. It read, 'THE EARTH DOES TOO REVOLVE AROUND THE SUN STOP N COPERNICUS.'"

He laughed boisterously. "He really sent it?" She nodded. "That's very funny."

"Probably not if you're the one receiving the telegram! But the point my father made is important. People who aren't willing to have open conversations with those who hold beliefs that are different from theirs are less likely to become mature believers; they're more likely to hold on to beliefs that are childish or just plain unsound. I resist the kind of protected, unapproachable believer my father sent his telegram to.

"If someone is telling me what he thinks about God and I have no chance to respond directly, I'm less likely to take him seriously. When I listen to a homily or sermon—something I don't do very often anymore—I carry on an internal dialogue with what I am hearing. I take from those internal conversations what seems believable to me, and pitch the rest. I don't feel obligated to accept anyone's whole package just because he's a pope or a preacher—even if that package is scriptural."

"I was with you until the last phrase." He looked concerned. "It suggests that there are parts of Scripture that don't seem true to you."

"Yes, there are—lots of them. The notion that God created the heavens and the earth rings true to me, but I don't buy the six-day schedule. I think that story and the one that follows it in Genesis are both poetic narratives, not history. Your Christmas Eve sermon describing Jesus as the mirror image of God rang true when I heard it, but I don't agree that he is the only flesh and blood embodiment of God there ever was or is. Then the whole Exodus story is full of problems for me. Especially what goes on at Passover seems totally out of character for God as I see God. The picture of God described in the Passover story not only seems inaccurate to me, it seems dangerous. To be blatantly honest, I find it repulsive."

He responded quickly. "I can understand why you doubt the scientific accuracy of the Bible's description of creation, but why the Passover story? Why would you question that?"

She sighed and looked straight at him. "Are you sure you want to keep going, Walter? This could get hairy."

"You said you believe in challenging conversation as a way to refine believing. I'm challenging."

She shrugged her shoulders. "Well, if you put it that way, I'll go on. Have you or anyone you know ever talked this story over with an Egyptian woman? I wonder if your missionary friend ever did."

"Probably not."

"That's why there need to be seats at the table for people like me. The typical questions one hears about the Exodus all have to do with how it happened mechanically: questions like how did God divide the waters so the Israelites could get across the Red Sea and escape the Egyptians? Those are guy questions. I can see a bunch of men sitting around the table, stroking their beards and speculating how God could have opened up the water so the Israelites could outrun the Egyptians. Probably you had conversations like that when you were in seminary?"

He nodded. "You're right; we did."

"That's what happens when only learned men are participants in the conversation. I want to reserve a seat at the table for an Egyptian mother. The learned divines aren't likely to represent her concerns or mine. I could care less how the wind blew the water apart. I'm stuck back in Egypt sitting with an Egyptian mother at the Passover."

He looked puzzled.

"You don't get my point, do you Walter?" He shook his head no. "Think about the story from her viewpoint. Think about the character of God in the story through the Egyptian mother's experience. It becomes a horrific story. God is obviously frustrated with Pharaoh. He's sends boils and plagues and locusts, but none of that is enough to convince Pharaoh to release the Hebrews from bondage. So, he takes one final terrible step. He slays *all* the firstborn children and animals of the Egyptians. He works out a neat door-post sign warning system that protects the children of the Hebrews from the holocaust. But that doesn't soften what God does to those innocent kids. And there's no doubt that the Lord did it; your God, Walter, if you accept the text as true. He murdered them all! It says so explicitly in the twelfth chapter of Exodus, verse 29. The verse haunts my memory: 'At midnight the Lord smote all the first-born in the land of Egypt.' The strategy worked. Pharaoh let the Hebrews go.

"But, if God killed all those Egyptian children, Walter, then God was wrong"—her voice became louder—"terribly wrong. God sounds like a modern general saying it was unfortunate that the raid killed a lot of innocent civilians, but it was of 'strategic importance'; it got the Israelites released from bondage. But my God, Walter, think of what happened from the perspective of the Egyptian mothers whose children God killed. How would they feel about this God that killed their kids? I can barely stay in the room when someone reads the story. All I can think about is those Egyptian mothers. I want to go away by myself and weep." She stopped suddenly; tears trickled down her cheeks. "You have your tears, Walter; these are mine." She wiped the tears away with the back of her hand. "I'm sorry. I didn't want to cry."

He reached out and took hold of her other hand. "Thank you," she said. Then she carefully withdrew her hand. "Please don't misunderstand; I appreciate your caring. But in this moment I want you to confront my truth, not be concerned about my feelings. Is this God your God? Do you believe God is like the God in this story?"

He was silent for a while. Then he spoke softly, "No, I don't think so. I can't believe God would do something like that—that God could kill all those kids."

"I am so relieved!" she said. "I was so frightened that you would say 'yes.'"

He continued in a soft but also clear voice. "If I were simply to follow my feelings, I would have to reject that image of God completely."

She leaned forward toward him. "Can you?" she asked. "Can you simply follow your feelings?"

He looked pensive. "I will have to see what happens when my head catches up."

For several minutes they sat and looked at each other. When he broke the silence he spoke carefully. "For a start, this much seems clear to me. I think the people who wrote the Scripture were inspired, but they weren't perfect. Most of the time they got it right, but sometimes they didn't. The Bible is an honest record that reports both what they got right and what they didn't. Interpreting the Bible is dangerous, but also essential. I definitely believe that most of it is inspired truth, but to protect that truth we have to ferret out misperceptions that compromise it."

She looked at him and nodded. "That's why we need people like Socrates and me at the table. We need them to ask the irreverent, unacceptable questions that no one else will ask. Without people like Socrates and me to challenge, people who want to believe tend to live in self-confirming boxes. They just keep reinforcing their beliefs—even horrific beliefs. Their undisturbed consensus insulates them from dialogue that challenges misbelieving." She paused and then spoke slowly, with determination. "I will never be a compliant believer like you are, Walter; I question everything—automatically. If you can't accept that in me, then I don't see how we can be together."

He noticed that her right hand had become a fist. He sat and stared at her fist. "I see that." He paused and pondered, then looked at her and smiled slightly. "It could be good for me."

She looked at him carefully. "I hope it could. But you need to know that I don't think I could ever become a compliant card-carrying Protestant Presbyterian Christian. I'm a committed skeptic; I am as passionate in the way I challenge as you are in the way you believe." She stopped abruptly. "You haven't been saying much; have I given you indigestion?"

"No," he said, after a pause. "You frighten me a little—and you intrigue me a lot. No one has ever talked to me the way you do."

She saw the intense look on his face and sighed. "That's what I do to men, Walter; I intrigue them, and I frighten them." Her face softened into a gentle smile. "Well, let's not talk about believing or not believing any more tonight. We'll find some ways to connect our worlds another time." Her smile broadened. "Right now I want to learn how to intrigue you better. Are you going to show me the rest of your house?"

He was reluctant to let go of the conversation, but he knew he needed time to think. "What more of the house do you want to see?"

"I want to see your bedroom. Then I can envision what you look like when you are asleep."

He looked at her and shook his head. "You really are bold!"

She smiled and took the combs out of her hair and shook it free. "You said you like my hair this way the night we went dancing. There it is—the way you like it." He watched her stand up. With her hair hanging loose on her shoulders she was startlingly beautiful standing before him in her almost zipped-up jumpsuit. She watched him look at her. "I'm ready; can we start the upstairs tour now?"

He grinned and nodded. He pushed his chair back, stood up and beckoned her to follow him into the hall. As they walked through the door from the kitchen into the hall he said, "I will take you up the front stairs; it's cold in the rooms up there, but the stairway is beautiful. Actually, during the winter it's cold even in this downstairs hall most of the time because when the temperature outside drops below fifteen or twenty above I have to shut all the doors to get the furnace to heat the rest of the house up to a livable temperature. The manse has an old, inadequate heating system and no insulation, so keeping warm when the weather is bitter is a real challenge."

He led her up the stairs; when they reached the top of the stairs he led her along the rail of the open hall to the front of the house. He opened the door to the bedroom above his study and switched on the ceiling light. The large room was furnished with an oak Victorian bedroom set. "What a beautiful bedroom set, but it's very cold in here," she said. "How do you sleep where it's so cold?"

"Actually, I don't sleep here," he said. "The furniture in this room came with the house; it's not mine. I sleep in a bedroom at the back of the house. My bedroom was probably used as a child's bedroom when a family lived in the manse; you'll find it much warmer in there. I'll show it to you." They walked back along the railing next to the stairwell. He opened a door that stood at the back end of the railing. They went through it into a back hall; he switched on a light and closed the door behind them. "The bathroom is at the back of this hall and there's a set of back stairs from the kitchen that lead up to this back hallway so you can keep the door closed to the front hall and heat the rooms back here without heating the rest of the upstairs."

"That's encouraging. I like it cool where I sleep, but I wouldn't want to sleep in a room like that front bedroom where there's no heat at all."

"I'll remember that for some future time." He reached through the open doorway next to them and turned on the ceiling light. "This is my bedroom."

She looked at his bed. "Your bed is made!"

"I make it every day in case someone should pay a surprise visit to my bedroom."

"At least you have a double bed."

"I do, but I'm so tall I have to sleep at an angle to stretch out completely."

"That could be a problem, if you can picture what I mean."

"I think we better go back downstairs."

"Oh, Walter, have you no spirit of adventure?"

He smiled and walked out of the bedroom and back into the hall. She followed him. He reached back into the bedroom and turned out the light. He opened the door to the front hall and they walked into that hall and back down the front stairs. When they reached the lower hallway they stood between the doors that led into the study and the parlor. She looked back and forth at the two open doorways. She walked through the doorway that led into his study. He followed her. She looked at the clock on the mantel over the bricked-over opening of what had obviously been a working fireplace in years past. "It's after eleven," she said, "too late for more pastoral counseling, don't you think?"

"Yes, it is," he said. "I usually don't have counselees this late at night—especially women."

She turned and closed the door to the hall and then walked across the room and turned off the light on his desk. The room was dark, except for light coming through the front windows from a streetlight. She came back and stood next to him in front of the large bookcase that held his Bible commentaries. "Well?" she said. "I just shut out the church and the world. You can do what you want." She tilted back her head and looked at him. He kissed her. "Walter, let go!" she said softly when their lips separated. "I've heard you preach so I know you can be passionate. Try it once more. Open your mouth a little more, put your right hand in the small of my back, put your left hand behind my head, and pull my head and body toward you like you really want me."

He did. He kissed her passionately. Finally she broke the kiss. "Whew! I need to breathe! If you keep that up, I'll have to ask you to take me home before we discover why priests never admit women past the public parlor in their rectories."

He looked into her eyes. "I'm going to do it again." And he did. When he relaxed his hold and their lips separated he started to say something, but was interrupted by the telephone ringing on his desk.

She made a face. "It's nearly eleven-thirty. Do you have to answer that?"

"I do." He reluctantly took his arms from around her, walked over to his desk and picked up the telephone. "This is Mr. Macdonald." The light coming through the window from the streetlight flickered on his face. She watched him listen. The expression on his face became grave. "I'm so sorry, Gert," he said when he spoke. "As it happens I am still up; I can go over to the hospital right away. No, it's no trouble. I need to be there—even if only for a little while. Thank you for letting me know. I will pray for Bob. God bless you."

"What's wrong?" she asked after he had hung up the telephone.

"That was Gert McCain; you probably know she is Molly Hutchins's mother. Bob had a heart attack earlier this evening. Molly called Erik and he called Burt Brundidge. They rushed Bob to Saratoga Springs Hospital by ambulance. Erik and Molly are still at the hospital. I have to go there."

"Right now?"

"Yes, right now."

"Can't we have just a few more minutes together like we just were?"

He shook his head. "I want to, but I can't stay; I have to go."

She became quiet and guarded. He stood motionless and watched her. When she spoke she measured her words carefully. "Walter, I was intrigued—as you were—from the first time I met you. Now it is my turn also to be frightened."

Her statement puzzled him. "Frightened? Why are you frightened?"

She looked at the floor and then raised her eyes to look at him. She spoke softly. "When we had dinner on Halloween and you talked about your believing I knew then that if we became more than casual friends we would have some significant differences to overcome, but what I just glimpsed is more frightening."

"I don't understand what frightens you."

"This is the way it would be if I were with you, isn't it? No matter what kind of moment we were having together a parishioner on the telephone could suddenly take you away from me, couldn't they?"

He was dumbstruck. Finally he stammered, "You're . . . you're right. Yes, they could."

She shook her head slowly side to side. "There would be no moments when I could be sure of being first for you; in your life I would always be second—like a mistress. It would be worse than being married to a doctor."

He could feel her pulling away from him. He wanted to reach out and bring her back, but he didn't know what to say. He glanced out the window at his car parked in the driveway, and then looked back at her. "I can see that you're upset. I would like to talk about it, but I can't now. I have to go."

"I know; you've already gone."

"I'll take you home."

"You don't need to. It's not far. I can walk."

"That's not necessary. I can take you home. It's on the way."

It was nearly one o'clock when he reached the hospital in Saratoga. He parked in the doctors' lot and entered through the emergency room. The nurse on duty recognized him and told him that Bob Hutchins was in the intensive care unit. He went upstairs to the third floor and found a very weary Molly sitting in one of the chairs in the waiting area outside the unit. When she saw him tears ran down her face. "I'm so sorry, Molly," he said. He stood and held her while she cried.

When she recovered they sat down next to each other. "It was so sudden, Walter. Bob ate a big supper. We sat and talked for a while and then he decided to read; he's really enjoying Allen Drury's *Advise and Consent*. I went into the family room and watched TV. About eight-thirty Bob stopped at the doorway and said, 'You're too good of a cook, Molly. I ate so much I have a bit of indigestion.' He grinned at me and said he was going to get a couple of Tums. A few minutes later I heard him moaning. I jumped up and ran to the living room and found him sprawled back on the couch with his hands on his chest. 'My chest hurts something awful, Molly,' he said. 'You better call Erik.' I called Erik and told him what was happening and he said he would come right over. I realized we might have to go to the hospital so I called my mom so she could come over to be with the kids. Erik must have had Becky call Burt Brundidge because the ambulance and Erik got to the house at the same time.

"As soon as Erik saw Bob he said, 'We need to get you to the hospital right away.' Burt and Jeremy put Bob on their stretcher and then into the ambulance. My mom arrived while they were putting Bob into the ambulance. Erik called the hospital and told them to let the cardiologist on call know that they would have a 'forty-seven-year-old male with an apparent heart attack in the ER in about thirty minutes.' I'll never forget those words. I rode to the hospital with Erik. I filled out some papers while Erik went into the ER to check on Bob. He was gone nearly an hour. When he came back he sat down next to me in the waiting room and said that Bob had had a serious heart attack and that they were transferring him to the ICU so they could monitor his condition. Erik said they probably will not know anything for sure for at least twenty-four hours. They'll just have to watch him and see how he does. There isn't much else they can do. Erik suggested I let him drive me home, but I can't leave Bob—even though they will let me in to see him only five minutes out of each hour. I called mom and told her I was going to stay here overnight. She said not to worry; she could spend the night and get Eddie and Jean off to school in the morning. I'm so scared, Walter."

"I know. I would be, too, Molly."

"He won't die, will he, Walter? His father and his uncle had heart attacks and died before they were fifty. But they know so much more about treating heart attacks now than they did twenty-five years ago, don't they? God won't let him die, will he, Walter?"

"Let's talk with him, Molly. Let's see if they will let us go in and be with Bob for a prayer." He walked to the desk and returned after he talked with the nurse. "The floor nurse checked with the charge nurse in the ICU; she says we can go in long enough to pray with Bob." He and Molly approached the doors of the ICU; they opened automatically and then closed after they had walked through them. Bob was in a bed on the left. He appeared to be sleeping. "I don't think we should wake him," Walter whispered. "Let's just pray for him."

He reached out and held Molly's hand. He bowed his head and shut his eyes. "Oh God," he said in a whisper, "Bob is so sick and we are so worried about him. He needs your care. We are frightened, but we are also confident. We have faith in you. We know that you care about Bob even more than we do. And we know that no matter what happens he will be safe with you. We ask you to be close by Bob and touch him with your healing grace. Make his broken heart whole again. Be close to Molly; let her feel your presence. Help her know that your love will not let her go. We ask you to hear us for Jesus' sake. Amen." They stood for a moment and watched Bob; he didn't stir. They turned and walked out quietly through the automatic doors.

Molly wiped tears from her cheeks with the back of her hand. Walter gave her his handkerchief. "You can keep it," he said. "I have a drawer full of them at home."

She smiled. "Thank you so much for coming—and for praying. I feel so much more confident. I'm not quite as scared as I was."

"You're very welcome," he said. "I will stay as long as you want me to."

"You don't need to stay longer. Not that I wouldn't be grateful. But I'll be all right. This is what a wife does, and I want to do it. You do understand?"

"I do. I'll stop back tomorrow afternoon to see how things are going. On my way out I'll ask the nurse if they can find a more comfortable chair for you to sit in. God bless you, Molly."

"Thank you, Walter. I am sure he will."

When he stepped outside into the parking lot it was snowing lightly. He drove cautiously along Route 29 toward Schuylerkill Falls; the road was slippery, especially in those sections that weren't sanded. It was after two-thirty when he arrived back at the manse.

He told himself he should go right to bed, but he knew he wouldn't sleep. He looked at the candlesticks on the table, the dishes in the sink, and the pots on the stove. The dinner with Mary seemed far away. He decided to clean up the kitchen. He washed the dishes, the silverware, and the pots. When everything was dried and put away he walked into his study. He didn't turn on the light that was always on; he just sat down in the desk chair. Light from the streetlight shone in through the front window and illuminated the tall bookcase. He shut his eyes and recalled the moments with Mary earlier in the evening; he could see her standing in front of his books with her head tilted back. He was kissing her; he could feel her loose, soft hair in his hand. Then the telephone rang and he had to rush away. Suddenly he felt sad. He opened his eyes, stared at the books, and thought about the sudden telephone call. That telephone call tore him away from her.

He sat up in his chair. "I wonder," he thought, "is God trying to tell me something? First Miss Simpson's stroke; now Bob Hutchins's heart attack. Both happened when I was with Mary. Maybe it was just a coincidence? At least this time I could respond right away when the call came. This time I feel okay with God—but not with Mary. I feel torn between them. I want to be right with both of them."

The wind blew through the trees outside. When the branches swayed they made the light coming in from the streetlight flicker on his books—the same as it had flickered on Mary when she stood in front of them. He recalled the look on her face when he told her he would have to leave to go to the hospital right away. "I wish she were here right now so I could explain. 'I didn't want to upset you, Mary, but I had to go. A parishioner needed me. It will always be that way. God called me to be their pastor. And that's who I am.'"

A gust of wind rattled the windows. He sat for a while in the quiet that followed, and then spoke to the silence: "I am their minister, God—and yours; I won't deny that. But I love Mary Kerrigan, and I won't deny that either."

———————— 9 ————————

IT WAS NEARLY NINE-THIRTY when Walter woke up the next morning. After he took a quick shower, ate a light breakfast and fed Willie he went into his study and telephoned the parents who had promised to be drivers for the youth group skating party on Sunday afternoon at Millerton Pond. Parents sometimes backed out of that kind of commitment at the last minute. But not this time; he was relieved: all of them were planning to go.

When he finished calling the parents he dialed Bob Hutchins's home. Gert McCain answered.

"Good morning, Gert, it's Walter. Any news about Bob?"

"Molly called a little while ago; she said he still seems to be holding his own."

"That's good to hear. I plan to stop by the hospital after lunch . . ."

Gert interrupted. "Now it's Molly I'm concerned about, Walter. She sounds very, very tired; she hasn't had any real rest since Bob was admitted. Maybe you can convince her to ride back home with you? I told her I'll be glad to go to the hospital and relieve her—even stay overnight there so she can get some sleep. But she insists that she is fine and that she won't leave Bob until it is clear that he is completely out of danger. I doubt I can convince her to come home even for a little while; she's been strong-willed ever since she was a little girl."

Walter laughed under his breath. "Sounds like she's her mother's daughter!" He paused to give Gert a chance to respond, but she didn't acknowledge his attempt at humor. "I'll do my best to convince Molly that she needs to conserve her strength. Bob may face a long recovery."

"Thanks, Walter. Thanks very much."

After he finished talking with Gert he read quickly through his sermon. No major issues; just a couple of places where he needed to refine the language. He could do that early Sunday morning. When he walked back to the kitchen he noticed that the two tall candlesticks were still on the kitchen table. Better get them back to the sideboard in the church parlor before anyone noticed they were missing.

He left for Saratoga just after one o'clock. When he came to a diner just outside the city his stomach reminded him that he had eaten only a small breakfast; he stopped and ate a hamburger and French fries. He arrived at the hospital just before two-thirty and walked quickly upstairs; Molly was sitting in the same chair in the hall outside of the ICU. Ellen Ward was with her. When he asked about Bob, Molly responded in a flat voice: "He's about the same. I spoke with Dr. Marino, the cardiologist on call, when he made rounds early this morning. He had nothing new to report, except that Bob will probably have to stay in the hospital for several more days; he's still having chest pains, so he's not out of the woods yet."

Walter tried to be positive. "But he seems to be holding his own."

Molly didn't respond. When it was time for her five-minute visit, he went into the ICU with her. Bob was awake. He smiled briefly when he saw Walter, but he was obviously uncomfortable. Walter returned the smile. "I'm sure, Bob, that you will soon be better." Bob managed another weak smile. He prayed with Bob and Molly, then excused himself so Molly could have some time alone with Bob. In the hall he told Ellen about his conversation with Gert. "Gert is really worried about Molly. Maybe you can convince her to let you take her home with you and get some rest."

"I'll try," Ellen said, "but I'm not optimistic that she will go with me. She's determined to stay here until the doctors tell her that Bob is out of danger—and that could take days."

When Molly came back out of the ICU, Walter sat down next to her. "You look completely worn out, Molly. Why don't you let Ellen drive you home so you can get a few hours rest? I'll be glad to bring you back whenever you're ready."

Molly shook her head no. "I won't leave until I'm sure he's going to be okay."

At the worship service the next morning the sanctuary was full; obviously the news of Bob's heart attack had spread throughout the village. Walter was struck by the sense of oneness he felt in the congregation when he prayed for Bob's recovery.

At the coffee hour after the service he drew Erik aside. "Can you stay behind for a few minutes and tell me what's really going on with Bob?"

Erik nodded. "I can; I checked this morning—and we really do need to talk." They walked over to the manse, took off their coats and sat down at the kitchen table.

Walter folded his hands in front of him and looked across the table. "Well, Erik, I'm no doctor, but it seems clear to me that Bob has had a 'serious' heart attack—to use your word. Can you tell me more specifically what serious means?"

Erik sighed and looked somber. "Well, Walter, serious is the right word to describe it; there's little doubt that he's had a 'serious' heart attack. I looked at Dr. Marino's updated diagnosis in Bob's chart early this morning when I made rounds; he wrote 'acute myocardial infarction.' In plain language that means an artery to someone's heart is entirely or mostly blocked. The lack of blood supply causes the heart muscle to struggle to keep working. We are trying to reduce the stress on Bob's heart by giving him oxygen and nitroglycerine, but the angina pain he continues to experience suggests that the ischemia is persistent, or in layman's terms that the blood supply to his heart continues to be restricted by the partially blocked blood vessels.

"I saw Dr. Marino after I read Bob's chart. He said Bob's EKG looks ominous to him—that's his word and he reads lots of EKGs, so he wouldn't say the situation is ominous unless it is. His concern is heightened by Bob's family history: his father and grandfather both died of heart attacks in early middle age—so did one of his paternal uncles." He paused and took a breath. "I wish I could be more encouraging, Walter, but if I am perfectly honest with you—and I assume you want me to be—that family history plus the ominous EKG bode a pretty bleak future."

Walter nodded his head slowly and looked at the floor. When he raised his eyes he said, "That's not what I wanted to hear, but it tells me how often I need to visit the hospital, and how much I'll need to be present to support Molly. Frankly, Erik, I'm concerned about Molly. She was exhausted when I saw her yesterday afternoon, but I couldn't persuade to go home and get some rest."

"Well, she's home now, and, hopefully, asleep. When I saw her this morning at the hospital I told her one seriously ill person in the family is enough. I said she was probably in for a long haul with Bob and had to take a break and get some rest. She tried to argue, but I cut her off. 'I'm driving you home and telling you to take eight hours of bed rest. Doctor's orders!

If any significant change occurs in Bob's condition, they will call me and you can ride back to the hospital with me.' So, I brought her home after I finished rounds this morning. When I dropped her off I saw Gert was still there —she spent the night at Molly and Bob's. She said she'd bring their kids to the skating party this afternoon and then bring them home afterwards so Molly can sleep."

"Are you going skating?"

"No," Erik said emphatically. "I'm great on snowshoes, but not on skates. That's Becky's department. I'm going to watch a football game and fall asleep."

In spite of his concern about Bob Hutchins, Walter enjoyed the skating party at the Rollins family camp on Millerton Pond. Ed Rollins built a roaring fire in the large stone fireplace in the camp living room. The kids sat on the floor in front of the fireplace, and sang camp songs, and roasted marshmallows after supper. It was a welcome break.

When he arrived home he tried to reach Mary on the telephone. No answer. After he watched Bonanza he tried to reach her again—still no answer. Monday after lunch he drove to Saratoga to the hospital to visit Bob. Bob was still in intensive care and Molly was back in her chair in the hall outside the door into the ICU. He went in with Molly to see Bob. Bob seemed more comfortable than he was the day before, though he was still on oxygen and talking obviously tired him. Walter offered a short prayer.

When they were back in the hall Molly said, "Bob does seem to be better, doesn't he?"

It was obvious that she hoped he would agree with her. He didn't feel as confident as she appeared to be, but he thought it was important to support her. "Yes, I think he does."

"Then maybe Erik is right that I don't need to stay here at night anymore. I'll ask Ellen to bring me home after she visits tonight." She paused and looked directly at him. "If something happens to Bob in the middle of the night, would you bring me back here?"

"Of course; please feel to call me any time, day or night."

After supper he tried again to reach Mary. As the phone continued to ring he was aware that he both wanted to talk with her and was apprehensive about talking with her. He was about to hang up when she answered.

"Hi Mary; it's Walter."

"I'm so glad to hear your voice. How's Bob doing?"

"He seems a bit better—not in as much pain today as he has been."

"That's good. Everyone at school is really concerned."

"Well, he's not out of the woods yet, but at least he seems to be holding his own. There was even some color in his face when I visited him earlier today."

"That's encouraging. I hope he continues to improve."

She sounded controlled—not at all like her usual animated self; there was hardly any spark in her voice. He wasn't sure how to continue. "I know you're concerned about Bob—we all are"—he felt himself stumbling, "but I . . . I didn't call to talk about Bob. I called to talk about us. I'm sorry our evening ended so abruptly on Friday. That wasn't what I planned."

She answered carefully. "I know you felt you had to go to the hospital when Gert told you about Bob. But the whole experience after you hung up made me wonder how I would do if we were together together."

He could feel her uneasiness; he wasn't sure what to say. Finally he said, "I hear what you say, but I don't know what it means."

She became more animated. "You're kissing me passionately, I'm totally enthralled, the phone rings, and I hardly have a chance to catch my breath before you tell me you're leaving! You say you're sorry you have to go, but hardly a word or even a gesture that shows me how you *feel* about having to go."

There was an awkward pause. "I didn't want that phone call to happen, Mary, but what could I do?"

"Maybe you couldn't *do* anything different, but you could have said how you felt about leaving. If you'd said something as simple as 'Oh, damn! I have to go'—and then kissed me again, that would have helped. Were you angry, or even disappointed, that the closest moment we have ever had was interrupted by a parishioner on the phone?"

He tried to recover. "I *was* disappointed. When I got back home from the hospital I felt really sad about the way our evening ended."

"It helps me to know you felt disappointed then, but that was three hours after the call. What about when the call came? Would it have made any real difference if you had stayed and spent a few more minutes of tenderness with me right after the call came? Would anyone's life have been affected adversely?"

He answered softly, "No."

She spoke gently. "But you couldn't stay, could you? Your heart *immediately* went away from me to the person on the other end of the telephone."

"You're right. It did. I couldn't stop it."

"What are you feeling right now, Walter?"

"I feel sad, very sad—and confused."

"So, do I." She paused. "Do you think you could find another way to respond when calls like that come in and we're together?"

"I'm not sure." He felt the impact of his equivocating response. When she didn't say anything he went on, "I need some space, Mary, to try to figure out what I can do. I feel uneasy when I say that. I don't want you to go away, but I am afraid you might. I don't want to step back; I just want to pause. My God, I don't want to screw this up and lose you, Mary Kerrigan. Can you wait for me? It may take a while for me to figure it all out."

"I can wait Walter. I don't want to go away, and I don't want you to go away, but my own feelings are confused, too. When we talked Friday evening I really felt we might find a way to live with our differences—until the telephone rang. What we stumbled into after the telephone rang raises a huge question for me. Now I wonder if I could be in a committed relationship with you and still have what I want and need. Could you ever be unconditionally mine? After what happened Friday night I'm not sure. Do you understand why I am concerned?"

"I hope so. Thank you for saying that you don't want to go away."

"You're welcome." She paused again. "Can I make a suggestion?"

"What's that?"

"I'd feel more confident if I knew you weren't going to try to figure it all out by yourself—if I knew you were going to talk it through with someone who is wise and caring. Do you know someone like that you could talk with?"

He thought for a moment. "Yes, I do," he said. "I do know someone like that."

On Wednesday and again on Saturday he traveled to Saratoga Springs to the hospital to check on Bob Hutchins. On Wednesday he discovered that Bob had been moved from intensive care to a private room. He was still on oxygen and having occasional chest pains. They were further apart and not as severe, but the fact that Bob was having any chest pains concerned him. When he talked with Molly he could tell that she was also concerned, but she insisted that though Bob's improvement was slower than she had hoped it would be, she was sure he would keep getting better. He wished he could be as optimistic as she seemed to be.

When he met Erik in the hallway following Sunday worship, he voiced his concern. "Erik, do you have a few minutes to update me on Bob Hutchins's condition? Molly insists that he's making progress, but it doesn't look to me like he's gaining as much as she wants to believe he is."

Erik glanced back into the sanctuary and said, "There's nobody in there; let's go back in there to talk." When they were inside Erik shut the doors that led to the hall. He spoke quietly. "Your hunch is correct; Bob is stable right now, but he's not improving. As you know his heart suffered a lot of damage; that's why he keeps having occasional chest pains. I talked with Dr. Marino when I made rounds Friday morning. He thinks Bob's chances of recovering are 50/50 at best. To be honest, Walter, we feel pretty helpless; there's little we can do besides watch and hope—and pray."

"Does Molly know what you just told me?"

"Yes, she does. Dr. Marino has been candid with her about Bob's condition all along, and so have I. I took a walk with her down the hall on Friday after I checked on Bob and we talked about Dr. Marino's prognosis. I told her I had to agree with him. She thanked me for being honest with her, but she's not willing to accept any physician's assessment as final. She's firmly convinced that Bob will recover. I suppose that's the way you see it when it's someone you love lying in the hospital bed. But if the worst happens, Walter, she may come crashing down. I hope the worst doesn't happen, but she'll really need you if it does."

Walter took a deep breath. "Thanks for the update, Erik. I will stay in close touch." He hesitated, and then continued, "If you have one more minute, I want to ask a favor." Erik smiled and nodded. "There's something personal I want to talk over with you. I'm not feeling sick so I'm not asking to see you as a doctor—I just need to talk over something with someone who is wise and caring. Would you have an hour or two sometime this week when you could be that someone and we could talk?"

"Well, when you put it that way," Erik said with a grin, "of course I do. Better than an hour or two, how about a whole afternoon?"

"That would be wonderful! Do you have one in mind?"

"Can you clear Wednesday? I don't have office hours on Wednesday afternoons."

"I don't have my calendar right here, but I'm sure I can."

"Do you snowshoe?" Erik asked hopefully.

"I do. In fact, I stopped at Goldstock's when I was in Schenectady one day a couple of weeks ago and bought some updated bindings for my Vermont Tubbs."

"Great! I own a share in a hunting and fishing camp on a pond near West Fort Ann. It's on a dirt road about half a mile in from the state road. We can drive from here to the intersection with the dirt road in about forty-five minutes. The snow is settled now so we can easily snowshoe in to the camp, enjoy a cup of coffee to warm up, have a couple of hours to talk, and then snowshoe back out before it gets dark. I'll be sure to get you back in time to lead the Lenten discussion group in the evening. I can come by for you after we close the office—probably just before noon."

"I'll be ready by 11:30 on Wednesday. I'll make some sandwiches we can eat in the car."

"It's a date. Now, I have to go before Eri drives away and leaves me behind to walk home!"

The weather on Wednesday more than fulfilled Walter's hopes; it was sunny and in the upper twenties by eleven o'clock, an ideal day for snowshoeing. When Erik drove into the manse driveway at five minutes past twelve he was ready with ham and cheese sandwiches, some cookies, and his snowshoes. The time passed quickly as the two of them drove north. They talked about spring training and the Yankees' prospects for the season, Eri's likely college choice, and where they might go fishing on the opening day of trout season a month from today. Just before one o'clock they stopped at an unplowed side road a couple of miles before West Fort Ann. A packed-down trail followed the snow-covered road into the woods. They strapped on their snowshoes and headed in on the trail.

In just three-quarters of an hour the hunting camp Erik had described on Sunday came into view. It was a small, very weathered cabin with a porch that stretched across its front. Three Adirondack chairs sat on the porch. They took off their snowshoes at the base of the steps leading up to the front porch. Erik took a key from his pocket, unlocked the front door, and they stepped inside. When Walter's eyes adjusted to the dim light he could see that the camp was clearly a guys' place. Erik found a couple of coffee cups turned upside down in one of the kitchen cupboards. He took a quart thermos from his small backpack. "This is leftover coffee from the big pot we have at the office. It'll be lukewarm, but hearty. Why don't we sit outside on the porch in the Adirondack chairs? It will be warmer out there in the sun than it is in here."

Walter shivered and nodded. "That's for sure."

They went outside and sat down. With only a light breeze blowing the sun soon warmed them. While they ate their sandwiches they talked about the pre-season forecasts for the Yankees and speculated about when the snow would melt enough so they could get away for an overnight to fish the Ausable River. After about half an hour Erik sat back in his chair, looked directly at Walter and said, "So, my friend, you wanted to talk today. What's up?"

Walter responded with a nervous laugh. "Well, when I proposed the idea, it seemed like it would be easier to talk about it than it does now!" He paused and took a breath. "You may not be aware of it, but Mary Kerrigan and I have become very close friends."

Erik laughed boisterously. "Walter, come on! You need to remember that Schuylerkill Falls is a small town, and you're a minister. People watch your every move, especially any moves with a woman. If someone notices you even glance at a woman, by the end of the day everybody's talking about it, and half of them imagine what it would be like if you were married to her! You may not think they're paying attention, and they would never say anything directly to you about it, but they're watching."

Walter sighed. "Well, there's definitely something for the people-watchers to see. The relationship is becoming serious. I asked to talk with you because she and I have run into some tough stuff and I don't know how to help us get past it." He paused and took a sip of coffee.

"Maybe the best place to begin is the night Bob had his heart attack. I invited Mary to the manse for dinner that evening. A lot of our conversation over dinner and afterward was just plain fun, but some of it was difficult, especially when we got to talking about differences in our believing—or to be more accurate, between my believing and her not believing.

"About ten-thirty she sensed we had gone as far as we could go for one night with that kind of probing. She'd been after me all evening to give her a tour of the house. So I did. We ended the tour in my study. She shut the door to the hallway, turned off the desk lamp that I always leave on, stood opposite me, and said, 'I just shut out the church and the world.' I kissed her. It was an incredibly beautiful moment." He paused.

"So, what's your problem?" Erik asked with a grin. "Or, maybe you don't want to tell me what happened after that?"

"The damn telephone rang! That's what happened! It was Gert calling to tell me about Bob Hutchins's heart attack. I don't mean to imply that I was sorry she called; I do want to know right away when a parishioner needs me. But as soon as I told Mary that I would have to leave to go to the hospital everything that was going on between us fell apart. I know most of that was my fault; after the phone call came I couldn't bring myself back to her. I told her I was sorry I had to leave. Her response was devastating. She said, 'You've already left.'"

Erik shook his head slowly back and forth. "That must have jabbed into you!"

"It did, though at the time I didn't completely get what she was talking about. But things quickly got even more unnerving. She said, 'This is the way it would be if I was with you, isn't it? No matter what kind of moment we were having together the parishioner on the telephone could suddenly take you away from me, couldn't they?' I couldn't say anything for a minute, then I said, 'Yes, they could.' It was an honest answer, but I didn't appreciate the impact it would have on her." He sighed and shook his head. "She looked straight at me and said, 'There would be no moments when I could be sure of being first for you; in your life I would always be second. It would be worse than being married to a doctor.'" He stopped speaking and looked directly at Erik.

Erik looked very sober. "What did you say then?"

"I told her I was sorry, but I had to go. I took her home and went to the hospital."

"That's it?"

"No, there's more. I called her early last week to apologize for leaving so abruptly Friday evening. I told her how badly I felt about it when I arrived back at the manse at two in the morning. But I still didn't get how *she* felt about it—until she spelled it out: I'm kissing her, the phone rings, and my concern for the person on the phone immediately overwhelms everything I am feeling for her. I realize now why she said I was gone from her even before I actually left." He looked off into the woods, then back at Erik. "She asked gently whether it would have made any real difference if I had spent fifteen or twenty more minutes of tenderness with her after the phone call came? Whether anyone's life would have been affected adversely if I had?"

He shook his head and spoke softly, "You know, Erik, it wouldn't have. But I couldn't do it; once I got the news about Bob, I felt like I *had* to go immediately. Nothing she could have said would have made me feel differently. If the scene were re-run again right now, I would feel the same and do the same." He stopped speaking and looked at the floor.

Erik nodded sympathetically.

"In some ways, Erik, the incident was just another encounter with an old issue. I've always had trouble letting go and having fun when there's something I ought to be doing. Ironically, I talked about that old issue with Mary when we were together at your Christmas open house. I made some decisions after that conversation and acted on them. And I think I've done a better job of protecting time for things and people I enjoy.

"But it all fell apart when the call from Gert came. After I got the news about Bob I couldn't bring myself back to Mary, even for a few minutes. I felt like I would be betraying someone if I stayed with her—even like there was something illicit about being with her." He looked directly at Erik. "And that thought makes me angry! Why am I having so much trouble feeling all right about protecting space in my life for this woman I love? What's going on?"

Erik leaned back in his chair and reflected for a while. He spoke carefully. "I'm that doctor it would be worse than being married to; I've been where you were the other night. It's not easy to learn how to protect yourself, but it could be as simple as not *what* you did but the *way* you did it. When patients or parishioners hurt and call and interrupt you, lots of the time they're aware only of their own pain, not about what impact the call might have in your life. You have to weigh that. Very rarely is the caller's need so critical that it's worth sacrificing moments like you gave away the other night when you were with Mary. But only you can protect those moments. You don't have to rescue parishioners, Walter, you just need to minister to them. Rarely is someone's need so critical that you have to immediately tear yourself away from someone you love and run out the door. Mary was right; it wouldn't have mattered if you had spent a few more minutes of tenderness with her and then gone to the hospital.

"It'll take some time, but you need to train your heart to honor both the woman you love and the parishioners you serve. You have the same right to a personal life as the rest of us do. And no one besides you has to give you permission to have it."

"You think I can train my heart?"

"I do. It may take time, but you can do it."

Walter grinned, "And if I can't, I'll be back to more therapy from you."

"I'll be available!" He paused and took a breath. "But I think there's something else we need to talk about that relates to what's happening between you and Mary." He leaned forward. "After my comment about people-watchers you can guess that I've known for a while that you and Mary are friends. I figure that what you do in your personal life is none of my affair; you have the same right to choose your friends as the rest of us have. But when you say that you and Mary are becoming more than friends that changes things. Even the possibility that she might become your wife could affect your ministry. Maybe you sense that and it's why you're somewhat uneasy about your relationship with her."

"Say more."

"For a long time you've managed successfully to keep Mary and your church separate, but the other night they collided. And I suspect you stumbled onto something much more difficult to cope with than learning better how you can protect time and space in your life for things and people you enjoy. I am a little hesitant to say this—I don't want to overstate, but I think your use of the word "illicit" to describe what you were feeling is very revealing. To put it bluntly: it makes it sound like you're having an affair with Mary. When the call came from Gert it was like you were kissing another woman and your wife was on the telephone."

Walter's shook his head decisively, "No! Not really!"

"Well, maybe not literally, but it's similar. Just think about it for a minute. You may not want to admit it to yourself, but I'm sure you know that Mary Kerrigan would have real difficulty fitting into your life as a minister's wife. I suspect that's why you've kept her and the church separate. She's all right as a friend you see occasionally, but you know even better than I do that the way she acts is miles away from what most church people could accept in a minister's wife.

"I know whereof I speak. My mother was a minister's wife; if she ever had any doubts about what my father or the members of his church believed, she never voiced them. That's what people expect in a minister's spouse. I don't think Mary would adapt to be that kind of spouse. I don't mean to imply that she's a troublemaker; she has too much integrity for that. But she would not hold her tongue; every time she couldn't accept something she would challenge it. That would really be tough on you . . ."

Walter stood up quickly, "It's already been tough, but that's not all bad! It's also been good for me! She's forced me to examine what I believe in ways no one else ever has. I think it would help us to have people like her participating in our church. I think her challenges could help strengthen our believing." He brushed away some snow and sat down on the porch rail.

Erik spoke quietly. "She *might* do that, Walter. But do you think most people in our church could contend with her? If she challenged their believing the way she does yours when you're alone with her, could they handle it? Are people in our congregation prepared to handle the *kind* of challenges she would bring?"

Walter looked away. "I'm not sure."

"Well, think about it. A church is not a place where we expect to face Mary Kerrigans. I don't mean to be pejorative, but a church is like a safe box where everything is designed to reinforce believing. When we're in the box we assume that *all* the questions that might challenge our faith have answers that will reaffirm it. So, even if we have doubts, we assume they're only temporary. Even when we can't think of an answer ourselves that supports believing, we assume there must be one—and if we can't think of it our minister surely could. Our church and minister are our safety net. We depend on it.

"But think what it would be like if Mary were your wife and in our church box. We wouldn't have a safe haven anymore. Your wife would be constantly challenging our faith. The fallout would be huge for us and especially for you, Walter. People would begin to wonder about the strength of your faith. If you couldn't convince your own wife to believe, you would lose some, maybe lots, of your credibility as our pastor. You would be compromised."

Walter sat for a while and watched the chickadees flitting among the branches of the pine tree next to the porch. "Well, Erik," he said finally, "I don't know what to say. I've been going along assuming that I will find a way to deal with Mary's disbelief, and that even if I can't, I can at least carve out a protected space with her in my life—and that doing that would be good enough. If what you've just said is true, all of that is just wishful thinking. To go on with her and go on in my ministry I will have to find a way to make what I believe credible to her."

Erik nodded slowly. "Or, you will just keep having incidents like you had with her the other night."

Walter gave him a puzzled look, "How so?"

"Walter, if Mary doesn't believe in God, when a call comes like it did the other night why would she think it's urgent for you to leave her to go and pray with a critically ill parishioner? So urgent that you would break away and leave immediately even when the two of you were having a tender moment? What good does is do to pray if there is no God to respond? How can you respect what someone does if you think that what they do doesn't have any reality? "

Walter sat and stared at the floor and then looked up at Erik. "That hurt, Erik! You just did surgery on me without giving me anesthesia." He shook his head slowly back and forth. "I don't have a reply that counters that. You know I don't."

"I'm sorry, Walter, but I felt like I needed to say it. I'm a doctor. I listen and analyze and then share what I think is going on with patients. Sometimes, what I think is happening to them is hard to share. When that's true I try to be gentle, but I never equivocate."

Walter nodded slowly, then he spoke. "When I was a boy and visited my Grandmother and Grandfather Richards at their farm near Ballston Spa I often sat on the back porch and watched the birds eat at the bird feeders they kept full all year-round. One sunny morning in the late fall I noticed how close the chickadees were coming to me. They'd land on the porch rail right next to me and crack the sunflower seeds they took from the feeders. I wondered if they would trust me enough to eat seeds out of my hand; I'd heard somewhere that they would. So, I reached into the covered can where my grandparents kept the extra sunflower seeds and scooped up a few in my hand. I pulled my chair up to the rail and sat back down and laid my open hand with seeds in it on top of the rail and waited. For a while the chickadees just flew around me, but then one of them landed on my fingers. For at least a minute she just sat there. We looked into each other's eyes and in that moment our worlds connected." He paused and looked at Erik. "I love Mary Kerrigan, Erik; every part of me loves her. In so many ways we already connect; it's only a matter of time until we find a way to connect the rest. And, by God, we are going to find it."

The two of them sat for several minutes in the quiet. Then Erik spoke, "I hope it happens, Walter, I really do—but something tells me she will always be a wild bird."

Walter realized there was no more to say. He glanced up and noticed how low the sun had fallen in the sky. He looked at his watch. "It's almost quarter to four. I guess we've done what we can do today, and we have to get back in time for the Lenten study group tonight. We should start snowshoeing out to your truck."

Erik nodded in agreement. He reached down and took some snow in his hand, and scrubbed out their coffee cups with the snow, walked inside the cabin, set the coffee cups on the shelves in one of the cupboards, came back out, and shut and locked the door. He put the empty thermos into his backpack and strapped on his snowshoes. Walter put on his snowshoes and followed Erik back down the path to the main road.

Later that evening, as Walter led the Lenten study group in a discussion of one of Jesus' last words on the Cross, he kept recalling Erik's description of why people participate in church. When he looked into the eyes of those present he could see that they hungered for reassurance that God could triumph over every adversity that life might bring, even such a colossal tragedy as the death of his own son. He was also aware that they were leaning on his conviction that God would carry them through any challenge that life might bring. They had faith in his faith. He looked into their faces. "I couldn't bear to disappoint them," he thought. "But I love Mary, and I won't give her up."

After the group broke up he dried the coffee cups as Gert McCain washed them. The two of them stood together in the church kitchen and he prayed for God to heal Bob's heart. After Gert left Walter locked the parish house doors and walked across to the manse. It was only quarter past nine, but he felt exhausted. He took a book to read up to bed with him. He read barely a page before he fell asleep.

The next morning he was aroused by the warm sun streaming through his bedroom window. He felt refreshed and energized. After breakfast he worked on his sermon. The writing went so well that he decided to have an early lunch and drive to the hospital in Saratoga to check on Bob Hutchins. He had just begun to eat a ham and cheese sandwich when the telephone rang. It was Gert McCain.

"The awful chest pains have come back, Walter. They've put Bob back in the ICU. Can you come to the hospital right now?"

"I'm on my way—and I'll pray for all of you!"

"Thanks, Walter."

He drove to Saratoga as fast as he dared. He rushed through the lobby and up the stairs to the ICU. He found Molly and Gert standing in the hall. They both looked distraught. He walked with them to the visitors' waiting room at the end of the hall.

"I was sitting with him when it happened," Molly said. "We were just chatting about the kids when he blanched and put his hand on his chest. 'It hurts terrible,' he said. I ran to the nurse's station. Lots of people came and they moved him quickly to the ICU. They called Dr. Marino. He's still in there with him. God, won't let him die, will he, Walter? Tell me he won't. I'm so scared. I need your faith. Please tell me Bob won't die!"

"Molly, I know God will be with Bob no matter what happens. Let's tell God how we feel." He took hold of Molly's and Gert's hands. "O God," he said, "we are frightened. We know that Bob is very sick and we want him to get better. We know that you can heal him. Please touch him with your healing hand. Please mend his broken heart. Most of all please be with him through whatever happens. Help us to feel your presence. Help us to know that you are close to us and caring for us right now. We trust you, God. We know that we will be in your tender care whatever may happen to Bob. Give us strong faith. For Jesus' sake. Amen."

Walter opened his eyes to see tears streaming down Molly's and Gert's faces. He smiled at them through his own tears. They seemed to relax. "Why don't you sit here for a minute and I will go find out whether they will let me go in and pray at Bob's bedside." He walked and stood before the doors leading into the ICU. They opened. He recognized the nurse at the desk inside and she recognized him. She motioned to him to come inside; the doors shut behind him.

"If you want to pray, you can stand at the foot of his bed, pastor," she said. "Just don't get in anyone's way."

"Thanks, Taffy." He stood three feet away from the foot of Bob's bed. Those on either side of the bed caring for Bob ignored him. He looked at Bob; he thought he detected a faint smile. He closed his eyes. He moved his lips but made no sound. "O God, please heal Bob. Please make his broken heart whole. I so want you to help my friend. Please heal him." No more words came. He stood for a few seconds and watched Bob struggling to hang on to life. There was nothing more to do. He turned and walked back through the automatic doors into the hall and faced Molly and Gert. "He smiled at me; I think he's going to be all right." He saw the fright on Molly's face. "Whatever happens, Molly, you have to believe that God will do what is best for Bob." She put her arms around him and held on to him tightly. He patted her back carefully and then helped her sit down.

He stayed at the hospital for another hour. When Bob seemed to be stabilized, he told Molly and Gert that since it looked like Bob was all right he was going back to Schuylerkill Falls. He promised to return in the morning, or sooner, if they needed him.

When he arrived back at the manse, he found a business card taped to his kitchen door. It was supervising principal Jerry Ward's. On the back Jerry had written, "Please call me as soon as you can." He went inside and dialed Jerry's direct line at the school. Jerry answered.

"This is Walter, Jerry. I just returned from the hospital. Bob has apparently had another attack, but fortunately at the moment he seems to be stable."

"That's good to hear, Walter. I do know about the attack; everybody at the school knows—the news spread very quickly. Some teachers came to see me after lunch. They would like to invite the faculty and anyone else in the community who wants to come to gather for a prayer service at our church late this afternoon. I told the teachers I was sure you would be willing to lead a service of prayers for healing for Bob. I tried to phone you but realized you must be at the hospital when you didn't answer. I checked with the elders I could reach and they felt you would tell us to go ahead, so I put out a notice to the faculty suggesting everyone gather at the church at five-thirty. I even turned the heat up in the sanctuary after I left you a note. I hope you're all right with what I've done."

"Of course I am, Jerry. I think it's a wonderful idea. I'll be glad to lead the service. Something simple, not formal, just some Scripture and time for prayer. Is that what you have in mind?"

"Exactly! I will let everyone know that the service is definitely a go. And thanks for doing this, Walter. We need to do it for Bob and Molly. I have never seen such deep concern among the faculty as I have seen today. See you in a couple of hours."

After Walter hung up he thought, "I wonder if anyone called Smitty." He dialed Gillespie's. Smitty answered. "Hi Smitty, it's Walter."

"You want me to play at five-thirty?"

"Then you know about the service."

"Walter, the whole town knows about the service. I'm going to close the store at five. There won't be any sense in being open; everybody will be at the service. What would you like me to play?"

"I didn't find out about the service until a few minutes ago, so I'm just beginning to plan it. I think if you can play some old hymns while people gather and maybe some appropriate music at the end, or maybe just silence at the end. Nothing maudlin, please, something upbeat that will help to set a mood of confidence."

"We think the same, Walter. I'll be there by five-fifteen."

"Thanks, Smitty."

He hung up the phone and picked up his Bible. The service seemed to plan itself as he leafed through the Scripture passages. In ten minutes it was all clear in his mind. "We need to close with a rousing hymn of faith," he said out loud. He picked up the Hymnbook. He paged through the hymns of faith and assurance section. "Number 374, 'Be Still, My Soul,' to Sibelius's tune 'Finlandia;' that's just right. Everyone will know the tune." He called Smitty back. "It's Walter again, Smitty. I'd like to use hymn number 374 at the end of the service today."

"'Be Still, My Soul.' Good choice; it will be familiar to everyone. I'll be ready to play it. Is it okay if I let the old Skinner organ go full voice on the last verse?"

"Of course, Smitty. We need all the inspiration we can get today. See you in an hour."

He hung up the telephone and typed out the order of service. He went upstairs, put on a fresh white shirt and tie and his dark blue suit. He went back downstairs to his study. He folded up the order of service and put it in the inside pocket of his suit coat. It was a quarter to five. He decided to walk over to the church to be sure the furnace was working properly. When he looked out the front window of his study he realized that wouldn't be necessary. Joe and Nancy Pritchard's car was parked on the street in front of the church. Rich MacIver's car was parked right behind it. Jerry Ward had obviously called session members and asked them to come early to welcome people. He walked into his kitchen and looked at the thermometer. It read forty-two degrees; he wouldn't need a coat just to walk over to the church.

When he opened the front door of the church Nancy Pritchard greeted him. "This is a wonderful thing we are doing," she said. "The whole community is coming together to pray."

"It is," Walter said. "It's a day we will all remember."

He was surprised to see Smitty come through the door. "I closed the store," he said. "There's nobody downtown. Even Butch closed his garage. I'll start playing as soon as my hands warm up."

People were beginning to arrive. He recognized many of them, but a surprising number of them were people he had never met. Smitty began to play familiar hymns. He remained in the entryway welcoming people, introducing himself to those he didn't know. By twenty past five the sanctuary was full. Someone suggested putting chairs in the aisles. Joe Pritchard said a firm "no" to the suggestion; it would violate fire regulations. They could leave open both the door between the parlor and the hall and the door opposite that led to the sanctuary. A few people could sit in the parlor and at least hear the service. At five-thirty the seats were filled, including those in the choir loft, and people stood across the back of the sanctuary behind the pews. He walked up the center aisle and took his seat in the large upholstered chair behind the pulpit.

Smitty stopped playing soon after Walter sat down. Walter took the order of service from his pocket, rose, and stood behind the pulpit. "Welcome to all of you. We gather here today to testify to our faith in God and to pray for our beloved friend and neighbor, Bob Hutchins. We come in faith that Almighty God will look upon us with kindness and hear our prayers. We are not afraid because we know that whatever may happen to Bob or to any of us, God will be with us.

"We begin our service with readings from the Scripture that remind us of the strong care our God promises to provide. He led the congregation in the words of Psalm 100: ". . . the Lord is good; his steadfast love endures forever . . . ," then Psalm 46: "God is . . . a very present help in trouble." He read from the book of Romans: "We know that in everything God works for good with those who love him . . ." His strong voice resounded throughout the sanctuary, through the open door and across the hall into the parlor, and through the open doors into the entryway.

At the end of the readings he prayed. "O God, we have gathered here today to pray for our friend and husband and father, Bob Hutchins. We ask you to touch his body with your healing grace. We know that you who made him in the beginning can mend his broken heart. We offer our prayers in faith and with hope, trusting your promises and your grace. Hear now the spoken prayers offered by those gathered here today."

For a time no one spoke. Then a woman spoke one sentence, asking God's healing for Bob. She was followed by the voices of women and men, old and young, offering simple, earnest prayers. When the prayers faded into silence, he invited the congregation to stand and sing "Be Still, My Soul." The mighty Aeolian Skinner organ lifted the singers' voices: "Be still, my soul: the Lord is on thy side . . ." Smitty added improvised harmony during the final verse. The mighty pipe organ undergirded the singers' resolution.

When the echo of the "Amen" died away Walter pronounced the bene-diction. "May the powerful God who gave us life in the beginning, protect and keep us and our dear friend now and forever more. Amen."

The sanctuary was mostly quiet as people left. They smiled at one an-other, but said little. Within ten minutes the church building was empty and Joe Pritchard was locking the doors. Walter thanked Joe for his help and walked to the manse. As he mounted the steps to the side porch he real-ized that he had forgotten to look for Mary in the congregation. He decided she must have been present. When he opened the door to the kitchen Willie followed him inside.

He fed Willie and then decided to fix a light supper. He cut some slices from a small ham he had cooked two nights before, made two sandwiches and poured a tall glass of milk. He glanced at the kitchen clock and realized the network news was on television, but he decided to eat in quiet; he didn't want anything to distract him from the mood set by the prayer service. When he finished eating he let Willie back out and went into his study and worked on his sermon for a while. The writing went very well.

At a quarter to nine he went into his living room and pulled the E. Power Biggs recording of Bach's Passacaglia and Fugue in C-sharp minor from its sleeve and placed it on the spindle of his Garrard record changer. Bach's passacaglia always fed his soul. He turned on the hi-fi and pressed the lever on the side of the changer. The record dropped on to the turntable. He stretched out on the floor in front of the speakers. The giant opening notes of the passacaglia coursed through his body. The dazzling counter-point of the fugue carried him aloft. When the music ceased he remained still. After lying there for a few minutes, he thanked God for the gifts of the day and went to bed.

He awoke the following morning at first light. He showered quickly and went downstairs. He was pouring boiling water into the top of his drip cof-fee pot when the telephone on the kitchen wall rang. It was Erik Peterson. "Hi, Walter," Erik said, and then paused. "I'm sorry to be the bearer of bad news. Bob Hutchins died about an hour and a half ago."

Walter sat down slowly in one of the chairs at his kitchen table.

"I came in early to do rounds. Tom Marino met me in the hall outside the ICU. He had tried to call me before I left, but I was already in my car. He said Bob's weakened heart finally wasn't able to keep up and he succumbed just after five o'clock this morning. Molly was with him. Jerry and Ellen drove to the hospital after the service last night. They brought Gert home when visiting hours ended, but Molly refused to leave. Maybe she knew? I don't understand how, but wives sometimes have a way of knowing."

He paused, but Walter couldn't say anything. "I'm about finished here and I'm going to bring Molly home. She did agree to an autopsy so it will be late today before Burt Brundidge can pick up Bob's remains. I called Nancy Pritchard and she said Joe can bring her in to work at the hospital today so she can drive Molly's car home after she finishes her shift. I'm sorry, Walter. But you could probably tell when we went snowshoeing the day before yesterday that I was afraid this is the way things would turn out."

It took Walter a while to find his voice. "I'm stunned, Erik," he said. "I don't think anyone expected this to happen. Not after last night's service." He was having difficulty keeping control. "Please tell Molly how deeply sorry I am, and that I will call her at home this morning to see when she would like me to stop by. Do you think you will have her home by then?"

"I do. I have office hours beginning at nine and I haven't had any breakfast. Again, after the magnificent prayer service last night, I'm so sorry to bring this news this morning." He paused. "I have to go now. I have one more patient to see here before I can leave. Please call me later in the day if there is anything you want me to do. I'll leave some medication with Gert that she can give to Molly to help her sleep. When I finish office hours I'll stop and check on Molly to see if she needs anything else."

"Thanks, Erik. I'll call if I think of anything." He hung up the telephone and sat in silence. He looked into his empty coffee cup. The minutes clicked by on his kitchen clock. He folded his hands and closed his eyes. But no prayer came. Instead he was carried back in time. It was before seminary, before college. He was sitting at a camp fire listening to his grief-stricken father who believed he had prayed in vain. "It doesn't work, Walter," his father said. "It doesn't work."

10

JUST AFTER NINE-THIRTY WALTER dialed Molly Hutchins's telephone number. He knew he needed to talk with her, but he dreaded it. He had no idea what more he could say than, "I'm sorry." And that felt hollow.

When Gert, not Molly, answered he was relieved. "This is Walter, Gert. Dr. Peterson just called me with the news about Bob. I'm so sorry. After the prayer service yesterday I was sure he would get better." He could hear Gert struggling; he waited quietly until she was able to speak.

"We were so sure God would heal him . . . but he didn't." Her words hung in the air.

The silence that followed amplified the inadequacy he felt. He moved the conversation on to another concern. "Dr. Peterson said he would leave some medication for Molly. I hope it is helping her sleep."

"She said she wouldn't take it. She's stubborn that way, as you know. But I convinced her to take a warm bath and assured her the medicine was just a mild sedative. She finally agreed to take one pill and lie down after her bath. In a few minutes she fell asleep. I hope she sleeps a long time. I don't think she's had a good night's rest since Bob went into the hospital."

"I'm sure you're right—and the next few days will not be easy."

Gert followed his segue. "I told her I would call Burt Brundidge at the funeral home to find out what we need to do about making arrangements. I talked to him just a few minutes ago. He said there is no reason to rush Molly; he doesn't have any commitments today or this evening. If Molly is up to it, we will get together with Burt later today. Would you be available later this afternoon to talk about the service?"

"I will. Why don't you ask Burt to give me a call when you decide what day and time you would like to have the service? Anytime is fine; I have nothing scheduled the beginning of the week that I couldn't change.

"Thank God, you came to us before this happened, Walter. I don't know how we would get through it without you. It helps so much to know we can count on your faith."

"Thanks, Gert. I'm sure God will help us all get through this. I'll wait for the call from Burt." After he hung up he sat in the silence and stared. "God, everybody is so sure about my faith; I hope *I* can count on my faith."

At three-thirty the telephone rang. It was Burt Brundidge. "This is Burt, Walter; Molly and I have worked out the services for Bob and we hope you can be available. Molly would like to have visiting hours at the funeral home at six Sunday evening, and then the funeral service at the church on Monday at four. I hope those times work for you. The late afternoon hour will make it possible for teachers to attend without disrupting the school day. No one in the family has to come from far away. And there's plenty of time to notify everyone. We can get the notices in tomorrow's newspapers, and you can announce the times in church on Sunday."

"That's fine. I can do the service Monday at four. I'll contact Smitty right away to be sure he's available to play the organ—but I'm sure he will be, and I'll let Joe Pritchard know the sanctuary will need to be cleaned Monday morning."

"Thanks, Walter. Can you hold on a minute? Molly has something she would like to ask you." He could hear Burt passing the phone to Molly.

"Hi, Walter." The flatness in her voice surprised him. He was about to speak when she continued, "Would you be able to stop by tomorrow morning around ten-thirty to plan the funeral service? I'd suggest we do it today, but I've done about all I can do today."

"Tomorrow is fine, Molly. Whatever is good for you is fine with me. When you wake up tomorrow morning, if you decide you want to meet later in the day, please feel free to call me and suggest a later time."

"Thanks, Walter. I'm sure that ten-thirty will be fine. Do you need to say anything more to Burt?"

"No, I don't think so. But I want to be sure that you are all right."

"I feel very tired, Walter, but I'm doing all right." She paused, then continued in the same flat voice. "Thanks for being there for us all those days when Bob was so sick and . . . I'll see you tomorrow morning." She hung up.

He puzzled over the conversation with Molly as he walked to Butch's garage where he had left his car for servicing earlier in the day. The one person he expected to be most openly upset was completely controlled. She was so different from the Molly who had wept openly and held on to him when Bob was in the hospital. He wondered whether the medication Erik gave her had dulled her emotions.

After supper he tried reading several different books, but none of them kept his interest. He turned on the TV. He realized again that Friday night programs weren't the best, but he sat in front of the set until the news came on at eleven. After watching the news for five minutes he switched off the TV and went upstairs. When he sat on the edge of his bed and took off his shoes and socks he felt Willie's absence. He missed that fickle cat! He was tempted to go back downstairs and look through the window in the kitchen door to be sure Willie wasn't waiting outside on the porch. But he didn't; he put on his pajamas, turned out the lamp on the stand next to his bed, and slipped under the covers. He tried to pray for Molly, but none of the words that came to him seemed adequate.

In the darkness his thoughts turned back to Willie. He wondered: What do cats know? Do they have faith? Who do they have faith in? He thought about a dead cat he had seen in the street earlier in the day. He wondered: does God care for cats any better than he cares for people? The question seemed silly, but it troubled him and it wouldn't go away. Across the back yards he noticed the lights of a passing car on the street in front of Miss Simpson's house. The quiet and darkness settled in again. The image of the unfortunate cat kept passing in front of his mind's eye. He wondered: was the cat simply unfortunate or not blessed? He knew what Mary would say.

The next morning he met with Molly over a cup of coffee at her home to plan the funeral. He knew she needed to grieve before she would be comfortable talking about the service. As they sat at the kitchen table he invited her to tell him how she met Bob. Being able to talk about Bob seemed to relieve her. Suddenly she seemed finished saying what she wanted to say; she stopped and looked directly at Walter and laughed quietly, "He was quite a guy."

"Yes, he was, Molly; he really was." He watched a tear trickle down her cheek. She quickly wiped it away with the back of her hand. He sensed it was time to move on. "Do you know what you would like to include in the service when we remember the wonderful guy he was?"

"Nothing much beyond what you usually do. I want it to be simple: the usual Scripture readings, especially the Twenty-Third Psalm. I do want to sing 'For All the Saints Who from Their Labors Rest.' That hymn was one of Bob's favorites. I love the way Smitty plays it to the Ralph Vaughan Williams tune." Her eyes sparked, "Tell him to play it with gusto! That's all I can think of. Except you may want to talk about how God could have chosen to let him die right after everyone prayed for him to get better." She stopped and looked directly at him. Her look froze him. Finally she looked away and continued. "Maybe I shouldn't have said that? But it is the big question that will be on everyone's mind."

For a moment he couldn't find words to respond with. "I'll be sure to include Psalm 23, and I will tell Smitty about the gusto request when I see him in the morning. And I will keep the big question in mind as I plan the service." His response felt weak to him; he wished he could think of something that seemed adequate, but he couldn't. As they sat together in silence he felt unprepared, like a student who hadn't done his homework.

Molly rescued him. "I feel tired, Walter. I'm ready for you to offer a prayer." She reached out to him across the table. He took both of her hands in his and prayed gently. "O God, we thank you for your sustaining presence during the long days of Bob's illness. Now he has gone from us to you and we don't know why. The pain of losing him is nearly unbearable. Molly's heart is broken—and so is mine. Please lay your healing hand on her and give her faith and hope. Please be a strengthening presence to her and Eddie and Jean and Gert over the next two days. Help all of us to trust you, even when we can't understand you. Amen."

When he raised his head and released her hands Molly wiped the tears from her face with the backs of her hands. He offered her his handkerchief.

"I really shouldn't take it; I still have the one you gave me in the hospital."

He smiled. "It's all right."

"I know; you have a drawer full of them." She wiped her face with his handkerchief and handed it back to him. "Thanks, Walter. Thanks for everything." He could feel her tears between his fingers as he placed the handkerchief back into his pocket.

Sunday morning he was awakened long before daylight by the sound of Butch's plow truck in the driveway. He got up and looked out the bathroom window. In the headlights of the truck he could see that at least six inches of snow had fallen. He had been so busy yesterday that he hadn't paid attention to the weather forecast. He realized he should have: early spring is a precarious season in upstate New York. Two days of almost warm weather had deceived him. He walked back to his bedroom and looked at the alarm clock on the table next to his bed. It read five a.m. It was due to ring in a half hour. He was awake now, so he might as well stay up. He shut the alarm button off.

The morning service was crowded—in spite of the snow. It seemed unnecessary to announce Bob's passing; everyone he talked with before the service knew about it. But he announced it anyway, and even though everyone had heard the news, there was still an audible gasp when he made the announcement.

After the morning service he went home to the manse and made lunch. When he finished his lunch he tried to take a nap, but he couldn't sleep. He kept thinking about what he might say in his sermon at the funeral service for Bob the next day. People would hang on his words; he would have to be clear and convincing.

He thought about an interview he saw on television with a young man who had survived a refinery explosion that killed two of his coworkers. The young man said he believed God preserved him because he had some important work for him to do in this world. He didn't know what that work was, but believed God would reveal it to him. It was a common response; those who survived tragedies often believed God had a direct hand in their survival. But that line of thinking was hazardous. It could suggest that God let Bob Hutchins die because he had no essential work for him to do in this life.

After getting up twice and going to his desk to make notes, he gave up on the nap. He went in and sat at his desk. By four he had chosen the Scripture he would read and filled three pages on a yellow pad with notes for a sermon. He felt relieved; in the morning he would be able to develop the notes into a strong sermon. It was time to make a sandwich and drink a glass of milk to gather strength for his weekly session with the youth group.

Finishing the funeral sermon the next morning turned out to be more difficult than he had anticipated. He kept struggling with the question he knew would be foremost in everyone's mind: why had Bob died only a few hours after the entire community prayed for his recovery. Nothing he was prepared to say offered a satisfying answer.

At three he folded the notes and put them in the inside pocket of his suit jacket and went over to the church. Smitty arrived just as he did. After thirty years as organist Smitty must have played every hymn in the hymnbook dozens of times, but he still arrived early before every service to practice the hymns chosen for that service. Smitty gave him a solemn look as he walked through the double doors into the sanctuary. " 'For All the Saints' with 'gusto,'" he said. "I need to practice the gusto."

Walter sat in one of the back pews and listened to Smitty practice. He loved to be alone in the church with the sound of the organ. The gusto Smitty worked out for the verses of "For All the Saints" brought tears to his eyes. He was glad to have an opportunity to weep before he had to lead the service.

When Smitty finished practicing Walter walked to the front of the sanctuary. As he stood behind Smitty he said, "I especially liked the alternate harmony you improvised for the third verse, and . . ." he stopped speaking. Smitty had turned around on the organ bench to face him. Tears stained his face. "I'm sorry," Walter said. "I didn't mean to intrude."

"It's all right," Smitty said. "I was thinking of a night many years ago when I came over to the church by myself and played that hymn. Some sorrow never goes away."

"I know," Walter said in a gentle voice, "I do know. I have some of my own that's like that."

Smitty nodded sympathetically. "And I left my pain-dulling companion at home so I would be sober and alert for this service." He put his hand into the inside pocket of his suit jacket and brought it out empty. "See!"

"Thanks, Smitty." He heard talking behind him. Burt had come in and was instructing the pallbearers and ushers. It was only a few minutes past three o'clock, but already people were beginning to arrive for the service. He walked among those arriving greeting those he knew and introducing himself to those he didn't know. By quarter to four, except for the pews reserved for the family and pallbearers, all the pews were full.

At ten minutes to four he walked down the hall past the parlor door to the choir room. He took his robe from the closet, put it on, walked back down the hall and stood before the closed door to the parlor. He took a deep breath and opened it slowly. Molly, Jean, Eddie and Gert were sitting inside. He reached out his hands to them. "Perhaps it would help all of us to have a prayer before we go in for the service."

"Yes, it would," Molly said.

Burt appeared at the door to the hallway just as Walter finished praying. "It's almost four o'clock," Burt said. "I would like to escort you to your seats now."

Molly took each of her children by the hand. "We're ready."

Walter watched them follow Burt out of the parlor and across the hall and through the door into the front of the sanctuary. Only once in his life had he walked in their footsteps. His heart reached out to them. After they were seated, he walked through the same door and up the steps and sat in the big upholstered chair behind the pulpit. When Smitty stopped playing he rose and stood behind the pulpit and spoke in a strong, confident voice.

"We gather today to remember and celebrate the life of Robert Barr Hutchins, husband of Molly McCain Hutchins, and father of Edward and Jean Hutchins. Bob, as all of us know him, was born May 5, 1915, in Sidney, New York . . . This past Friday, March 3, 1961, early in the morning he passed on to be with his Lord . . . Though Bob has died and departed this life, we know that he lives on and shall never die."

After he prayed for God's presence and comfort he read several Scripture readings. When he finished the readings he closed the Bible and looked into the faces of those gathered before him.

"Today we gather together to mourn the loss of Bob Hutchins, our husband, father, teacher, friend, and colleague. We will miss him. We already miss him in so many ways." (He paused and managed a slight smile.)

"Who will ever be able to undo the wire puzzles in the collection he left behind? He threw away the instructions!"

There was a titter of laughter in the congregation. He could feel people beginning to relax. He described several humorous incidents from Bob's years as a teacher and as a leader in the church. After the laughter died away he continued in a more serious tone.

"Today we give thanks to God for Bob's wonderful life. But as we do so we are haunted by a nagging question—a question that Molly and I agreed would be on the minds of all of us today. Why did God let Bob Hutchins die when he was only 45—and right after we had all gathered here in this very sanctuary to pray for his healing? Did God want Bob Hutchins to die at such a young age?"

He stopped speaking. Fixated faces in the silent sanctuary waited for his response. He saw Mary among them; she was looking directly at him. For a second panic reigned inside of him: he doubted that he could answer his own question. The pause became awkward. The congregation stared at him. Finally he spoke:

> *The answer is a resounding "NO!"* Bob Hutchins's death does not reflect either some tragic mistake on God's part or, worse, some punishment meted out to us or to him . . . Though we are sometimes tempted to think so, our faith does not give us some privileged status. We are subject to the same hazards of life in this world as all humans are.
>
> But even if we understand why there is suffering in our world we still wonder: Are the particular adversities we suffer personally the result of some moral failure on our part? Again, the answer is a resounding 'No.' The afflictions we suffer are not a punishment for some sin we committed. God does not send illness or let us die to teach us something.
>
> But whatever we may suffer, there is good news: *no affliction we suffer is final.* God can and will overcome all our suffering. Even death is not the end. At the end there is God who will not be defeated . . .
>
> Bob Hutchins died last Friday of a heart attack that was neither deserved nor fair. But that was not the end of him; God has raised him up. Our prayers were answered. Bob Hutchins may not have recovered from his sickness, but by God's grace he lives. That knowledge gives us peace that surpasses understanding.
>
> In the confidence that faith brings to us, let us pray.

After several moments of silence he offered prayers of thanksgiving for Bob's life. After he finished praying he invited the congregation to stand and "with 'gusto' sing a hymn that Bob Hutchins loved, that great hymn of faith, 'For All the Saints Who from Their Labors Rest.'" As he watched a tear-stained Molly listening to the singing and slowly nodding her head he thought, "This is what she hoped for when she said she wanted the hymn sung 'with gusto.'"

After the benediction he walked to the back of the church and greeted the worshippers as they left. One of them was Mary Kerrigan. As he shook hands with her she smiled through her tears and took his hand in both of hers and said, "Thank you; thank you for your words of hope." Her words surprised him. He was surprised and pleased. He said, "You're welcome, Mary." He wanted the moment to last.

After the family left he took off his robe and hung it back in the closet in the choir room. He walked through the building and checked the thermostats and the doors. He knew Joe Pritchard always secured the building before he left, but he liked to check anyway. When he came back into the vestibule between the front doors and the sanctuary, Smitty was standing there. "Hi, Smitty," he said, "I thought you had gone." He noticed a bit of a grin on Smitty's face.

"No," Smitty said, "I've been waiting here for you."

"Is something wrong?"

"No, just wondering if you have anything planned for the next couple of hours?"

"No, I don't."

"Remember the bet we made Christmas Eve?" Walter nodded. "You lost. You owe me a steak dinner. How would you like to pay up?" He paused and the grin faded. "Walter, I need a friend tonight."

Walter looked at him with understanding. "So do I," he said. "It is a good night to pay up. Where shall we go? You're the winner so you get to choose the restaurant."

"The Falls Diner, of course. It's our only gourmet restaurant. Their fare ranges from pizza to steak dinners. Frankly, Walter, I never thought a Greek could cook an excellent steak, let alone make an acceptable pizza, but Stephanos does both. Of course, he worked at Leonardo's in Saratoga before he bought the diner. That little restaurant hidden away in southwest Saratoga is a real treasure. You can't find better Italian food anywhere than you can get at Leonardo's."

"I know," Walter said. "Their sauces are excellent."

"How do you know about Leonardo's? Who took you there?"

"My friend, Mary Kerrigan."

"Ah, yes. Your Mary—such a good guide; she definitely knows the territory. Meet you at the Diner in an hour."

The dinner with Smitty was great fun. At the end of the meal they were the only customers left in the restaurant and he invited Stephanos to join them for coffee. Stephanos bought each of them a rich dessert and refilled their coffee cups. Smitty and Stephanos told increasingly bawdy jokes—obviously Smitty was a regular. When they stood by their cars at the end of the evening and shook hands Smitty refused to let go of his hand. He looked directly at him. "Thanks, Walter, for the dinner—and for the 'therapy.' It helped a lot. I feel much better than I did two hours ago. Let's do it again soon."

Walter nodded. "We will, my friend; it was good for me, too."

As he drove home he felt re-energized. It was refreshing to spend an evening with someone who just wanted to be with him. When he drove around the corner from Main Street on to Church Street he noticed a silhouette of the Presbyterian Church's steeple towering over the tops of the houses in the moonlight. He spent most of his sleeping and waking hours in the shadow of that steeple. How different his daily experience was from most people's. He was surrounded most of the day, every day, by symbols and routines that reinforced his believing. He lived in the shadow of a church steeple in a house made of the same brick as the church. Three nights of most weeks he went to meetings in the church building where they discussed church affairs. He spent three hours nearly every morning in his study, surrounded by books that supported the faith he espoused. Everywhere he went people knew him and treated him as "Reverend Macdonald," a minister of God.

When he approached the manse driveway, for the first time in years he recalled a poem with motions that his Grandfather Richards taught him when he couldn't have been more than five or six years old. He remembered watching his grandfather carefully and copying the shapes he made with his hands as the two of them sat together on the big swing on the front porch at his grandparents' farmhouse. His grandfather began by placing his hands in front of him with the palms turned up, fingertips touching. He nodded at Walter, "Now you do it."

Walter did the same.

Then grandfather moved his hands together and interlocked his fingers. With the fingers still interlocked he turned his hands toward himself so the palms were inside now and the backs were facing out. "Now you do it," he said to Walter.

Walter kept trying until he could do the same.

Grandfather then extended his index fingers upright together like a church steeple; his thumbs were together below the "steeple," side-by-side like church doors.

Walter worked his hands into the same position.

"You've got it!" Grandfather Richards laughed and then began: "Here's a church," he said, nodding at his and Walter's hands; and as he nodded at their upright extended fingers he said "and there's the steeple," then as he folded his thumbs back revealing the fingers inside he said, "open the doors"—Walter did the same—then Grandfather wiggled his fingers and said, "and there's the people!"

Walter remembered laughing and trying again and again until he could do the motions with his hands while he recited the poem.

Then grandfather taught him a second version. This time when he began he interlocked his fingers so that only one finger was inside, the rest were outside. He varied the ditty as they went through the motions together. "Here's the church/ and there's the steeple/ open the doors/ and there's only the minister." He wiggled the single finger inside. "It's a weekday!" he shouted and laughed.

Walter stopped the car in his driveway, stepped out and looked up at the church steeple towering over the manse. He formed his hands to match the second version of the poem and wiggled the lone finger. "It's a weekday and I'm that minister," he thought. "How different my life is from everyone else's. Everything around me tells me that God is real. Everyone treats me as someone for whom God is real. They assume that I know that God is real and present everywhere. But their lives aren't filled with markers like mine is that say it's true. Or, if they are, they don't see them. Or believe in them. Unless they see everything through lenses shaped by ingested believing like Miss Simpson and confirmed believers like her do. It's the box Erik talked about." He shook his head, walked up the drive, across the walkway, up the porch steps and went inside. He took off his jacket and went into his study. He stood and looked at his books.

11

As Easter approached he was busy with additional services that entailed additional preparation. He marveled at the stamina of his Calvinist predecessors who had prepared three sermons every week year-round. On Easter Sunday he was glad that he had accepted Becky and Erik's invitation to join them for Easter dinner. He apologized for "eating and running, but I'm exhausted." They understood: he looked very tired. Even though he took a long nap when he arrived back home, he fell asleep on his big couch shortly after nine and missed most of Bonanza on television.

On Monday Mary was very much on his mind as he trout-fished on the Schuylerkill Creek. He had been so busy with pastoral work and preparations for Easter that he had neglected to call her. And, after the difficult evening when he'd had to rush away from her to go to the hospital, he felt like he had neither the wisdom nor the courage to talk with her. But enough time had passed now that he felt able to do it. When he reached home late in the afternoon he went straight through from the kitchen to his study and sat down at his desk and dialed her number. No answer. Then he remembered: it was a school vacation week. She was probably away. He kept calling all week. He didn't reach her until the following Monday evening. When she answered the telephone he said, "Hi, Mary, it's Walter."

"Walter?" she said, obviously a put-on questioning in her voice, "Walter who?"

"Okay, Miss Kerrigan," he said. "You're right. It's been a very long time since I called."

"I was beginning to wonder if you had lost interest."

"That will never happen!" he said emphatically. "With you I might lose my nerve, but I will never lose interest. And to prove that I haven't yet lost my nerve, I called to see when we might get together. Are you free this Friday?"

"Unfortunately, I'm not. On Saturday my mother is presenting a paper at the Mid-Atlantic regional meeting of the American Academy of Religion in New York City and she's asked me to go along with her. I'll take the train down there with her late Friday afternoon. I'll listen to her presentation on Saturday morning because she's my mother and I care about her. But I'm not particularly interested in the rest of the sessions so I'm going shopping in the afternoon and then I'm going to hook up with some old friends from my Barnard days and do the town with them. Want to come along? We could even take in a Yankees game."

"Sounds like fun—and I might even be interested in the Academy sessions. Unfortunately, I have to work weekends."

"Too bad. You'd have fun on a weekend with me."

"With your mother along?"

"She could get her own room. She wouldn't mind."

"Miss Kerrigan, you are scandalous."

"Mr. Macdonald, you are not—sadly. You pray, 'Lead me not into temptation,' and that prayer is always answered—in spite of my attempts to interfere."

"So, what about the following Friday, the twenty-first?"

"That seems so far away." Her voice brightened. "I have an idea. I coach the debating club. Melanie and Eri are on opposite sides of a debate a week from Wednesday. You could come to the debate and we could order take-out pizza from the diner afterwards. There's a deal for you! You earn credit for supporting two kids from your church and get a date with me in the same evening. How can you resist?"

"I won't. Where and what time?"

"In the school library at three-thirty. We use the Mace style of debate so we keep very strict time. We should be finished by five. You'll be interested in the topic."

"What is it?"

"At the high school level, girls' sports should receive the same support as boys' sports."

"I bet I can guess who suggested that topic. Melanie Chase."

"None other. Then you'll come?"

"I will." The lilting tone left her voice as she continued, "I'll be glad to see you Walter. I've missed you."

When she said, "I've missed you," her longing touched his. "I've missed you, too," he said. "I've missed you a lot. The next ten days can't go by too quickly."

The ten days did not go by quickly or easily. Walter hoped to at least listen to the Yankees opening game against Minnesota on Tuesday, but he had to attend a Presbytery committee meeting in Schenectady that lasted all through the game. To make matters worse, when he caught the news and sports on his car radio, as he drove home he discovered the Yankees had lost six to nothing. The next day he decided to attend to the pastoral calling he had neglected during the weeks leading up to Easter. He committed the remaining weekday afternoons to catching up. By the end of Friday afternoon he had, with varying degrees of patience, endured six elderly parishioners' complaints about their ailments. The one exception was Miss Simpson, now back in her own home, with whom he had a spirited conversation about the similarity between correct believing and correct grammar.

Saturday morning he finally worked out Sunday's sermon. After lunch he took a nap and then went for a long walk. He caught the end of the Yankees game when he returned. He was pleased that they recovered from their opening-day loss to Minnesota and beat Kansas City.

Sunday was cold and rainy, and church attendance was poor. "Just as well," Walter thought as he walked to the manse after the post-service coffee hour: the sermon felt disappointing when he preached it; it was not one of his better offerings. Monday and Tuesday dragged by; Wednesday finally came. He worried all day that some emergency would take him away from his date with Mary. He was grateful that the telephone was silent.

Mary was obviously pleased when she saw him in the small audience that gathered in the school library to watch the debate. The four students—a boy and a girl on each team—had taken their assignments to heart; they were well-prepared. But as soon as she spoke it was clear that Melanie's team would prevail; debate was definitely her forte. She was a formidable contender. She obviously loved challenging and being challenged. Eri had all he could do to hold his own against her. She won the hearts of the audience as well as the votes of the judges. When the debate was over Walter congratulated each of the debaters. They seemed genuinely pleased that he had attended.

The room cleared quickly; by quarter past five Mary and Walter were alone in the library. "The debate was great!" Walter said. "You did such a good job of coaching the debaters. Even the boys spoke in strong and convincing voices."

"Thank you," she said as they walked down the hall toward the door leading to the teachers' parking lot. "It took real work! At least Eri has been in some plays, but this was Fred's first foray into the world of public speaking. It took hours to get him to look somewhere besides at his shoes when he speaks! But enough rehash. I'm hungry! How soon can we order something to eat?"

Walter raised his shoulders and cocked his head to one side. "Well, I'm ready now," he said.

"Tell you what," she said. "I'd like to stop at home and change out of these schoolmarm clothes. Why don't you order the pizza and pick it up and I'll meet you at your house in an hour?"

"Sounds like a plan. Want me to pick you up?"

"No, you don't have to do that. It's not that cold out. I can walk over and you can drive me home later."

"You're right," he said when they stepped outdoors; "it is a mild evening for this time of year. I'll look for you in an hour." He started to walk toward the visitors' parking lot. Suddenly he turned around and walked back toward her. He called out to her. "What do you like on your pizza?"

She turned around. "Everything," she said. "How about you?"

"Everything but anchovies."

"Real men eat anchovies," she said. She gave him that Mary Kerrigan smirk.

He stood and looked at her intently. "I'll not be out-smirked!" he said. "Large pizza to go with everything—including anchovies. See you at my place in an hour." She grinned at him and walked toward the sidewalk leading down School Street. He felt buoyant and confident as he watched her walk away.

It was six-fifteen when Mary walked up the steps to his side porch. He opened the door before she had a chance to knock. The smell of pizza keeping warm in the oven greeted her. He had searched through the linen drawer in the dining room until he found a white tablecloth to cover the kitchen table. It was too big, but it had the desired effect. A burning candle he had inserted into the spout of an empty wicker-covered Chianti wine bottle sat in the middle of the table. There were two place settings, each adorned with a folded red cloth napkin.

He helped her off with her jacket and hung it on one of the hooks on the wall next to the door. She turned and faced him. He put one arm around her waist, the other behind her head, and pulled her to him and kissed her passionately. "My God, I've missed you," he said when he finally relaxed his hold.

She looked into his eyes. "I thought you invited me to eat. You keep kissing me like that and we will eat very cold pizza!"

"That wouldn't be all bad," he said with a grin.

She laughed. "You sound like me!"

"Maybe you're rubbing off on me."

"I hope so." She turned and looked at the table. "Your table looks just like our table at Leonardo's."

"Thank you," he said. "We had such a great evening that cold night when we danced and had dinner there. We need to do it again soon." She smiled and nodded. He noticed that she had on the same over-sized varsity crew sweater she had worn the first time he saw her. "The sweater is familiar," he said and quickly added, "but I like it."

"I know you do," she said, "because you kept staring at it when I wore it to Erik and Becky's picnic." He felt himself blush. "Besides it's always cold in your house. But enough about my clothes. The pizza smells wonderful. I'd like to eat."

"Please be seated, madam," he said as he pulled a chair out for her.

"Thank you, 'Dr.' Macdonald."

"Will you be having wine, this evening?"

"What are you offering?"

"We have a bottle of that Ruffino that you like so much. We have been saving it in anticipation of your visit."

"By all means, please serve it!"

They continued the friendly banter during supper. They caught up on the news from each other's lives; her father had a book coming out in May—there would be a reading and reception at the college. Maybe he would like to attend with her? It would be an excellent opportunity for him to meet her parents; her father was bound to be in a good mood. He agreed. He talked about his relief that the frenzied Easter season was finally past. The only sober moments occurred when he shared his concern about Molly; Mary became very quiet when he talked about her. In other circumstances he would have thought she was jealous, but wasn't sure enough to ask.

As he set their dishes into the sink she said, "You look so much better than you did the last time I saw you."

"You mean at the funeral—I think that was the last time."

"It was. You looked completely worn down that day."

"I was. When Bob died the morning after we all prayed for his recovery I felt like I was forced into the position of a debater representing God's team. My sermon at the funeral represented a massive mustering of emotional and spiritual energy."

"Your sermon was very convincing," she said. "For a few seconds in the middle of it you looked like you had forgotten your lines, but you recovered and went on to make a strong case."

Her implication that he was like an actor playing a part troubled him, but he chose not to challenge it.

"It seemed much longer than a few seconds to me," he said, "but I was all right when I recovered. I felt confident as I shared the clear, well-defined believing I gained in seminary."

She looked puzzled. "I'm not sure what you mean by 'the clear, well-defined believing I gained in seminary.'"

He looked at her soberly. "You really want to talk about this? I thought we were just going to have a fun evening."

"I thought the same, but what you believe and how you came to believe it matters to me—because you matter to me."

Her comment encouraged him to continue. "Thank you, I'm glad you care." He took a moment to reflect before he went on. "I'll try to be concise. Theological education provided me with disciplined believing. In seminary you learn that true belief in God rests not on speculation but on revelation. What God is like is revealed in Scripture—the Word of God. The historic creeds and doctrines of the church are products of that revelation."

She gave him a quizzical look.

He smiled, "I recognize that look! Let me try to explain. Just the other day I was discussing faith with a parishioner. She seems more rigid in her believing than I am in mine, but she described the way of believing I learned in seminary very well. She said that, just as there are rules of grammar, there are rules for believing; sound faith comes from honoring these rules. For example, she reminded me that her minister father believed, just as I do, that Christian faith is a revealed faith. I thought she illustrated this point very well. 'We must never use the subjunctive when speaking of God,' she said. 'We must never conjecture, if God *were* such and such . . . Scripture reveals what God is. It enables us to speak about God always in the indicative.'"

"Sounds like someone who used to have my job."

"It is someone who used to have your job."

"And you believe like she described believing."

"I do."

She responded with the same quizzical look.

"You look uncomfortable with my answer."

"I am."

"Why?"

"Well, if I understand correctly, for you all the fundamental questions of believing are settled. You have the answers; they were given to you in seminary. That's what theological education did for you. For example, you believe God is like a good and caring cosmic parent. That's the primary question and the answer is clear and settled. That fundamental belief was the foundation for your sermon and it supports all your dealings with Molly. No matter what evidence to the contrary might appear, it doesn't shake your fundamental conviction that God is a good and caring God. Right?"

He responded cautiously. "I'm not sure where you are going with this, but for now I will say, 'Right.'"

She smiled and sat back in her chair. "So, only secondary questions remain, that's where I'm going. When something bad happens, like Bob's death or your brother's death, it doesn't undermine your conviction that God is good and caring. It may challenge your faith, but it doesn't shake it because if you can't see why it happened, you assume the problem is not that God's goodness is somehow compromised, you assume that the problem is your lack of understanding."

"That's correct; it most likely is my problem. God is much bigger, far beyond our ability to imagine God."

She sat up straight and looked directly at him. "But doesn't that seem too easy, Walter? No matter how horrible things get you assume there is some explanation that would dissolve the apparent conflict between the horror that has happened and your belief that an unfailingly good God is in charge. So what happens doesn't always reflect what God wants. Bob Hutchins has a heart attack and dies because unfortunately he was born with a flawed heart, but that's not what God wants. So, you can have a creation that includes both beautiful sunsets and children who die in accidents and still have a good God."

He rubbed the back of his neck. "I wouldn't have said it exactly that way, but I think that is essentially right. Things that happen may shake my faith, Mary, but they don't do it in." He paused. "I can tell by the look on your face that you don't accept what I just said."

"Walter," she said shaking her head back and forth, "I love you and I wish I could accept it, but to me theological education sounds like a kind of brainwashing. You learn these fundamental beliefs handed to you by the church. You keep on believing them even if there is no convincing evidence to support them—even when you encounter evidence that argues overwhelmingly against them. Once you swallow the church party line it's like you wear a set of blinders that prevent you from looking around and seeing things as they really are."

He sat up and looked straight at her. "No, this time I wouldn't say it that way. I would say 'that evidence sometimes *appears* to argue against what I believe.' I think 'appears' is an important addition. I feel God's care even when I don't understand why something happens like Bob's unfair death. I can keep my faith when something like that happens because I believe there are limits to what we can know." He saw she was ready to speak. "Give me one more minute before you respond."

She leaned forward and looked at him intently. "Okay, go on."

"I believe this world is a corrupted version of what God created. We don't know exactly how it got that way or why God permits it to continue that way. But our ignorance doesn't preclude continuing to believe. Faith offers remedies not explanations. Forgiveness and peace are remedies. We don't pray for answers to the question 'why,' we pray for grace. We don't plead 'tell me why,' but 'help me get through it.'"

She waited for a moment, then reached out and took hold of his hand; she spoke carefully. "Walter, I respect what you propose when you say faith offers remedies, not explanations. That possibility even gives me some comfort, but it doesn't satisfy me. I'm just not the kind of compliant believer you seem to be. Remedies may comfort me, but they don't content me."

"So, you think all beliefs should be open to questioning."

"They have to be. There's too much conflicting evidence. Sometimes a good God seems to be in charge of what happens and other times no one seems to be in charge. I think the best any faith can offer is theory, a tentative theory that is always subject to revision. Even popes hold erroneous beliefs."

He felt himself struggling to respond; he let go of her hand. "I agree that there has to be room for questioning, but not in basic matters of faith." His voice had become strong. "When believing becomes only a theory it loses its power. It takes more than a theory to comfort people like Molly Hutchins and my father. My father can't believe so he has no consolation."

"You believe," she said gently, "and you still have tears." She regretted the comment as soon as she had made it. She reached out and touched his hand. "I'm sorry, Walter. I didn't mean to hurt you."

He responded softly, "I know you didn't." He searched her face carefully, then continued, "For me tears are a sign of grieving, not evidence of a lack of faith. We cry because we are human, not because we believe or don't believe. You had tears while I was preaching at Bob's service. I saw you. When I looked at you I thought you were agreeing with what I said. I barely kept control of myself when I looked at you."

There was a long pause. She sat back in her chair and looked into his eyes. "Are you sure you want to go on? I'm afraid this conversation could become even more painful than it already is."

He nodded. "Yes, I think we need to continue, even if it is painful." He sounded more determined than he felt.

She was reluctant to go on, but she agreed. "All right, I did believe what you said when I was there inside the church. When I said 'thank you' at the door it was an honest expression of gratitude."

He ignored the last part of her statement. He went back to the first part. "You just said you 'did believe' when you were 'there inside the church'? What happened to change that?"

"I really feel uncomfortable, Walter; I don't want to be hurtful."

"It's okay; I know you don't."

She paused and waited for him to say something more, but he didn't. So she went on. "When I go to a worship service that touches me like Bob's funeral service did, I often feel like I am in the audience at a very moving play. At Bob's funeral I felt like that. I felt like I feel when I watch a great classical drama. For a few moments I was completely taken in. I suspended my disbelief; I was a believer."

"*Was* a believer?" he said loudly.

"Yes, 'was' is accurate. For those few moments my disbelief was suspended, but then it came back. At the end the music stopped, the performance was over, people chatted with one another, you took off your costume and we all went back out into the real world."

He was speechless. He sat in silence looking down at the table.

She could see how uncomfortable her comment had made him. She reached out and placed her hands on top of his. She spoke quietly in an attempt to soften the impact of what she had said. "I know the play is still there, Walter, waiting for someone else to perform it. That's what believing seems like to me, like a serious drama that some people take for real life." She could see the pain in his face. "I'm sorry. I've probably said too much."

He looked resigned. "No, you didn't. It's what you don't believe. I needed to hear that." He paused in an effort to regroup. "Why isn't the message convincing?"

She withdrew her hands. "When the music stops and you take off your costume and we go outside, we are back in a world that is disconnected from the church. It's like there's a huge gap between the church world and the real world.

"There are moments when I want to believe that what you say is true when we are in church could be true out there. But in the real world the Bobs (she paused and looked at him tenderly) and the Bills still die young. The inspiring answers you give in the sanctuary don't seem to hold up. I can't find God there. You say he is involved, that he's still in charge, but I don't see it. Most of the time your explanation seems like a salvage operation: no matter what happens God will help you pick up the pieces. That's not enough for me. I want more than solace after the fact—more than consoling 'peace that passes understanding.' I want understanding. I want a God who is more than a cosmic ambulance attendant."

He cringed. "So do I. I think God is so much more than that."

She spoke gently. "But, Walter, can't you see that there's a huge gap between the God you talk about when we are safely tucked away in a church sanctuary and the real world? Except for rare moments like those I spent in the service for Bob I live on the far side of the huge gully that separates the church sanctuary from the rest of life. The evidence where I live argues overwhelmingly *against* believing. No matter how hard I try I can't pretend not to see that evidence." She sighed. "And there are times I have tried very hard."

"Maybe there is evidence you haven't seen yet!" He spoke urgently. "I believe that if we could see the whole picture, we would know that God is really in charge. Sometimes it just doesn't appear that he is."

She took a deep breath. "I'm sorry, Walter—I seem to be saying that a lot, but I really am sorry. I'm not just arguing to be difficult; I just can't accept that kind of explanation. I heard it a lot when I went to church while I was growing up, but it has always seemed weak to me. It may satisfy people who want it to work—like Molly and Adele; it may even work with people who defer to the church like Erik does, but it doesn't satisfy people like me. It may seem convincing when we are closeted in a church sanctuary, but it doesn't hold up when we go back into the outside world. In that world a million Irish starve in a potato famine—including most of my great-grandfather's cousins. A century later six million Jews die in the Holocaust. That leaves millions of weeping wives and fathers. It's Passover all over again."

Her voice was becoming strident. "When I think of all those Irish and Jewish and Egyptian weeping wives and mothers I can't believe there is a gracious and omnipotent God running things. And I can't accept some sappy explanation that God must have a purpose in letting that kind of horror prevail. What happened to Molly and her sisters in sorrow isn't fair, and in the light of day nothing you said or can say about God makes it fair. I'll never find peace without understanding."

He could see that she was becoming upset. He started to interrupt. She didn't let him.

"You asked me to tell you how I feel. Please hear me out."

He sat back in his chair.

She hit the table with her fist and started to cry. "God damn it, Walter. Look at the evidence. Bob Hutchins never had a chance. Just like his father and his uncle he wasn't fit enough to survive right from the start. God, or whatever created him, made him that way in the beginning. What's the purpose of God in that? If I were Molly, I would be screaming that question right now. And a well-modulated 'I-don't-know-but-put-your-faith-in-God' response wouldn't diminish my grief. I heard that kind of crap from priests when I was a kid."

He felt helpless as he listened and watched the tears flow down her face her; he wanted to comfort her, but he didn't know what to say.

"When my cousin, Jenny, discovered that Richie, her little boy, is retarded, the priest told her that God gave this 'special' child to her because he knew she would love him. That's sick! It may be a way to keep believing intact, but it's sick." She struggled to continue. "You and I can theologize or philosophize about what happened to Bob Hutchins, but that's the luxury of detachment. Molly can't do that. The husband she loves is not in her bed anymore. He's dead and she has to face the cold nights alone."

She was sobbing now. She looked at him watching her helplessly. "For God's sake, Walter, I'm falling apart; please hold me!" He got down on his knees next to her chair and put his arms around her. After a few minutes she stopped shaking. "I'm not hungry anymore. Can we go sit on your big couch?"

"Of course," he said. He took her hand and led her into the dark parlor. She sat in the middle of the couch. "I'll be right back," he said. He walked through the door into his study, and took the telephone receiver off of its cradle. and laid it on the desk. He came back and sat down next to her. "I just shut out the church and the world," he said.

She turned, put her feet up on the couch and lay down with her head in his lap. "Walter, I don't want to think or talk anymore, just kiss me."

He leaned over, slid his arm under her, pulled her up to him and kissed her. Her face was wet and warm with tears. He let her back down into his lap. "Your nose is running."

She laughed. "Do you have a handkerchief?"

"I do."

"Then wipe it!"

He reached into his back pocket, pulled out his handkerchief and gently wiped her nose.

"Walter, I love you, but I will never be able to believe like you do. Is loving you enough?"

"I hope to God it's enough—because I love you so much."

"Let's not try to figure out anything more tonight. Just kiss me again."

He lifted her toward him; she wrapped her arms around him and pulled him toward her. He could feel every part of her when she pressed her sweater against him. Her open mouth and the warmth of her body drew him out of himself. He felt his inhibitions slip away. She became all that mattered to him. It was strangely beautiful.

When he relaxed her into his lap she looked at him impishly.

"How long have you been thinking about doing what we are doing now?" he asked.

"From the moment I saw you at the picnic table that October day I met you at Becky and Erik's."

"That long ago? You didn't even know me."

"You're right, but it didn't matter. When you stood up as I walked up to the picnic table I thought, 'I would do anything this tall, beautiful man wanted me to do.'" She laughed.

He shook his head and smiled. "You're scandalous, Mary Kerrigan."

"Only with you. Kiss me again!"

When their lips parted he searched her eyes. The early anguish had subsided; she seemed completely at peace. He watched her face and gently caressed her hair. She smiled. For a while they were just quiet together. Then she said softly, "I had no clue that tonight might be the night we might . . ."

"I didn't either."

"I really want to, right here on your big couch." She paused and then continued slowly, emphasizing each word. "I want to right now."

"So do I." His breathing quickened.

She turned her eyes away from him. After several seconds she looked back at him; a tear trickled down her cheek. "I just had a frightening thought. As much as I want to make love with you, I don't think we can—not here where someone needing help from you could suddenly appear at the door."

"That hardly ever happens at this time of night."

"But it does happen; someone could show up unexpectedly. And, if they found us together, people would no longer accept you as the minister here. We can't risk that."

He thought of the night they were together and Miss Simpson had her stroke and Erik came to the manse looking for him. He nodded reluctantly. "You're probably right." ("Just this once we could take a chance!" he added in his head, but he couldn't bring himself to press her by saying it out loud.)

She could see the disappointment in his eyes. He couldn't speak. She reached up with her hand and touched his face. "Somewhere, someday, when we can be sure no one will intrude, we will; I promise." Through her own sadness she watched as sadness spread over his face. "I'm so sorry. I'm so sorry we can't tonight," she whispered. "Just hold me now and we'll be here together." He watched her eyes close. He leaned over and put his arms around her; in the quiet they drifted into sleep.

After a while she sighed deeply; he rose up. She opened her eyes, and sat up slowly and shifted her feet on to the floor. "The conversation we had earlier really drained me. I feel better now, but I'm exhausted and I have to be at school early tomorrow morning. It must be almost midnight. Probably you should take me home."

He wanted to argue, but he didn't. "In a minute I will. Right now I want you to lie back down so I can kiss you one more time." She did and he kissed her gently. He raised himself up and gazed at her lying across his lap. "I love you, Mary Kerrigan—and I will remember your promise."

She looked at him intently. "I love you, Walter Macdonald—and I will keep my promise."

She was so tired that she almost fell asleep as they drove the two blocks to her apartment. He walked her to her door. When they stepped inside, she gave him the familiar standing-one-step-up good-night kiss. She said, "Call me soon," as he stepped out onto the porch.

When he arrived back at the manse he put the cork back in the wine bottle, wrapped the cold pizza in foil, washed the dishes and set them in the rack to dry. He reheated the leftover coffee, poured some into a cup, walked into the dark parlor and sat down on his big couch—at the end where he sat earlier in the evening. He set his coffee cup on the big coffee table and lay against the back of the couch. Mary was right: the conversation early in the evening had been very difficult. As believers they were centuries apart. He was a contemporary of sixteenth-century John Calvin; she was a twentieth-century modern. He believed; she disbelieved. The gully that separated them was huge. He had no idea how they would bridge it.

The magnitude of his dilemma seemed overwhelming: he was in love not just with an unbeliever; she was a disbeliever—a beautiful, exciting, caring, competent disbeliever. He felt utterly vulnerable. He cared more for Mary Kerrigan than he did for anything or anyone else in this world. He turned his head and glanced at the door that led into the hallway and across into his dark study. He turned back and looked at the cushions on the couch. They still held the outline of her body. He spoke slowly and softly, like someone confessing. "It's true. I'm in love with someone who doesn't believe in God—and I don't know how to help her. But I'm not going to stop loving her."

------------ 12 ------------

THE NEXT MORNING IT was snowing when he woke up: nothing formidable, just enough cold, wet snow to be aggravating on the eve of the first day of spring. After lunch he drove to Saratoga to visit a parishioner in the hospital. The snow had almost melted by late afternoon when he returned. Mary would probably be home from school by now, but to give her a chance to recover from the school day he decided to wait until five-thirty to call her. The telephone rang six times before she answered sounding breathless. "It's Walter," he said when she managed a "Hello." "Obviously I made you run for the phone; I'm sorry."

"It wasn't your fault; we had one of those endless teachers' meetings after school."

"I can call back later, if you would like me to."

"No, I've waited all day to talk with you. I don't want to wait any longer. Just give me a minute to take off my coat and boots." He could hear her put down the receiver. "That's better," she said when she came back. "How are you today?" He noticed a concerned tone in her voice.

"Missing you," he said. "You've been in my mind all day."

"Same for me," she said. "I had trouble concentrating; I know I didn't teach very well." She paused. He was ready to speak when she continued, "I'm sorry I was so difficult last night when we talked. Today it seems like I pushed too hard. I hope I didn't push you too far out of your comfort zone."

"No, I need that kind of nudging!" He tried to sound convincing. "But the conversation feels unfinished to me. I think we quit because we were tired, not because we had resolved the issues we talked about."

"And where we went afterward?"

"That was wonderful, Mary."

She paused. "You're not going to bolt, are you, Walter?"

The question surprised him. "No, I have no intention of bolting," he said. "Why do you ask?"

"That's been my experience with men. If I let a man get close to me, he becomes frightened and leaves."

"I admit I'm a little frightened, but I'm not going to leave."

"I need to hear you say that today, Walter. I need some reassurance. I know it may not make any sense to you, but as much as I want you to be close—very close—when you are actually there, when I feel you touching me, it frightens me."

Even before he spoke she could tell he was confused. "You seemed so much at peace when we were close and fell asleep last night. I'm surprised that today you feel uneasy about it. Why are you uneasy?"

She spoke slowly. "I'm afraid I will disappoint you, Walter. I'm afraid that if I let someone see and touch all of me, he will think that it's not enough and leave. That's what happened with Darryl; I let him touch and see all of me—and it wasn't enough to keep him."

He could feel the alarm in her voice. "I wish I could see you and hold you right now and you could look into my eyes and know that will never happen with me. I was disappointed last night, but that wasn't your fault; you were right about needing to be cautious." He paused and took a breath. "Mary, I have my own fear when you get close to me. Though it may seem like a strange juxtaposition, whenever I let you get close to me I feel afraid that you will expose my believing. My believing is like a protective covering. I get scared when I think someone might reach beneath it and discover that it's not enough."

She spoke carefully. "So, we want to be close, but when we are close we threaten each other. I feel threatened when I feel you touching my body; you feel threatened when you feel me touching your faith." Her words hung between them. As the silence continued she became more and more uneasy. Finally she broke it, "Perhaps I was too blunt?"

'No," he said quickly, "no, you weren't. You spoke the truth. I feel threatened with exposure every time you and I talk about believing."

"Are you all right now? Do you still feel threatened?"

"No, when you say it back to me it sounds too strong. I misspoke. I don't feel threatened; I feel . . . *vulnerable*, Mary, very vulnerable." He had to catch his breath before he could continue. "In church we dress our believing in proper Sunday clothes; we never take the clothes off of our believing. We are afraid to let others see what our believing looks like without them.

We pretend to believe what we're supposed to believe even when we don't—because we think we have to. When I'm in church no one ever demands that I become a naked believer."

"But with me . . .?"

"The relationship I have with you is different. I know you love me. But I'm still uneasy when you disrobe my believing. I'm not equipped to answer the kind of challenges you bring to my believing. In seminary I learned to view people who don't believe as empty or needy or unable. You're not any of those; you disbelieve and you're strong. In conversations with you—especially the one last night—I have begun to see why you disbelieve as you do." He sighed deeply. "And I have no idea how to respond—not only as a minister, but as me. That scares me." He paused. "Sometimes . . . I wonder if I could live next to you and keep my faith. Your disbelieving is actually a believing—as solid and passionate and vital as my believing."

He realized he was running on. He was having difficulty keeping up with his feelings. "Mary, I love you so much, but I don't think I could survive for the long haul if I can't find a way to be together with you and keep my faith. I'm scared."

She responded softly. "Is there some way I can help?"

"I wish I could think of one, but I can't. I guess I need to do some work on it on my own." He stopped speaking. He could sense by her silence that he had made her uncomfortable. He attempted to reassure her. "But I promise to stay in touch. I'm not going to withdraw from you!"

"Thanks for saying that. It would be hard for me to feel cut off."

"Please trust me, Mary; I'm not going to bolt. I just need some time and space to reflect. I need to find out how I could be naked with you and keep my faith."

"You don't have to be afraid to be naked with me, Walter. I would never hurt you. I love you."

"Oh, my dearest Mary, no one has ever loved me like you do."

"My love is tough, Walter."

He hesitated a few seconds. "I hope mine is as tough as yours!"

"I believe in you, Walter . . . Have you got a plan?"

"Yes, I do. My seminary offers post-Easter weeklong residency opportunities for ministers. I'm going to take advantage of their offer. I called them late this morning and they have an opening the week after next. I will have a room of my own and I can take my meals in the commons. I will have both the seminary and the university libraries at my disposal. I will have a whole week to read and think and pray. I know it's a safe place where I can get my bearings again.

"My contract with the church provides for one week of study leave each year. Tonight at our monthly meeting I'm going to ask the session to approve the week away as a study leave. I'm sure they know it's been a hard winter and spring for me and that I could use a break. I'm sure they'll give me the time off."

"I'm a little concerned that you're going to try to work everything through by yourself. Is there anybody down there who can help you look critically at what you believe, or are they all card-carrying Presbyterians? Is there anyone you could talk with at the seminary who might be helpful to *us*?"

"There is! A new professor of New Testament, Dr. James Frieslander, came on the faculty during my last year at Eastminster. Dr. Frieslander followed a much-beloved teacher who suddenly took sick and died the year before. So, it was not easy for him to gain respect from the students. I was one of the few who got on with him. I came to know him not only an excellent scholar, but also as an understanding person with a deep faith. And what's most important now, he's a little irreverent—not quite as much as you are (he heard her laugh), but he has a background in science and philosophy as well as biblical studies. He was a biologist before he turned to biblical studies. A lot of his writing addresses the interface between traditional faith and modern thinking. I wasn't ready to talk about that interface when I was a student, but I'm ready now. If the session approves my request, I'm going to call him and see if he can find some time for me."

"The possibility that you will have a conversation with even a slightly irreverent professor makes me a little more comfortable with your plan, Walter. I just wish you would take me with you. I want to be close to you."

"The rooms have only single beds."

"So?"

"You really would enjoy scandalizing them, wouldn't you?"

"Yes, but since I can tell you won't let me come along, I want to send something with you."

"What's that?"

"When you said you would be talking with a biblical theology professor who began as a biologist I thought of something for you to read—something that might help you to understand me and people like me."

"What?"

"Darwin's *The Origin of Species*. Have you read it?"

"No," he said with a slight chuckle. "I know about it, but no one ever suggested that I read it."

She ignored his chuckle. "I know it's an old source and probably not on the usual theological school reading list, but it should be. I discovered it when my father suggested that I take a philosophy of science course when I was at Barnard. He said that familiarity with the scientific revolution that occurred during the nineteenth century would help me appreciate why so many Victorians lost their faith—and why so many moderns and postmoderns find it difficult to believe.

"I'm glad I took his advice. Darwin's *Origin* was one of the books I had to read for the course. The book threatened a lot of believers when it came out—still does; some believers, especially the Fundamentalist variety, still see Darwin as a villain. Actually, he was a gentle man who became a disbeliever reluctantly—like I did—because he couldn't reconcile what he saw in nature with belief in a loving God. The mass of evidence he presents in *The Origin* and the thinking it led him to still shape the way lots of people see reality on my side of the gully. I don't mean to be arrogant, but I think that part of the reason you're so sure that God is in charge of everything in spite of the overwhelming evidence to the contrary is that you haven't really looked at the evidence to the contrary. If you read even half of *The Origin*, I think you will begin to appreciate the obstacles that stand in the way of believing for people like me. Will you read it? For me?"

"Yes, I will. For you and for me."

"I still have the copy I used in the course. If you don't mind reading a book that has my underlining in it, I'll drop it off sometime early next week. I'll turn the corners down on pages that seem most important to me."

"I would love to borrow your copy. It will give me something that smells like you to take with me."

"What a good idea! I will spray it with my perfume and bring it by in a plain brown wrapper. That way if you're not home when I come by, you won't have to worry that some church member who stops to see you will find a copy of Charles Darwin tucked inside the storm door on your side porch."

"I promised to read your aromatic Darwin carefully. Do you know when you will stop by?"

"I'm sorry, but I don't. My family is getting together to open and clean our camp on Lake George this weekend. We call it a camp but it's really a very nice, spacious house. My lumber-baron grandfather built it just after the turn of the century. We need to get it ready for our annual beginning-of-summer gathering on Mother's Day Weekend. It's always a big job to clean after it sits vacant all winter, so I'm not sure when I'll get back to Schuylerkill Falls on Sunday."

He paused. "I hope I'm here when you come by because if I'm not I probably won't see you before I go. I'll have to hustle next week to get everything done ahead." He stopped and took a breath. "I promise to call you as soon as I get back. I love you, Mary Kerrigan. I will miss you."

"I love you, Walter Macdonald. Take care of yourself, and come back to me."

That evening the session enthusiastically approved his request for a study leave. They assured him that they were grateful for his hard work and knew that he needed some time for personal renewal. The next morning he called George Holland, the retired pastor of Albany Street Presbyterian Church in Schenectady, and asked him to cover the service the Sunday he would be away. He was relieved when George said he was available and would be happy to take his place in the pulpit in Schuylerkill Falls. He promised not to tell too many stories from Walter's childhood during the sermon.

Sunday evening when he returned home after going to the diner for pizza with the youth group he found a small, plain brown bag inside the storm door on his side porch. He felt heavy with disappointment as he picked it up and carried it inside; he had missed seeing Mary. He hung his coat on one of the hooks next to the door. He opened the bag. Inside was a thick book. He turned to the title page. It read "The Origin of Species By Means Of Natural Selection, Or The Preservation Of Favored Races In The Struggle for Life." He turned back to the first blank page. "Mary Kerrigan" was written at the top; the signature was bold and free-flowing. The book smelled like her. A handwritten note was tucked inside the front cover. "Enjoy my book. I hope you find answers while you are away. Call me as soon as you are back. I love you. Mary." He tucked the note back into the book. As he walked into his study he said, "I already miss you, Mary Kerrigan." He put the book into his briefcase along with the other books he planned to take with him to Eastminister. He looked out the window at the church next door. "Please, God," he said, "this time try to be a help, not an obstacle." The prayer surprised him, but he didn't dwell on it.

The drive from Schuylerkill Falls to New Jersey on Sunday afternoon felt like the beginning of a long-anticipated pilgrimage. As he drove south on the New York Thruway he could feel the tension going out of his body. A sense of comfort and safety enveloped him as he drove on to the Eastminster campus.

He had never felt more secure as a believer than he did during the years he spent as a member of the seminary community. Everything here testified to the reality of the faith: chapel service every morning, prayers before every meal, long conversations debating fine points of theology, buildings like Knox and Witherspoon Halls named after Calvinist saints, the wisdom that reposed in the faculty, the massive library with its collected history and defenses of the Christian faith. As he parked his car and walked toward the dorm where he would stay, he realized how much he had missed it all—especially the reassuring smell of books in the library.

The week passed quickly. Every day he went to the library after breakfast. Except for a short walk after lunch he studied all day. He read sections of several theological books—including chapters in the first volume of Rudolf Bultmann's *Theology of the New Testament.* On Wednesday he read the first four chapters in Mary's copy of Darwin's *Origin.* He read the sections she had marked carefully and pondered why she had marked them. Several times he wondered what passing students and faculty would think when they saw him reading controversial authors like Bultmann and Darwin. But he relaxed when he recognized that most of them would conclude he was reading them to refute them.

In truth, he found both Bultmann's "demythologizing" of Scripture and Darwin's argument that "natural" selection rather than God's providence is the controlling force in nature unsettling. Two long conversations with Dr. Frieslander helped him to recover his bearings—especially the second one on Thursday evening at the Nassau Tavern. It began with dinner and lasted until nearly midnight. When they parted Dr. Frieslander had become "Jim"; the former professor had become a colleague. As he loaded his suitcase into his VW Monday morning and drove away from the campus, he felt refreshed and energized. He promised to give himself another week of study leave next year.

The sun was setting on Monday when he drove into the driveway next to the manse in Schuylerkill Falls. He pushed up the seatback of the front seat and retrieved his briefcase and suitcase from the back seat of the VW and set them on the driveway next to the car. When he stood up and shut the car door he glanced up into the sky and noticed that the swallows had returned while he was away. He stood still and watched them do their end-of-the-day fly-around. They chattered and swooped along the peak of the church roof searching for insects.

He smiled as he followed their aerial antics. His thoughts traveled back to a summer evening when he was a boy sitting on the porch at his family's camp in the Adirondacks watching other swallows do their fly-around. His dad walked over and sat down next to him. For a while they sat together in the quiet of twilight and watched the birds. Then his dad said, "Walter, we should give thanks for the swallows because if it weren't for them, we'd be eaten alive by mosquitoes and black flies."

At the time he felt grateful for the birds. But this evening he recalled the passage Mary had marked on the third page of chapter three, "Struggle for Existence," in Darwin's *Origin*. When he first read it on Tuesday during the past week he pondered it for so long that he could still recall Darwin's exact words: "We behold the face of nature bright with gladness . . . ; we do not see or we forget, that the birds which are idly singing round us mostly live on insects or seeds, and are thus constantly destroying life . . ." "Those beautiful swallows eat bugs," he thought to himself. "They're part of the violent culling of life that Darwin calls 'natural' selection. They can fly and sing because they destroy life."

He watched the birds circle the tall steeple of the church swooping up small insects that he could not see. "That's the way it is throughout all of nature," he said out loud. He realized that he would never again be able to view songbirds with the same innocence he had felt as a boy. He looked at his briefcase; he was sorry that he had read Darwin's words. He picked up the briefcase and his suitcase and walked around the back of the car and up the walkway toward the side porch. Willie jumped up on the porch in front of him. He looked intently at the big orange cat. "You leave the birds alone!" he said pointedly. Willie ignored the sermon; he was hungry.

He felt a sense of relief when he looked at the worn wooden storm door: there were no notes tacked to it. He walked down the hallway and pushed up the thermostat. When he walked back into the kitchen Willie was scratching on the storm door. The cat obviously thought the manse was his second home. Willie bolted into the kitchen when he opened the outside doors. He took a can of cat food from one of the cupboards over the kitchen counter and placed it in one of the small bowls that had been assigned to Willie, filled the other bowl with water and, set both of them on floor. It was almost six o'clock; Mary should be home by now. He walked into his study and dialed her number on his desk phone. She answered on the second ring. "Hi, Mary," he said. "It's me."

"Oh, me," she said. "It's so good to hear your voice. I missed you. I missed you a lot. How was your trip? Did you find what you needed to find?"

"I missed you terribly," he said. "There were times when you were so much in my head that I couldn't concentrate on what I was reading."

"Good!" she said. "I want to be more engaging than anything you might read."

"Well, the plain fact is that you are!"

"Good," she said. "Did you get a chance to talk with Dr. Frieslander?"

"Actually Jim and I had two wonderful conversations; the second one lasted from supper until nearly midnight. Thursday night we sat at a back corner table at the Nassau Tavern and drank an entire pitcher of beer."

"So, it's 'Jim' now. Obviously the two of you connected very well."

"We did. We really did."

She hesitated a few seconds. "So, did you talk with him about me? Is that what kept the two of you talking until midnight?"

Walter laughed. "I did tell him about you. And we did talk about you. But most of the time we talked about Darwin and a German theologian by the name of Rudolf Bultmann."

"What did Jim say about me?"

"He said I must be brave to even think about marrying a woman like you."

"Oh, Walter, you didn't really tell him the truth about me?"

"I did. It was pertinent. I told him that you gave me your marked copy of Darwin's *Origin* to read and that you are the main reason I decided to read Bultmann's theology."

"So, now I am driving you to theology!"

He laughed. "You are. Love can do wondrous things." He became serious. "I think Bultmann would suit your theological taste—and finding a way you can believe matters a lot to me." He paused.

"Thank you for caring."

He could feel warmth and gentleness in her voice. "I thought maybe Bultmann might help me figure out how to build a connecting bridge over our gully, that he might help me make believing credible to you. He tries to address the conflicts many people now see between Scripture and modern science. He thinks that modern science makes many of the images and stories in Scripture improbable—like the creation of the world in six days and Jesus ascending into heaven. Bultmann views these images as 'myths'—that's his word. He suggests that we 'demythologize' the Scripture—that we look through or behind the myths to find the meaning or essential truths the biblical writers wanted to convey. He believes that struggling to defend the myths as literally true gets in the way of what they can teach us." He realized he had talked nonstop and she hadn't said anything. "Am I boring you?" he asked.

She laughed. "Almost, but go on anyway."

"You really want me to?"

"Yes, I suppose theology is what ministers talk about when they get excited, so I guess I better get used to hearing about it. To be honest, it's more interesting than football. And, besides, it matters to you so it matters to me. So, go on."

"The problem is that once you start demythologizing, where do you stop? It's not always apparent which stories describe historical events and should be taken literally, and which are myths. With some stories—like Adam and Eve in the Garden of Eden—it's not difficult to decide. With others, it's not so cut and dried—like Passover and the Virgin Birth. It's not clearly preposterous to believe that Mary was impregnated by the Holy Spirit, and that's how we can be sure the child she bore was both human and divine."

"If you and I had gone ahead the other night and I had become pregnant and three months from now you told your church that the Holy Spirit did it, they would find your explanation preposterous."

"Your name may be Mary, Miss Kerrigan, but no one could believe you would ever be as compliant as the Virgin Mary—even if you could prove that an angel appeared to you."

"Touché! The week away was obviously good for you."

"It was, very good. When can we get together? That's really what I called to find out. I want to see you as soon as possible. I have lots to share with you from my reading and my conversations with Jim Frieslander. And we have to finish the discussion we started and didn't finish the last time we were together. What about Saturday? Are you busy Saturday? I'm sure I can get the whole day free. I've had a whole extra week to think about a sermon so I am sure I will be done writing next Sunday's before Saturday."

"I would just need to be off to my family's cottage by four o'clock or so. We always get together there for supper on Saturday of Mother's Day weekend and then stay over to celebrate Mother's Day on Sunday."

"That may interfere with what I had in mind. I was going to call Erik and see if he or any of his buddies plan to use their hunting camp on Saturday. If they aren't and the weather's good, we could pack a lunch and hike into the hunting camp. But we'd have start walking out by two to get you back here to pick up your car in time for you to drive to back up to Lake George to help make supper."

"The camp is near Fort Ann, isn't it?"

"Yes it is, West Fort Ann."

"In a roundabout fashion that's on the way to Lake George. On Saturday I could follow you in my car. We could park both cars by the dirt road that leads to the camp. That would give us most of the day together for the hike. Even if we don't get back to our cars until four o'clock I can still get to Lake George in time to help make supper. I don't want to wait another week for us to have a day together."

"What about tonight? Have you had supper? I could get a pizza from Stephanos."

"I can't. I have to go back to school for parent-teacher meetings."

"What about tomorrow night?"

"I have compositions from two classes to correct by Thursday. I'm sure it will take me both Tuesday and Wednesday evenings to read all of them. The junior prom is Friday night and I have to chaperone. What about Thursday?"

"I have a property committee meeting Thursday. They always drag on and on. Damn! Looks like Saturday is the first possible day. Can you be ready by nine or nine-thirty?"

"Let's say ten-thirty. The prom goes until midnight, so it'll be one-thirty or two by the time I get to sleep."

"Well, I do want you to be rested so you'll enjoy the hike. I'll be in front of your house at ten-thirty on Saturday. Right now that seems like a long way away. It will be hard to wait."

"We could pack all the things that really matter to us into my station wagon and run off in the middle of the night tonight and never come back. I have enough money to keep us forever. If you will come with me, I'll give you my body night after night after night forever."

Her proposal took his speech away.

"Well?" she said when he didn't answer.

He wanted to say yes, but he suspected that if he did, she would call his bluff. He stumbled a response, "My agreement with the church requires me to give two months' notice."

"Walter, that is so incredibly responsible! Is there no romance in you?"

"There is, but I guess you have to wait until Saturday to see it."

"This is so disappointing, Walter. I offer a man my body, and he tells me he needs two months to respond. I must be getting old and losing my appeal." She sighed. "Well, you have thrust me back to mundane reality. Instead of packing up the few things that really matter to me, I need to be off to a parent-teacher meeting. In the meantime, think about my body, and call me in the middle of the night if you change your mind."

"I will!" He paused. "Mary, tell me the truth, no kidding: if I call you at midnight and say that I am ready to go off with you, will you go with me?"

"Yes."

"Really?"

"Yes."

"I love you, Mary Kerrigan."

"I love you, too, Walter Macdonald. See you Saturday. You bring wine; I'll bring lunch. Bye for now."

He hung up the phone slowly. He looked out the front window and across the lawn and stared at the brick church next door. As much as he wanted to he knew he wouldn't call her in the middle of the night.

13

SATURDAY MORNING BEGAN CHILLY, but the forecasters promised a clear and warm day—temperatures in the sixties. It would be an ideal day for a hike: late enough in the spring to be warm, but not late enough for the miserable biting black flies to be out. At ten-twenty Walter placed one of the bottles of wine he had purchased in Saratoga in a brown paper bag, set it on the back seat of his VW and drove to Mary's house. He parked in front of the house and walked up on the porch. Her car was parked in the driveway; the door to the back seat was open. He could see her suitcase on the back seat. When he reached the front door, before he had chance to ring the doorbell he could hear her running down the stairs. She opened the door so quickly that it banged against the wall next to her. She threw her arms around him and kissed him. "My God, I missed you," she said when their lips parted.

"Not as much as I missed you," he said. "It's been awful to have to wait all week to see you. Let me look at you." He took hold of her hands and stepped back. "I want to get the full effect." He gazed at her. "Ah, yes, jeans that cling, a tightly tucked oxford-cloth shirt with buttoned-down collar—sexy and serious all at the same time."

"That's what I want to be when I'm with you: sexy and serious!"

He reached out and touched the choker around her neck. "And this wide, silver choker—it was made for your neck. I've never seen it before. Did you just get it?"

"I did, from a little shop in Saratoga, but it came originally from Mexico."

"And the dangling silver earrings?"

"The same."

He cradled her chin in his hand and looked at her face. "You're beautiful, Mary Kerrigan, but your eyes tell me that you're weary."

She smiled and nodded.

"How was the prom?"

She sighed. "Thank you for calling me 'beautiful'; I love to watch you look all around me. You're right; I am tired. It was nearly two in the morning by the time I got to sleep. The dance was mostly fun. There was only one difficult incident. About eleven-thirty someone came in to report two boys and two girls out in the parking lot necking and drinking beer. Confronting them was unpleasant, but I had the presence of mind to wait until Chief Pete Haines responded to my call and could go with me. He gave the boys a ride home and I took the girls home to their houses after they helped the clean-up crew take down the decorations in the gym. Fortunately, the girls hadn't been drinking. That was the only incident. I just wish I had invited you to chaperone with me. The band was great and we could have dazzled everyone with our dancing."

"Funny you should say that," he said. "I thought about crashing the dance, but decided it wouldn't be appropriate."

"Oh, Walter," she sighed, "with you propriety always wins—except when I'm around to sabotage it."

"Well, you're around today so let's head for the woods and see what happens!"

She grinned. "I'll follow your lead, Dr. Macdonald. Just let me go back upstairs and get my jacket and the knapsack with our lunch and we can be off." She came back down quickly wearing her jacket. She placed the knapsack on the back seat of her car next to her suitcase. After she shut the door to the back seat she looked at him and said, "Try not to drive so recklessly that I can't keep up with you!"

He grinned. "I think you think I could use more reckless abandon in my life."

"I'm trying my best to help that along."

The drive north in separate cars seemed longer than the forty-five minutes it actually took. Walter turned on his car radio to help pass the time, but he soon tired of the disk jockeys' chatter and turned it off. It was nearly eleven-thirty when they arrived at the turn-off to Erik's camp. The narrow dirt road leading to the camp looked mostly dry and they might have been able to drive on it, but they decided to hike. They locked their cars and left them parked by the state highway. Walter placed the bottle of wine inside Mary's knapsack. He shouldered the knapsack and they began a leisurely walk up the road to the camp. As they walked along they held hands and joshed with each other and caught up on the news from each other's lives. At the prom one of the seniors had asked Mary to dance. It was fun at first, she said, but then as they danced a slow dance he started to get seriously close. "What was he thinking, Walter!!?" she burst out. "In July I'll be thirty and he's only eighteen."

"If I had been at a dance with you when I was eighteen, I would have tried the same. It's just hormones. Boys can't help themselves."

"Walter, you don't really believe that hormone crap! It just a lame excuse boys use to justify rubbing against girls. Besides, some chaperone would have seen what you were doing and they would have expelled you from the dance!"

"So, did you expel the young man?"

"No, I pushed him away and said, 'Stop that!' He looked embarrassed, but he got the point. He held me at arm's length while we finished the dance. So, what adventures have you been through since we last talked?"

He told her about a young couple he had married. "The young woman was very pregnant, but I could see that she and her man were very much in love. There were just the four of them for the wedding in the big church: the couple and the two friends who stood up with them. We lit the candles and did the ceremony like there were a hundred guests."

"I would have cried, if I had been there."

He nodded. "I almost did." He paused and she watched a tear fall from one of his eyes. He brushed it away quickly. "After they drove away from the church I stood outside and watched them go down Church Street and turn on to Main Street, loudly honking the horn on their car. I wondered if I would ever drive away from my church in a car honking the horn to tell the world I had married the love of my life."

"You could do something to make that happen, Walter."

"I hope to," he said. "That's why I spend so much time with you." He stopped and pointed, "Well, there's the hunting camp. It's not much to look at, but it has a great porch that faces south. We can sit on the steps and enjoy the warm sun while we eat our lunch and drink our wine." They walked to the cabin and sat down on the steps leading to the porch.

"Did you bring a corkscrew?" she asked.

He blanched. "No, I forgot."

"I did," she said quietly. "It's in the bottom of the knapsack." She took out three sandwiches, a bag of chips, two wine glasses wrapped in tissue paper and a dessert wrapped in foil. She pulled out a corkscrew and held it up the triumphantly.

"What would I do without you?"

"Suffer!" She laughed and handed him the bottle of wine. When he popped the cork loudly she said, "Hooray for corkscrews!" She unwrapped the wine glasses and held them while he poured wine into them. He set the bottle down. She raised her glass toward him in a toast: "May we dance together forever!"

He raised his glass toward her, "To you who freed me to dance!"

Over lunch they relived the evening at the Gideon and Leonardo's. Walter ate two sandwiches while Mary ate one. When she unwrapped the foil he was delighted to see two pieces of chocolate cake with chocolate frosting—one small and one very large. The bottle of wine was nearly gone when they finished dessert. He was just beginning to tell her about his dinner with Smitty when suddenly he stopped talking. "Did you hear that?" he asked.

"Hear what?"

"That bird call. Listen! It's the one that runs up and down the scale like someone running the hammer back and forth across a xylophone." They listened intently. "There it is," he said.

She smiled. "I hear it. It does resemble someone playing on a xylophone. It sounds like there are two of them calling back and forth."

"They're veeries. When I was kid we had them around our camp in the Adirondacks. We used to call them the 'xylophone birds.' I love to hear them." He fell silent again.

"You seem pensive, Walter. Do you want to talk about what you are thinking?"

"Yes," he said softly. "I do. It's important that I do." He spoke slowly. "It was almost dusk when I got home from Eastminister last Monday. As I walked from my car to the porch, I noticed the swallows had returned. People say they come back on the same day every year. I stopped and watched them do their evening fly-around. They chattered and swooped high in the air. As I watched them I was reminded of evenings when I was kid and used to sit on the porch at my family's camp and watch the swallows do their fly-around at sunset." He stopped and looked straight at her. "But, as I watched them last Monday, I thought about what they eat.

"My dad said one time that we should give thanks for the swallows because if it weren't for them we'd be overrun by mosquitoes and black flies. I laughed when he said it. But I didn't laugh when I watched the swallows over the top of the church roof on Monday. They eat bugs; they're part of that violence-filled order of nature that Darwin describes. The beauty of the swallows and the veeries depends on their eating bugs. From the bugs' perspective they don't seem beautiful at all." He stopped abruptly.

She reached out and touched his arm. She could feel his sadness.

He went on. "Reading Darwin on my study leave forced me to see things for the first time from the bugs' perspective. When we see nature as beautiful and peaceful like we did a moment ago when we listened to the veeries' call, we overlook the violence that regulates the natural order, the struggle for survival that Darwin describes. I know you meant well when you suggested I read Darwin, but in some ways I'm sorry I did." He paused and looked at her. "It was like reading the Passover story for the first time from the perspective of an Egyptian mother. It was painful." He stopped and looked at the ground.

She took hold of his hand. "But you did read Darwin," she said softly, "and . . . ?"

He took a deep breath. "I not only read large sections of *The Origin*, I went over to the Princeton library on Thursday and scanned some sections of Darwin's other works as well. I didn't have time to look at everything—he wrote a lot, but what I read convinces me that the evidence Darwin offers is overwhelming. He painstakingly studied a huge array of living specimens and fossils: beetles and birds and fish, and monkeys and apes and humans. He describes the same underlying chaos everywhere. In the world he sees, *everything* is engaged in a struggle for survival."

As she held his hand she could feel him struggling. She spoke carefully. "And . . . ?"

"If I were to consider only Darwin's evidence, I would have to conclude that through all the eons the earth has existed survivors have survived because heredity favored them with stronger bodies or stronger beaks or better hearts or better minds. There's no evidence in Darwin that some cosmic Creator favored a chosen few, much less rewarded them for some kind of exemplary moral behavior or preserved them to serve some divine purpose."

"So, what does all of that evidence do to your believing?" She was direct but also gentle.

He squeezed her hand and let go of it. "It sure does challenge it, my love! But, fortunately, I had Jim to talk with during the week. As you know, he studied biology before he turned to biblical theology. He's lived on both sides of the gully we are struggling to bridge. He thinks that the disciplines that guide science and believing are different. He says we can't use the tools or insights of one to prove or disprove the conclusions we draw from the other. Sometimes they seem competitive and sometimes they seem complementary. In the end they are just different." She wanted to respond but she knew he needed to say more.

He stood up. "After talking with Jim I don't see Darwin and the Bible offering competing explanations of evolution. The world of perceiving is full of gullies—at least of what seem to be gullies—that sometimes defy bridging. Darwin doesn't offer evidence for faith, not only because he was not a believer, but also because defending faith was not his purpose. His purpose was to elucidate the mechanics of evolution.

"Jim pointed out that the Bible is not a science text, that it doesn't answer mechanical questions about how the creation works. The mechanics the ancient writers believed in are not the mechanics we believe in today. Even the ways scientists view the mechanics of creation change over time: the physics Newton theorized are not the physics of Einstein that most physicists affirm today. It's the same with biology, he said. We shouldn't expect to find evidence in the Bible that supports the theories of either Darwin or Einstein. And we don't."

"What your new friend says is all very neat, Walter. But you haven't made it clear where we do find *evidence* for believing."

He looked at her and nodded. "I had a whole week to think about that question." He sat down and took her hands in his and looked into her eyes.

"I think there are different kinds of evidence, Mary. There are some very significant realities that are not proved with the same kind of evidence that Darwin offers. There is no objective evidence that does or could demonstrate that I love you. Right?"

She looked at him and smiled warmly. "No, there isn't, but it's definitely real!"

"The way I act and what I say demonstrate my love for you. But there is no way to prove I love you by some evidence-based trial. Relational 'evidence'—and I include believing in this category—is always soft, inconclusive. You become convinced of it by continuing in a relationship. Its reality becomes convincing as you go along."

He watched her listen as he spoke; there was a gentle caring in the way she looked at him. He paused to give her a chance to respond, but she didn't. She said simply, "Please go on."

He stood up and took a deep breath. "Mary, I think we need to respect both scientific knowledge and relational knowledge, and recognize that though they are complementary sometimes they lead to conflicting conclusions. If I look only at Darwin's evidence, I don't see any evidence of a guiding hand at work in the creation. When I read your copy of Darwin I realized that his method does not reveal any evidence for a caring God who governs everything."

"I agree," she said softly, "I wish it did, but it doesn't."

"But that does not mean that there is no evidence at all that supports belief in a caring God, Mary. If believing can be verified only within a believing relationship, it cannot be verified—or disproved—apart from that relationship. Those who aren't willing to enter into a relationship with God won't get it."

He leaned over, took her hand in his, and looked directly at her. His voice was soft, but also intense. "That you and I should fall in love with each other is not rational. It's beyond understanding, Mary, yet it's real. We know it's real, and so do others who watch us. Faith that perceives God as a guiding force in the creation is like that. It's verified in the accumulated faith experiences of billions of people over thousands of years. I am one of those billions who know that God's care is real. I am as certain of that as I am of my love for you."

He watched her eyes fill with tears. "I feel your love, Walter; I really do . . ."

"But what?" He sat up and let go of her hand.

She shook her head slightly. "But I'm still not convinced, Walter. Don't you see that your entire argument is based on an analogy—and like every analogy it breaks down? I can see you and you can see me, and other people can see us. We know we are not illusions. But no one can see God. The supposed 'evidence' of faith is not real evidence, evidence that can be *independently* verified; it's based on what you and others *believe*, not on what you *know*. I respect what you believe about God's role in the world—I really do. But I don't see any evidence for it like there is for the love you feel for me. To me it seems like the product of collective imagining, handed down through generations of people who were ignorant of the actual workings of nature.

"Darwin's evidence challenges that wish-dream. The colossal suffering that surrounds us seems to me to rule out any possibility that the whole show is run by some good, caring God. When I listen to you talk about a caring God I'm thrown back to the trolley in your grandfather's store: the prayers of the faithful go up to God on some cosmic trolley and once in a while a little change comes back—sometimes someone gets better or is spared from tragedy. But it's a sop; there's no real fix. The suffering just goes on and on."

He started to respond. She interrupted him. "I want to hear what you have to say, Walter, I really do, but I haven't had a chance to get my thoughts together like you have. I'm just now seeing clearly why I can't accept what you believe. I need to say it out loud."

He leaned back against a post.

She stood up on the bottom step. "I know as a minister you see a lot of suffering and it doesn't shake your faith that a caring God is in control. But, when you talk about it using theological language, to me it sounds like a physician talking clinically. I don't mean to imply that you are without feeling—I know you're not, but suffering you watch is different from suffering you suffer. You can choose not to watch it—like you do when you shut your eyes because you don't want to watch a violent scene in a movie, or you can put it out of your mind when you go home.

"My cousin can't do that with her retarded boy. He's always there. She knew when he was little that he was too much for her to care for. But when the priest told her that God had chosen her to be the parent of this special child that damn priest set her up. She couldn't let him go to a home for kids like him because she would have been overwhelmed by guilt the rest of her life. So her little boy has become a big boy—and for fifteen years she has given up whatever life she might have had of her own, including her marriage, to be his caregiver. She survives by believing she is doing a good thing—and maybe she is. Who's to know? But the explanation the priest gave her seems to me to be sadistic, Walter. The bastard protected his God at the expense of my cousin." She sat back down on the top step. Her fists were clenched.

He stared at her clenched fists, then looked up. "Mary, I don't know why God permits evil and suffering to continue in the world. Honest to God I don't. I believe that some time, somehow, the whole thing became flawed. I don't believe the Adam and Eve story in Genesis is factual, but I do believe it is a myth that reflects reality. The creation is not what it was in the beginning when God made it. It is definitely flawed.

"I would never have told your cousin what the priest told her. If I believed she was going to give herself to care for her boy of her own free will, I would have told her, 'You are doing a beautiful thing by giving up so much to take care of someone God loves.' I wouldn't have pushed her to sacrifice her own life unless she wanted to. But I do believe that sometime, somewhere, her suffering and the suffering of her boy will be healed."

Tears trickled down her cheeks. He reached out to hold her. "No, don't," she said as she took hold of his hands and gently pushed them away, "I appreciate your gesture, but I don't want to feel weak right now." She wiped her face with the back of her hand. Her eyes were filled with sadness. "What you believe doesn't work for me, Walter. I don't see how it ever will. I think we're at a draw. You believe; I disbelieve. That's just the way it is and I don't see how it can ever be any different. You will always believe God is in control no matter what; I will not believe that is so no matter what. And, as hard as it is to say it, I don't see how I could ever overcome my disbelief enough to be either a helpful partner to you or to be an acceptable minister's wife." She shook her head slowly as she spoke. "Your God is the center of your life, Walter. If I'm to be with you, you *need* me to believe in him; you need me to cross over and fit in your world of believing and I can't. I just can't."

He didn't say anything when she finished. They sat in silence for several minutes. When she spoke her voice and eyes were filled with sadness. "I don't see how we're ever going to resolve this disagreement. We go over the same ground again and again. You keep probing, hoping you can find some convincing evidence that will prove to me that a God like yours exists out there. But it never works for me. And, as much as I love you, I don't see how it ever will."

He stood up. "All believing is hopeful, Mary. It flies in the face of the evidence. It challenges us to look beyond evidence. *All* believing is hopeful believing. I believe in God because I feel the reality of God deep within me. It's as real to me as life itself."

She answered slowly, shaking her head. "I think 'hopeful' is the wrong adjective, Walter. I think all believing is wishful." He slowly sat back down. She looked directly at him and spoke softly. "All the passion in me wants to be with you for the rest of my life, but here in the bright light of day I know I couldn't do it; I couldn't spend the rest of my life pretending. I couldn't spend the rest of my life sitting in a front pew Sunday after Sunday—smiling at everyone and pretending to believe—and that's what I'd have to do be an acceptable minister's wife. Walter, I love you, but I won't pretend to believe to have you. I can't do it."

She looked at the ground and shook her head back and forth slowly. When she looked up there was a mixture of pain and caring in her green eyes. "I had so much hope for today. I really hoped that what you learned when you were away would help us build a bridge. I hoped we wouldn't end up at an impasse—on opposite sides of a huge gully without a bridge. But we have—again."

She stood up next to him and touched his cheek with her hand. "That day we met at the picnic table if we had known how we would end up, we wouldn't have gone on." He looked up at her. She sighed deeply, "But we did, Walter—and now we've hit a dead end. You can't betray who you are to have me; I won't violate who I am to keep you." She slowly shook her head back and forth. "We're so in love, but we're different, Walter—in ways that matter. I couldn't ever change myself enough to become what you need me to be to fit into your life—and if I don't and I'm with you, I might hurt you. I won't risk that."

He felt the meaning in her words; he couldn't think of anything to say.

She wiped the tears from her eyes with her sleeve. She looked at her watch and spoke in a shaky voice, "I have to go." She took the tissue paper out of her knapsack and began wrapping the wine glasses in it. "We need to pack up and start walking back to our cars. I don't want to be late for supper."

He didn't move. "So you think there's no way over the so-called gully?"

"Not if it means I have to become a believer."

"Maybe we should take a breather for a while to give ourselves a chance to sort things out? Maybe we can still find a way to make it work?"

She looked at him in disbelief. She smiled and shrugged her shoulders in a gesture of futility. "You just won't give up, will you, Walter?"

"No," he said softly. "No, not yet."

"Okay, I'm willing to give it a little more time. I'm not going anywhere—at least not right away, but you need to know that I don't think more time will help. What is is. We've gone back and forth over this issue again and again for months and gotten nowhere. The evidence seems pretty clear to me. I think we've found our limit. We always come up against the same impasse. I can't believe; you can't not believe."

She finished packing the knapsack. She put her arms through the straps. "You carried it in," she said, "I'll carry it out." She started down the path leading back to their cars. He followed her.

They said very little as they walked out to the paved road. When they reached their cars, she unlocked hers and placed the knapsack on the back seat next to her suitcase. She stood and faced him.

They both felt awkward. Finally he said, "I knew the day would not end well when you didn't wear your crew sweater."

She laughed a little and looked at him. She stood on her tiptoes and kissed him on the cheek. She stepped back and looked at him lovingly. "We're stuck, Walter, and there's nothing we can do about it."

He held the door as she got into her car. "But I love you, Mary." He closed the car door. It took all the will power she could muster to turn the key in the ignition. After she backed her car on to the pavement and turned it to face the west, she leaned over, smiled though her tears and waved. He waved back. Tears rolled down his cheeks. He watched her drive up the road over the top of a distant hill and out of sight.

"Oh, God," he cried out, "I couldn't do it! Why can't I convince her? Why aren't you helping me? Is there something I'm not getting? Tell me!"

The wind blew softly into his tear-stained face, then stopped. He stood for a while and listened. There was no sound in the silence. Then the wind began to blow and he heard pouring rain coming across the trees. When it began to fall on the road he quickly got into his car.

As he backed the car into the turnaround and started toward the road, lightning struck the rocks where he had been standing.

$$14$$

ON THE SURFACE WALTER'S life as a minister seemed much the same as it had been before Mary drove away. His efforts as a volunteer pitching-coach at the high school bore fruit: the boys' baseball team won most of their games. After calling ahead to make sure that Eddie and Jean would be home he made a pastoral call at Molly Hutchins's house late one Friday afternoon. In a few minutes Molly excused herself and went outside to work in her garden while he talked with Eddie and Jean about their dad. It was a difficult conversation—especially at the beginning; neither they nor he quite knew what to say. Then suddenly Jean began to sob and Eddie blurted out that he was so angry with God for taking his father that he would never be able to forgive him.

Walter mostly listened for the next forty-five minutes. When he spoke he tried to speak directly and honestly to their hurt and anger. He knew Eddie wanted to cry but he didn't know how to help him do it. He felt clumsy during most of the conversation. He was surprised that Eddie and Jean hugged him and thanked him for listening when he stood up to leave. As he drove away he was disappointed in himself; he doubted that he had really been helpful to them.

The VFW invited him to offer a prayer on Memorial Day at the ceremony honoring local veterans. The keynote address was offered by a past state commander. Walter looked at the faces of those gathered as the speaker recalled battles from World Wars I and II and Korea by name. He could see that, for many of the veterans, life had never been the same after Argonne or Normandy or Okinawa or Inchon. After the address the local drill team fired a salute. Walter stood at attention while a bugler played taps. The notes echoed across the hills—and for a few moments he was again back at Bill's funeral.

He saw Mary at a distance several times, but never close enough to talk with. He thought several times about calling her, but he never did. He was afraid he wouldn't know what to say to her if she answered. Besides, he rationalized, she was the one who broke off the relationship; any movement to restore it was hers to make. He was encouraged when she came to a couple of baseball games, but during the games he was too occupied with coaching to seek her out. He looked for her when the games were over, but she always left right away. She drove out of the parking lot at Jim's Market as he drove in one day. She waved and smiled as she passed him. When he looked in his rearview mirror he thought she was pausing at the exit. He parked quickly and jumped out of his car, but she continued driving away.

He hoped she might come to a church service some Sunday, but after three Sundays of not seeing her he gave up hoping. He had a cynical moment when he walked back to the manse after the communion service the first Sunday in June: he concluded that he, not God, attracted her to the few services she attended at his church in the past. As the days passed he resigned himself to their situation. But resignation didn't cure his longing; neither prayer nor will power made the longing go away. He was busy—and hurting most of the time.

The high school baccalaureate service was held each year in a local church on the second Sunday evening in June. This year it was the Methodists' turn to host it. Walter sat on the platform and did his part as one of the local clergy by reading a Scripture lesson. After the service he moved among groups of graduates and their families standing in the sanctuary and the vestibule, shaking hands and congratulating them. He glimpsed Mary several times in the crowd, talking with students and their parents. Once he thought she caught his eye and smiled at him, but he wasn't certain, and they never were close enough to talk. He looked for her when people began to leave, but she was gone. As he walked home he thought not only about how she had acted this evening, but also about how she had acted ever since the day she drove away after their hike. The conclusion seemed inescapable: she was avoiding him intentionally.

When he arrived at the manse he took off his suit jacket and necktie and hung them on one of the hooks next to the kitchen door. He looked in the refrigerator. He was usually very hungry after a service, but not tonight. He was too tired. He took out a piece of left-over chocolate cake and reheated the coffee left over from the morning. After he finished the cake and coffee he thought about watching Bonanza, but decided not to. He shut off the lights in the downstairs and went up to bed.

As tired as he was he didn't fall asleep. He couldn't stop thinking about Mary. She seemed so determined to avoid him. He knew they had come to an impasse the day of the hike, but why was she avoiding him? He thought about the last words she said before she drove away, "You love me, but you will protect what you believe no matter what the cost . . . and there's nothing we can do about it." The words reverberated. "You will protect what you believe . . . There's nothing we can do about it."

Suddenly he sat up and spoke to the dark. "There is something *she* can do—and she's doing it! I know why she's staying away. She's protecting me! She's staying away because she thinks she has to—because she knows the effect she would have on my side of the gully. It's like Erik says: disbelievers like her have to stay on the other side of the gully, away from the church. They somehow sense we can't deal with them over here. I think she's staying away because she cares! About me. About my church." He lay back down. It all made sense. Erik's perception of her was accurate: she was too formidable for the people in the church to deal with. Churches couldn't deal with disbelievers like her.

Yes, it all made sense. Yet, it didn't seem right. Needing to keep disbelievers like her away from the church seemed like a cop-out. The thought unsettled him. He wondered: would he be copping out if he stayed away from her? He wasn't sure what he should do. He couldn't decide. How could he know what to do? "Who is she, God?" he wondered out loud. "An angel I have to wrestle? Or a siren that will draw me on to the rocks? I have to find out." He shut his eyes and watched a swallow circling the church steeple. Thoughts of Mary and God and swallows whirled around inside his head. Finally he fell asleep.

He felt it was important for him to attend the high school graduation ceremony; several members of the graduating class were from church families. The day was clear and sunny—warm, but not humid like the previous Sunday evening at the baccalaureate service. He decided to walk to the school. When he arrived at nine-thirty the graduates' families were scattered throughout the parking lot and along the walkway that led to the auditorium. Everyone was waiting until the last minute to go inside. The large auditorium in the new school building had ample seats for the graduates, their families and guests, but it was not air-conditioned. Fortunately, it had a high ceiling. Even with the favorable weather, by the time the two-hour ceremony was over everyone would be grateful for the high ceiling; with so many people in attendance the air inside the auditorium would be very close.

He congratulated the graduates and their families as he walked among them. He looked for Mary, but didn't see her until the ceremony began and he stood up with all those gathered to honor the graduates and faculty as they marched into the auditorium. For an instant he didn't recognize her. The familiar ponytail was gone; she had cut her hair. Her hair hung just to the collar of her black academic gown. He followed her with his eyes as she made her way in the procession through the auditorium and onto the stage. She smiled when she passed by him. Her lovely face and eyes still looked the same. But the haircut changed her: she looked more like a woman than a girl.

After the ceremony he made his way through the crowded auditorium, congratulating graduates and their parents. He lingered outside, hoping he might see her, perhaps even walk with her to her house. But even after most people had left she still didn't appear. He looked up at her house when he walked down School Street, but there was no sign of her. He decided she must have gone somewhere besides home. He turned the corner onto Church Street and walked back to the manse. He went upstairs to his bedroom and changed into slacks and a sport shirt. He came back downstairs and ate some cheese and crackers and drank a glass of leftover iced tea. He didn't want to spoil his appetite; the food was certain to be plentiful and delicious at the barbecue Erik and Becky were hosting to celebrate Eri's graduation.

It was just after two-thirty when he turned into the drive at the Petersons' farm. The invitation said two, but he decided to wait an extra half-hour to arrive because he didn't want to appear gauche. When he saw the large number of cars already parked along the drive he realized he had no cause for concern. After he parked his car he walked across the yard and joined those gathered at a table full of hors d'oeuvres and drinks. As soon as she saw him Becky Peterson came from behind the table, greeted him with a hug and handed him a Coke. He joined a group of men talking about the Yankees-Detroit game. Everyone hoped the Yankees would do better than they had the day before when they lost four to two. It was the usual after-the-game post-mortem, based on information they had all gleaned from the sports pages in the morning paper. None of them had actually listened to the game.

But his heart was not in the conversation about the Yankees; he kept glancing away, looking for Mary. Finally he saw her at the buffet table filling her plate and talking with a group of students. He wanted to walk over and join her in line, but he thought it would be rude to walk away abruptly from a group talking about his favorite team. The group finally broke up and he was able to move to the buffet table. Mary was gone when he arrived. He filled his plate and looked around for her. He saw her sitting at the picnic table under the apple tree next to the garden by the pasture fence. She was alone. His heart was pounding as he walked over to the table and stood opposite her. She looked up and smiled. He returned the smile. "Hello, *Ms.* Kerrigan, I'm Walter Macdonald, may I sit down?"

Her smile broadened. "I would be delighted to have you join me, *Reverend* Macdonald."

He returned the smile and sat down opposite her. For a moment he didn't know what to say. Finally he said, "You cut your hair."

"Do you like it?" she asked.

"I do. I like it a lot. It makes you look . . ."

"Older?" She looked concerned.

"No, that's not the word I was going to use. I was going to say 'more serious.' I like the way it turns at the ends. It's smart, even sassy." She was smiling now. "But it definitely says, 'Take me seriously!'"

"Well, after what that boy tried when he danced with me at the prom, I decided it was time I looked more serious."

He laughed. "Your hair may have changed, but you haven't." She smiled. He sat for a moment and watched her eat. "My God, I've missed you, Mary." The sentence burst from him.

She put her fork down on to her plate and sighed. "I've missed you, too, Walter—a lot."

"Do we have to live this way—apart and hurting because we don't think we can be together?"

"Have you thought of a way I can be in your life?"

Her directness threw him. "No," he finally admitted. She looked away and continued to eat. After a pause he said, "Mary, look at me." She did. "Are you staying away from me because you want to or because you think being with me will jeopardize my ministry—because that's what I think?"

She stopped eating and gave him a very sober look. "The day I drove away, Walter, I left because I realized that if I stay in your life I will probably wreck your ministry. I still love you and I believe that you still love me, but I know that you won't do anything that might jeopardize your ministry. So, if I can't figure out how I can be in your life without wrecking your ministry, then because I love you I have to stay out of your life."

He shook his head back and forth and sighed. "I was afraid of that. The other night when I thought again about that Saturday before Mother's Day I realized you went away because you thought continuing our relationship would be too costly to me—because you thought I would have to abdicate my ministry, perhaps even my believing, for us to go on together."

She responded in a quiet voice. "I thought I needed to leave." She paused and looked away like she was pondering what to say. She looked directly at him when she spoke. "I took care of you like people do with ministers; I'm sure you know that they do. They're careful not to swear and they don't talk about sex when there's a minister around." The sentences were barely out of her mouth when she regretted them. She stopped talking. When she continued her voice had a softer, almost apologetic tone. "That seems arrogant to me now—at least presumptive—to think that I need to take care of you. I acted as though you can't take care of yourself. That wasn't right." She looked away.

He didn't say anything for a moment. His voice was strong when he responded. "Mary, look at me." She did. "If I can keep my believing only because you take care of me—because anyone takes care of me—I will always feel weak. I don't want to feel weak." He reached out his upturned, open hand to her across the table. Slowly she laid her hand in his. He grasped it tightly. "Mary, I love you. If we have to go our separate ways because we can't find a way to be together, I want to stand up and look straight at you when we make the decision. If we go down, I want us to go down trying. I want to try one more time to see if we can find a way we can be together. To be honest, I don't know how we will do it. Sometimes I despair when I think about all that is against us, but I want us to try one more time—and I don't want you to restrain yourself. I'm not weak; I can take care of myself"—he grinned slightly—"even in a head-to-head with a smart disbeliever like you." He realized she was looking at him carefully; he was determined to look confident.

She smiled and spoke gently. "Oh, Walter," she said, "you can be such a persistent fool! I do know that you are not weak. But if you tell me not to restrain myself, whether believing or disbelieving will prevail might not be the greatest concern. If we are together and I let myself go and you let yourself go, you might not want to turn back. You might cross over to the other side of the gully with me and never want to come back."

"I'll take that risk." He sat back and smiled. "Luther once said, 'Sin lustily that you may be lustily forgiven.'"

"But you're a Calvinist!"

"I have my Lutheran moments. When can we get together?"

"I think there's even a bit of the devil in you!" Her smile broadened.

"There's a bit of the devil in all of us," he said. "When can we get together?"

"How about tomorrow?"

"Tomorrow is Sunday."

"I know. I'm going up to my family's camp on Lake George this evening. No one is there this weekend. You could drive up in the afternoon tomorrow. We would have most of the afternoon and evening together. Can you do that?"

"I can," he said. "Once the morning service is over I'm free. I'll need directions."

"It's not hard to find. You already know how to get to Erik's camp." He nodded. "It's easy from there. I can write directions and draw a map on my napkin. Do you have a pen?"

"I do." He took a pen from his shirt pocket and handed it to her.

She wrote directions and drew a map on her napkin. She walked him through the directions: "If you actually get into Cleverdale, you have missed the Shore Road. Just turn around and look for the Shore road on your right. Then you will be taking the Shore Road south instead of north and my driveway will show up on your right about half a mile south of the village. There's a signpost that says 'Kerrigan' on it near the fence gate that opens to the drive. The address is 55 Shore Road. If all else fails, find a pay telephone and call me at this number. I'll look for you around two-thirty. Bring your bathing suit. It's supposed to be a very hot day."

"I'll be there." he said.

She stood up. "I have to go. I have to put in an appearance at two more graduation parties this afternoon."

"I understand." He stood up and looked at her. "I am really looking forward to tomorrow."

She nodded. "So am I."

He looked around at the groups of people scattered about the yard. "Did you notice that no one bothered us the entire time we sat here and talked? That's surprising, isn't it?"

"Not really," she said. "When we're together we give off vibrations that frighten everyone away, but they still watch us—especially when we hold hands." She grinned. "Preach well in the morning; I will be thinking of you."

15

HE DID PREACH WELL the next morning. At the coffee hour after the service worshipers went out of the way to tell him how pleased they were with his sermon. They called it inspiring and said they enjoyed the humorous anecdotes he used to illustrate his points. When they thought he couldn't overhear them they told each other that he seemed to have gotten past whatever was pulling him down. He was obviously much happier than he had seemed during the past few weeks.

He was polite and tried to be interested in his conversations with church members at the coffee hour, but inside he was impatient for it to be over. When he arrived back at the manse he ran up the stairs to his bedroom and changed his clothes. It was so hot he was tempted to wear shorts. But he didn't. He never wore shorts except when he was somewhere where he was sure no one would see him. With his long legs he thought he looked ridiculous in shorts. He came back downstairs, made himself a sandwich, poured a glass of milk, and ate quickly. He took a bottle of wine out of the cupboard, placed it in a paper bag and took a thin jacket off one of the hooks next to the door—in case it turned cold, which didn't seem likely, but he wanted to be prepared just in case. He turned the knob so the door would lock when he went out.

As he walked down the steps he thought about leaving a note on the door explaining where he was and a phone number where he could be reached, but he decided not to. The idea of leaving a note revealing where he was going made him uncomfortable. "Besides," he told himself as he walked toward his car, "I'll be back in the late evening." He opened the door of the VW and placed the jacket and the bag with the wine in it on the back seat. He was about to get in when he remembered that he didn't have his bathing suit. As he walked back to the house and unlocked the door the fact that he might have gone off without his bathing suit struck him first as funny and then as erotic. He fantasized skinny dipping with Mary Kerrigan as he ran up the back stairs. "Maybe I should just leave it home? Maybe I won't be able to find it?" But he did, in the bottom drawer of his dresser.

The drive up Route 40 seemed overly long; the road was crowded with slow drivers. It took him at least ten minutes longer to reach the turn-off to Erik's camp than it had the Saturday before Mother's Day. He had the Yankees-Detroit game to listen to on his car radio for part of the journey, but today was one of those few days in his life when a Yankees game failed to engage him—in spite of the fact that they had lost to Detroit both Friday and Saturday. The turn onto Route 9L, Ridge Road, was easy to spot; so was the turn onto Cleverdale Road. He almost drove past the turn onto the Shore Road, but he saw it in time. In less than a quarter of a mile he saw the driveway, the fence, and the signpost with "Kerrigan" on it next to the gate. It was twenty minutes to three.

When he drove through the gate and saw the house he was startled by what she had called a "camp." His family had a camp; this camp looked more like an estate than a camp. He should have taken a clue from the stone wall that ran all along the side of the property next to the road. The wall appeared to be at least two hundred feet long. The entrance gate located toward the north end of the wall was framed by sloping ironwork on either side. Hedges ran down both side of the property. The gardens next to the hedges were gorgeous. The two-story natural wood-sided house was well set back from the road; he guessed the house was fifty feet wide.

He parked his car in the turnaround at the end of the driveway; the Volkswagen seemed paltry next to the four-bay garage. When he stepped out of the car he saw Mary in shorts and a tank top, running barefoot across the lawn. She jumped up, wrapped her arms and legs around him, and kissed him. Open-mouthed, for a long time.

"I have never had a warmer welcome!" he said when she finally let go.

"I should hope not!" she said. "I'm so happy you're here. I've been waiting for you to get here ever since I got up this morning."

"Let me get the wine I brought and my bathing suit and you can show me this magnificent house."

"I'm glad you brought your bathing suit; it's hot."

"I almost forgot it," he said. "I had to go back into the house to get it."

"That wouldn't have been a problem. It's Sunday and the neighbors will all leave in the late afternoon. So we could still go swimming."

"You are wicked!"

"I know; you've told me that before."

As they walked toward the house he said, "The gardens are gorgeous."

"I'll tell my mother you said so. They're hers. They were originally my grandmother's, but now they're my mother's. She tends them all summer. We have spent our summers here ever since I can remember. That's an advantage that college professors have: they are free in the summer, ostensibly to think and write and prepare for the coming year. My parents do study and write some of the time; they each have a study in what used to be a live-in cook and handyman's apartment over the garage. But they don't work all the time. My mother gardens and my dad golfs and plays tennis. Even at sixty-two he's still a formidable opponent. I rarely beat him."

She walked up the steps and through the back door into the kitchen. "Welcome to the house that grandpa built," she said. He set the bottle of wine on a kitchen counter and his bathing suit on one of the benches in the breakfast nook. She led him through a swinging door into the dining room. To his left on the inside wall he saw a long oak buffet. A large, rectangular, expandable oak table stood in the center of the room. Six matching chairs sat at the table and four more sat along the walls of the room.

She led him through an archway into the middle of the living room. He turned from side to side and surveyed the room. It stretched across the entire front of the house. There were large opened windows at both ends and across the front that faced the lake. A round oak table covered with a half-worked jigsaw puzzle sat to his right toward the outside corner of the room; at the other end of the room an open staircase led to the second floor. A large stone fireplace dominated the inside wall. Two matching sofas sat in the center of the room—one on each side of a long coffee table in front of the fireplace. Tables and comfortable overstuffed chairs were scattered throughout the room.

On the outside wall directly across from the fireplace a double door led to a screened porch that also stretched across the front of the house. The floor to ceiling screens on the west side faced the lake. A door in the center opened onto an expansive lawn that sloped down to the water. The porch was furnished with wicker furniture, except for a large picnic table at the south end. She watched him take it all in.

"Want to see upstairs?" she asked.

"I do! Your house is magnificent."

"Thank you." She smiled and led him back into the living room and up the stairs to the second floor. A long hallway ran two-thirds of the width of the house. They walked down the hall, through the door at the end of the hall, and into a huge bedroom that ran from the front to the back of the house. The room had large turn-out windows that faced out to the lake, the north side and the back of the house. "This was originally my grandparents' room. My grandfather had it built this way so grandma could see both the lake and her gardens from their bedroom. It's on the north side so it's away from the sun, which was important because they didn't have air conditioning in 1920 when the house was built. Now that both my grandparents are gone this room belongs to my parents. You won't get to meet them tonight because they are in New York City for a long weekend attending my mom's fortieth high school reunion." She watched to see how he reacted to what she said; she couldn't tell.

"Actually, my grandmother moved to the downstairs bedroom off the living room after grandpa died. He died of a heart attack, the same kind Bob Hutchins had. Of course grandpa was sixty-eight, but it was still devastating; I had just finished my freshman year at Barnard." She looked at the bed and then at Walter. "He was the love of her life. She couldn't bear to sleep in their old room without him. She never did." She stood and looked melancholy. He put his hand on her shoulder. She looked up at him and smiled.

She led him out of the room and back down the hall and through a door that led to the other front bedroom. "And this is where I sleep," she said as they walked into the room. This room matched the front half of the room on the other end of the house; it had the same large open windows across the front and down the side. The furniture was similar except for a very Victorian red fainting couch. "Don't you love the couch?" she asked. "I bought it at an auction last summer." He smiled weakly and nodded. She shook her head. "I can see you're not into Victorian fainting couches."

They walked back out into the hall. She paused in the center of the hall. "There are two guest bedrooms on the back of the house and a large bathroom." She pointed to a more modestly furnished corner bedroom on the southeast corner of the house. "When I was a kid this room was mine, and"—she gestured toward front room they had just left—"this room was my parents. But after both grandparents were gone my parents moved over and I moved forward. It's nice to have your own walk-in closet."

She opened another door on the side toward the back of the house. "And here are back stairs you can use to sneak down into the kitchen for late-night snacks and trysts. Want to see the grounds?"

"I do!" he said enthusiastically.

"Well, I can tell you're more interested in grounds than furniture and walk-in closets. Since you're a man we'll skip the flower gardens." She took him down the front stairs into the living room, through the door onto the porch, out the front screen door, and down a set of stone steps onto the lawn. They walked across the lawn and on to the dock. He could see a float about thirty feet from the end of the dock. They walked out farther stood at the end. It was hot, but a breeze off the lake helped to make the heat tolerable.

He looked down. "The water's deep."

"Yes, but you swim, right?"

"Oh, yes, I grew up summers living in the lake at my family's camp on the Sacandaga Reservoir." He looked down again into the water. "There are no rocks; there are always rocks in Adirondack lakes."

"Grandpa had them removed when he built the house. A bunch of them are piled over there."

He looked up the shoreline to the north where the rocks were piled on the far side of a small building with a large door that opened onto the water. "You have a boathouse."

"Yes, and a boat. Want to see it?"

"I do." He sounded eager. She looked at him and smiled as they walked to the boathouse. She led him in through a side door. "That's it," she said as they stood on the ledge next to a sleek wooden speedboat with chrome trim and red upholstery. "Grandpa loved this boat. It's a 1940 twenty-five-foot Chris Craft Sportsman—a classic mahogany 'woodie.' It has a 327 engine. It really goes! I learned to water ski behind it. Grandpa loved to take me; he would tow me for hours. I'm really good. Do you water ski?"

"I do. We have a boat with a big Evenrude outboard on it at my family's camp. But it would be no match for this one."

"I love to go fast!" She looked at him and grinned. "You want to go fast with me? In the boat, I mean."

He pursed his lips and looked at her. "I knew what you meant."

"I have one more place to show you before we go out in the boat." She led him along the ledge to the back of the boathouse and up a ladder that led to a loft. When he reached the top of the ladder he saw a sparsely furnished room. There was a double-bed mattress on the floor. It was covered with a zipped-open sleeping bag and two pillows. A folded blanket and a pile of folded towels sat on the floor next to the wall. Next to the mattress there was a small table with a kerosene lantern on it. Several paperback books were piled on the floor next to a well-worn, hardcover a copy of *The Great Gatsby.* A large screened window at the front of the loft opened onto the lake; another at the opposite end faced the lawn.

"This is my lair," she said. "When I was in high school and college I used to sneak up here at night and read. Sometimes I would turn off the lamp and pretend I could see a green light across the lake. I would take off all my clothes and lie on top of the sleeping bag and imagine what it would be like to bring a man up here."

"Did you ever do it?"

"Not yet, but someday I'll get lucky." She gave him the Mary Kerrigan look. "Let's change and take the boat out. It's full of gas and ready to go." They climbed down the ladder and walked along the ledge. "Just a minute," she said. She climbed into the stern of the boat and turned the lock on the overhead door. She grasped the handle and pulled. The spring-loaded door clattered up. She walked to the middle of the boat and lifted a cushion and opened the cover over the engine. She climbed back up onto the ledge. "Grandpa always let the boat and boathouse air out before he started the engine—in case there might be some collected gas fumes. He'd read about some poor guy who started his engine without airing out his boat and boathouse and blew the boat and himself to kingdom come. I don't know whether his theory is accurate, but I do it every time—just in case. And I never light my lantern upstairs unless the door to the boathouse is open."

Walter grinned. "Sounds like believing to me; I thought you didn't do that."

"So!" she said, nodding and returning the grin. "You're not going to restrain yourself either today, are you?"

"No, I'm not. As they say, 'what's good for the goose is good for the gander.'"

"Come on, gander, let's change and see how fast the boat will go."

They walked back to the house. She pointed to a door to the right of the fireplace. "That's the downstairs bedroom; you can change in there. I'll go upstairs and change into my bathing suit and be back down in a minute."

He walked to the kitchen, picked up his bathing suit from the bench in the breakfast nook, went into the bedroom, and changed. He decided to leave his tee shirt on; he hadn't been out in the sun very much and he didn't want to risk getting a bad sunburn. When he opened the bedroom door she was standing there. He was startled. She was wearing a black, strapless bathing suit. She had the familiar white oxford-cloth man's shirt on over it. But the shirt was unbuttoned and he could see the full outline of the bathing suit—and her—underneath.

She smiled. "Do you like it?"

"You look beautiful—I mean the bathing suit looks beautiful." He paused. "That was awkward, wasn't it?"

"I get your drift. Let's go boating." She took his hand and led him to the boathouse. They untied the boat. She started the engine and backed the boat out. She turned toward the open water; once they were clear of the shore she opened the throttle. She was right; the boat really did go. For the next hour they sped around the lake. She took him north, around the point and down into another bay, and showed him the marina. They went back up that bay and out into the middle of the lake. His eyes kept coming back to her as they flew across the top of the water. She took her shirt off and handed it to him. He looked at her arms and shoulders. He watched the wind blow her hair. He had never been close to anyone so free and happy. He envied her. He wondered if he could ever be that carefree. It was a freedom he had never known. Maybe it was a freedom he never could know? Maybe it was a freedom he never should know? Did he have the right to be that carefree? Did anyone have the right to be that carefree?

After a while she switched seats with him and let him take the wheel. Out of the corner of his eye he saw her lie back across the cushion and look at him. He wondered what she was feeling. Did she want him as much as he wanted her?

It was nearly five o'clock when they slowed and came past the point above Cleveridge and into the bay, and a quarter past when she eased the boat back into the boathouse. After they secured the lines she said, "I'll leave the door open; we may want to go back out later. Right now I'm hot; let's go for a quick swim before we cook supper." She reached into her shirt pocket, took out a small strap, and threw her shirt on to the lawn. She put the strap around her neck and buttoned one end into the top of her bathing suit on one side and the other end into the top of her bathing suit on the other side. She saw him watching her. "I need the strap so the top of my bathing suit won't come down when I swim. You wouldn't want that to happen, would you?" He smiled, but didn't say anything. She cocked her head and grinned at him. "Race you to the float!"

She ran across the lawn, down the dock and dove into the water. By the time he had his tee shirt off and dove in after her she was already halfway to the float. When she arrived at the float she turned and watched him swim toward her. It struck her that he swam like he preached: one determined stroke after another. "The water's cold, but it feels good, doesn't it?" she said when he was next to her.

"It does feel good. It always takes until the Fourth-of-July for the reservoir to warm, so I'm used to swimming in cold water in June. But, as good as the water feels, I'm really hungry. It must be quarter to six."

"I figured you would be hungry. I bought two big T-bone steaks and four ears of trucked-in corn at Jim's last night, and two bottles of good red wine at the Schuylerkill liquor store—in case you didn't have any to bring. It seems ridiculous that you still can't buy wine in New York State on Sundays; we have such archaic blue laws. Let's swim for a few minutes. Then you can fire up the charcoal while I make a salad. Is steak and corn and salad enough to eat?"

"It will be plenty," he said.

"And I did make a surprise dessert."

"What is it?"

"A surprise!" She splashed water in his face and ducked under the water. She surfaced in front of the dock. He dove under and swam toward her, but she was gone when he surfaced. Somehow she had eluded him. It took several attempts before he caught her on the far side of the float toward the open water. They splashed water furiously at each other. He grabbed her and dunked her. When she was under water she pulled at the bottom of his bathing trunks. She nearly got them down before he wiggled free.

"Almost got you!" she said when she surfaced.

"But you didn't!"

"I will next time!"

He abandoned himself to laughter. He held on to the float with his left hand pulled her to him with his right arm, and kissed her. She wrapped her legs around him. When he let her go she looked at him impishly. "You said you were hungry," she said. "You feel hungry."

"I am!" He kissed her again.

"If you keep kissing me like that, we won't eat for two hours!" She laughed raucously, splashed water in his face, and swam to the dock.

In less than half an hour she had made a salad, he had uncorked a bottle of wine and started the charcoal, and they were sitting in chairs on the screened porch. She had on the familiar unbuttoned oxford-cloth shirt over her bathing suit. "I like the way you dress," he said. He leaned over and refilled her wine glass.

She smiled. "Why, thank you," she said and took a sip of wine.

"Okay," he said, "I can't hold back my curiosity any longer." He made a circular gesture toward the house and then toward the yard and the lake. "Where did all this come from?"

"From my grandfather; he built it in 1920. He and my great Uncle John founded the Adirondack Lumber Company in Glens Falls in the early 1900s. The business was a huge success. Grandpa bought the land just after World War I and built the camp a year later. Uncle John managed their timber holdings up north. Grandpa said my Uncle John was a marvel; he could walk through a tract of wood and know how much he could pay for it and turn a large profit when the trees were cut. They bought thousands of acres of timber; we still own most of it.

"When grandpa accepted the fact that my dad would always be more interested in literature than lumber, he made my Uncle Frank the president and general manager of the corporation. When grandpa died my cousin Jenny and I each got five percent of the company stock. That doesn't sound like much, but it turns out to be plenty. Adirondack Lumber has been good to all of us: we have always been able to have what we wanted—including this camp."

"When I saw you in your apartment in Schuylerkill Falls and driving your yellow Rambler station wagon I would never have guessed you are . . ." he paused, trying to find an appropriate word—

". . . an heiress." She finished the sentence.

"Yes," he said smiling, "an heiress. Do people in Schuylerkill Falls know about . . . your origins? Am I the only one who somehow doesn't know about your secret life?"

"No, you're not alone. Most people don't know. I don't talk about my 'origins'. Most people know me only as the English teacher who replaced Miss Simpson. Jerry Ward knows all about me because he and my dad grew up together in Glens Falls. They've always been best friends; they played varsity basketball together all through high school. He and Ellen still spend at least one long weekend here every summer. Erik knows because he knows everything about everybody in Schuylerkill Falls; he's the town doc.

Erik may be self-made, but he has too much class to say, 'Oh, by the way, Mary Kerrigan grew up rich so she'll never be content to live in a Presbyterian manse.'" He winced. She saw him wince. "I'm sorry," she said. "That was kind of crude, but it gets at the truth. I'm lucky. I've always been able to have and do whatever I wanted. I teach English not because I have to, but because I want to."

For a moment he said nothing. "Well, could you?" he asked when he spoke. "Could you be content to live in a Presbyterian manse?"

She sighed. "It would be difficult. If I married you, the money wouldn't go away. And you know how I am. My mouth wouldn't go away either. I could try to restrain it, but that wouldn't last long, so I would probably irritate many, maybe most, of your church members. And I am used to having what I want. I could still buy whatever I want to have. So, I know it's not fair, but I'm going to turn the question back at you. Now that you know where I come from, as well as how I am, could you stand me living in your manse?"

He looked straight at her. "I think I could deal with it. I'm not sure the church could."

"Ah, yes, the church. I always forget that I can't have you without getting the church. It makes me feel like a mistress in love with a man who can't get rid of his wife." She paused. "That was crude, too, wasn't it? But it's how I feel, and we said we wouldn't hold back today." She watched him.

He looked somber. "Yes, it was crude, but it is how you feel."

She sighed and stood up. "If we keep going in this conversation, we won't eat. The charcoal must be ready by now. I suggest we take a break. You cook the steaks and I'll put on a pot of water and cook the corn. Let's have fun talk while we eat and save any more talk about the intrusive church until after dessert."

He stood up and smiled. "Good plan! How do you like your steak?"

"Rare, with lots of red juice running out of it."

He smiled and nodded. "I should have known. Dry red wine, strong black coffee and bloody red meat."

By the time the water boiled and the corn cooked the steaks were done. After they had eaten salad, steaks and corn she brought out the surprise dessert: chocolate cake with chocolate frosting. "I love chocolate cake with chocolate frosting," he said.

"I know. I saw how much you like it the first time you came to my apartment for dinner." She cut the cake and placed a large piece on a plate and handed it to him.

He set the plate down and cut a large bite of cake with his fork. "It's delicious," he said. He watched her put a piece of cake into her mouth. "That seems like a long time ago, the first time I came to your apartment." He looked pensive. "We were pretty naïve then, weren't we? We had no idea what we were getting into."

She looked equally pensive. "But now we are into it and we aren't naïve." Neither of them said anything for a few moments. The sun was low on the far side of the lake. A bird sang in the distance. "That's a veery's call," she said. "You taught me about veeries the day we walked together to Erik's camp."

He smiled and nodded. Then he grew serious. "We've been having such fun today. I've worried all day that today will end up like the day we went to Erik's camp. I felt so free and happy when we hiked in and sat on the porch that day. But then everything fell apart." He folded his hands in front of him on the picnic table and leaned toward her. "I said yesterday when we sat at the picnic table at Erik and Becky's farm that I have no idea how we could ever reconcile my believing with your disbelieving, or how we could live together in a manse when you would be so uncomfortable as a minister's wife." He paused. "I still don't have any idea how we could." She didn't say anything.

"I should probably tell you that I had a long conversation with Erik the Saturday after you and I came to our impasse. It not only didn't help; I came out of it feeling less hopeful that you and I could have a future together. Erik thinks that, even if you could somehow fit into the role of a minister's wife, your disbelieving would undermine my ministry. He doesn't say it straight out, but I'm sure he thinks I have to choose between having you and being a minister. And he's very sure that God wants me to be a minister and he doesn't think you could ever fit into a minister's life."

"That's not surprising. Erik tries to straddle the gully that separates the church and rest of the world, but when it threatens to get too wide, he comes down on the church side. He always will."

He took in her words. "So do I," he said. He watched her carefully. She didn't flinch. He went on. "I've decided that you think the gully is already too wide to straddle. I think as far as you're concerned the gully is a huge chasm. And you've come down on the opposite side—not my side."

"That's true." She matched the serious tone in his voice. "I have. I don't see any alternative. That's the inescapable reality that became clear to me the day we hiked." She spoke carefully. "There are beautiful moments when we connect personally. But when it comes to believing we are worlds apart, and I wonder if the beautiful moments we have will ever enable us to bridge the chasm that separates us. At the end of the day we hiked I drove away and didn't look back because I realized that the chasm will only become wider and deeper as time goes on. It already seems impossible to bridge."

She could see how bleak he looked, but she still continued to speak. "Walter, let's face it. The world you experience is very different from the world I experience. The world you experience is filled with evidence of God's care; the world I experience is filled with evidence that argues against a caring God. Every day you expect to find more evidence of God's care, so you look for it; every day I don't expect to find more evidence of a caring God, so I don't look for any. We each find what we expect to find. We each believe in the realities we have constructed and there's no way to connect them. When you look at evidence I think is convincing, you discount it; when I hear you talk about what convinces you to believe, I think it's wishful thinking. You think of the evidence I see as only a challenge that someday will be overcome; I think of your believing as a wish dream that will never be more than an imagined reality."

She could see that he wanted to respond, but she didn't let him. "We each have our lapses: you question God's care when something happens like your brother being killed; I attend a moving worship service like I did Christmas Eve and am inspired and almost believe. But these are only lapses. You say a prayer and recover your believing; when the music stops I go back outside and recover my disbelieving. Each of us goes back to our real world. In a way it's like a self-fulfilling prophecy: we each accept the evidence that supports our perspective and reject evidence that could challenge it. And so it continues on and on. Different evidence that supports our different perspectives accumulates in our different memories and encourages us to hold fast to our different convictions." She sighed deeply. "Now I can't believe and you can't disbelieve. We're stuck on opposite sides of a Grand Chasm."

He stood up and walked over to the screen door. The sun was setting across the lake. He turned and looked at her. "Everything you cite as evidence describes only the mechanics of nature, nothing beyond. You assume that there is nothing beyond. But your evidence doesn't *prove* there is nothing beyond, only that you can't see that there is.

"There is so much more than you can see from the other side of the chasm. Deep in my bones I know that beyond what our minds can fathom there is something called God sustaining this universe. Giving up that belief would rob me of hope. I can't let it go. Even if I can't offer any evidence that will convince you to accept what I believe, I won't let it go. It's my assurance of things hoped for." He paused. She didn't respond. It was his turn to talk.

"I admit there are personal and cosmic flaws evident all around us. My believing doesn't deny or overlook the flaws. My faith sees them, but it also reaches beyond them. Christian faith is the conviction that there is a redemptive power at work both in the universe and in our personal lives; I believe that life for all of us does not end on Good Friday but on Easter."

He sat back down and reached across the table and took her hands in his and looked at her. Tears welled up in his eyes. "Mary, God weeps for Bob and Molly, and for Jenny and her retarded boy—and for your great-grandfather's Irish cousins who starved and the millions who died in the Holocaust. But that cosmic weeping is not the final word. The world we live in is not the end; the end is a culmination, a new creation where they and all of us are raised up into a new life. That's hope. I admit it's not empirically based, but it's not a myth. It may be in some ways a metaphor, but it's not a myth. It's not all smoke and mirrors; it comes from the certainty that conviction provides. I will always believe it even if I can't explain it. Faith is like that—mine and millions who stand with me. I don't keep my faith because it answers all the questions. I keep it so I can live with the questions."

She carefully withdrew her hands. She spoke quietly and firmly. "Walter, for me it is all a myth. And I have to keep it a myth. Whatever happens is the luck of the evolutionary draw. I was lucky; they weren't. I'm sorry they weren't. But I'm not sorry I was. I feel for them; I'm willing to do what I can to help them. But I don't feel guilty that I have what I have. I don't subscribe to that 'there-but-for-the-grace-of-God-go-I' crap. Do you really want a world run by a God who hands out grace to some and lets others suffer? I can be happy in a world that includes Bobs and Richies and starving Irish, and Jews sent to gas chambers because I *don't* believe. If I did believe there was an all-powerful God and he didn't fix things so there would be no Bobs and Richies and starving Irish and Jews sent to gas chambers, it would make everything worse. It would mean that the creation is run by some kind of callous and capricious Higher Power. That kind of believing *would* throw me into despair."

He could barely contain himself until she finished. He stood up quickly and spoke in an urgent voice. "But suppose there is an all-powerful God and for some reason we can't fathom, but that is for our good, he doesn't fix everything?" His words hung between them for a moment.

"That's a nice idea," she said gently, "but you have no evidence to support it. All the evidence points to nobody in charge. What each of us gets is the luck of the draw; there's no evidence to the contrary." She looked directly into his eyes. "The truth is, Walter, I don't need to believe—and I don't think I'll suffer some horrible consequence because I don't. Believers think everyone *needs* to believe in God. It's not true. I don't and I'm all right. I really am. I'm okay on my side of the chasm. And you aren't—and never would be."

He sighed and sat back down slowly. "This is futile; we're getting nowhere."

"No, we aren't."

"I had a prof in seminary who said you can't argue someone who doesn't want to believe into believing. He's right. You can't make someone believe what they don't want to believe—even if it's someone you love." He looked at the floor and then up at her. "I knew that was true for us months ago; I just couldn't accept it."

She got up and walked around to his side of the picnic table, lifted one leg over the bench, and, straddling, it sat down next to him. "Walter," she asked, "do you have to win this argument? Is there some colossal cosmic reason you have to win this argument? Is winning this argument the only way you can let yourself love me and be together with me? When it comes to believing why can't we just agree to have an ongoing conversation like the one depicted between Socrates and Jesus in the mural on the ceiling of that church in Maine?"

He didn't look up. She laid her hand on his arm and pleaded with him: "I don't love you as a believer, Walter; I love you as a human. Why can't you just love me as a human? Why do I have to believe in your God to have you? Why can't we just be two humans in love?"

She waited for an answer. He just kept staring at the floor. "Damn it, Walter, look at me!" she shouted. The outburst startled him. He turned his head and looked at her. "There's so much more human in you than you let out most of the time. I've seen more glimpses of the person you really are today than I have since the night we went dancing at the Gideon. You've been so relaxed. Is that because you're away from the church? Do you have to get away from the church and away from being a minister to be yourself?"

He didn't respond. He started to get up. She reached up and placed her hand firmly on his shoulder. "Don't go away!" she said. He settled back down on the seat. She took her hand off of his shoulder. "You told me yesterday that you wanted me to let go today, to hold nothing back. I'm going to do that. I'm going to tell you what I think about when I look at you and what I want with you. If you don't want me to do that, you better go now!"

He made no attempt to get up. He sat up straight and tried to look confident. "Okay," he said. "Give it to me—all of it. I'm ready."

His statement wasn't quite convincing. She spoke slowly. "Well, here it is, straight out." She took a deep breath. "I'm not sure that believing is good for you—at least not the way you do it. I feel like believing for you is some kind of relentless discipline that has taken over your life. It hardly ever lets you have fun like we did when we danced last winter and when we had the water fight a little while ago. I loved the way you laughed and splashed water at me when I tried to pull your bathing suit off. I never see you laugh like that when you're in Schuylerkill Falls, when you're being the minister. I sometimes see you smile, but I never see you let go and really laugh. I don't think your believing ever lets you be free. Your God seems like an ever-present, hovering parent with whom you have to check every feeling, every impulse, every inspiration to be sure it's okay to have it. The only moments you seem free to live—to really live—are those moments when you forget about your God." He looked frightened, but she didn't stop.

"Walter, when I see you act out what it's like to be a believer, I don't want any part of it. I don't want to be like that and I don't want you to be like that. It's not just that I couldn't tone myself down enough to live in a manse; I don't want to live the rest of my life with someone who thinks he has to throttle down his humanity to be a minister. If I could pray, I would ask God to help you strip off your ministerial veneer so you could be all the time the wonderful man I glimpse when we dance and when we have a water fight.

"I don't want you with your robe on, Walter." She was crying now. "Other people may want you that way, but I don't. I want you with your robe off—as just plain, beautiful, naked Walter." Tears ran down her cheeks. She leaned over on the table in front of him and looked directly at him. "I want to love you and be human with you, Walter. That's what I want." She stopped talking and wiped her eyes with the back of her hand. "There," she said. "You have it. Is what I want enough?"

Her outburst overwhelmed him; for a few minutes he couldn't find words to answer her. He struggled even to look at her. Finally, he managed to speak; he spoke slowly and carefully. "I can take off my robe and be naked with you, but my faith is not something I can take off. It's not imposed on me; it's inside of me. I still believe when I'm naked; I can't take it off." He stopped and looked into her eyes. "Can you love a naked believer?"

She stared at him for a while and then a gentle smile spread slowly across her face. "Walter, we'll never find the answers by talking. Let's go swimming!"

"It's dark!" he protested.

"I know," she said. "Dark is the best time." She stood up. "Come on! Beat you to the float!"

He laughed and grabbed her shirttail. "No, you won't!" She wiggled free of her shirt and bolted out the door. He stripped off his tee shirt and ran after her. She ran to the end of the dock and dove into the water and swam toward the float. He was right behind her. He caught up to her and grabbed her foot when she was halfway to the float. She turned and splashed water furiously into his face. He dunked her and swam to the float. She came in just behind him. "I won!" he said.

"Next time, I will," she said. She climbed up the ladder and lay down on the float. He climbed onto the float and stretched out next to her. They stared up at the stars; a warm breeze blew across them. "Thank God for the breeze or the mosquitoes would be all over us."

He turned and looked at her. "Thank God for you."

She smiled and turned over on to her stomach. She looked across the lake. "See that light across the bay?" She pointed. "It's right there, straight across from us."

He turned over and looked. "I see it."

"When I was in college I used to lie here on the float by myself at night and watch it. Sometimes there would be music and you could hear people laughing. And I would imagine it was a green light."

"Daisy's light?" he asked.

"So, you do know!" she said excitedly.

"I do, from reading the book a long time ago when I was in college. But the music and the party should be here—at Gatsby's, not at Daisy's."

"Smarty!" She stood up and jumped into the water folded up like a cannon ball. When she came to the surface she swam over to the dock. She looked up at him. "Let's have a party like Gatsby never had. Let's go skinny dipping!" She slipped off her bathing suit and placed it on the float next to him. He looked a little frightened. "Come on, chicken," she said. "I won't look at you while you take it off." She dove under the water.

He slipped off his bathing suit and jumped into the lake. When he came to the surface he listened carefully, but he couldn't tell where she had gone. Then he heard a voice behind him around the corner of the float. "Over here," she shouted, and when he turned, he got a face full of water. He lunged at her, but she ducked under the water. He ducked under the water, but it was dark and he couldn't see her. He surfaced and held on to the float, listening. He began to worry. Then he heard her. "Over here," she called to him, "by the rocks." He let go of the float and swam toward her.

When he reached her she was standing with her feet on the bottom of the lake; only her head was out of the water. He stood in front of her. She smiled at him. "Kiss me!" He did, and she wrapped her legs around him. Her entire body embraced him. He stopped thinking; she was all that mattered.

When their lips parted she tilted her head back and motioned with it toward the boathouse. "Let's go to my lair!" He looked concerned. "Don't worry, Walter. All the neighbors have left; we can run naked across the lawn and no one will see us. This is not your parish, anyway; here you can do whatever you want to." She took hold of his hand and led him through the water to the ladder on the side of the dock. He followed her up the ladder. When he stood up on the dock she stood in front of him and grinned. "Isn't this fun?"

He grinned back at her; it was a very wide grin. "Yes, you imp; it is fun. It's a lot of fun!"

"I think you'd like to have even more fun." She gave off a wicked laugh. "But you have to catch me first!"

She ran to the boathouse. He was right behind her. He followed her through the side door and up the ladder to the loft. It was so dark he could barely see. "Wait there," she said when he reached the top of the ladder. "I know where the matches are." In a few seconds he saw the match flash, and then the steady light of the kerosene lantern. She stood still and let him look at her. She smiled and picked up a towel and held it out to him. "Would you like to dry me?"

"I would love to dry you—all of you."

He walked over to her and took the towel. He carefully worked his way around her body, gently drying her. She picked up a towel and did the same for him. When they were dry, she lay down on the sleeping bag. She watched him look at her. "Well, you aren't going to just look, are you?"

He kneeled down carefully next to her. She reached up toward him with her arms. "Come on." She drew him to her. The feel of her consumed him. He had stopped thinking; he was only feeling and wanting. He raised his head and looked at her. She could see the hunger in his eyes. "Go on; but first you have to kiss me." He placed his mouth against hers and let her devour him. After a long moment he raised his mouth barely away from hers; she could feel his lips brush against hers when he spoke. "I love you, Mary Kerrigan."

"I know."

He kissed each side of her neck. She ran her hands up and down his back and through his hair. "Oh, my God, how I love you!" he whispered. "I have never wanted anyone or anything more in my life than I want you."

"Then do what you want, Walter! For God's sake, do it! Do it now!"

He did.

For a long time afterward they lay together with their arms around each other. Then he rolled over and alongside of her, facing her. He looked into her eyes. "You are unbelievably beautiful."

"Unbelievably?" She gave him an impish look.

He realized what he had said. "You are the most *believably* beautiful person I have ever seen." He looked at her longingly. "I don't ever want to go home."

"Don't. As the Scripture says, 'Take, therefore, no thought for the morrow.' Just lie here and hold me and we will go to sleep."

He had no idea what time it was when he woke up. She was asleep wrapped around him. At some point she had awakened and put out the lantern and covered them with a blanket. When he stirred, she turned over. He sat up carefully so that she stayed covered. The moon was in the west—moonlight coming through the open window shone on her face. A gentle breeze blew through the open window; he could hear waves breaking against the rocks below. He sat still and watched her sleep. She looked so beautiful and peaceful. He started to lie back down next to her.

Suddenly he thought about the screen door at the manse. Suppose there was a note tacked to it? Suppose someone needed him and no one knew how to find him? Probably no one did need him, but he couldn't be sure. There was no way he could stay here and be sure.

He looked again at Mary sleeping. Slowly he let himself down next to her and shut his eyes and tried to sleep. He basked in her warmth as the moments passed, but the image of the screen door still pulsed in his brain. It wouldn't go away.

He rose up slowly. Mary stirred. He stood still and listened to her breathing until it was relaxed again. He picked up a towel from the floor and walked softly to the back of the loft. The moonlight shone on Mary's face; he remembered what he said to her: "I have never wanted anyone or anything more in my life than I want you." A surge of desire came over him; he wanted desperately to wrap his body around hers and fall back to sleep, listening to the gentle waves breaking against the rocks—to "take . . . no thought for the morrow." But the image of the manse screen door with a note tacked to it asking for help and no one there to respond came at him like a sword stabbing his soul.

Slowly he grasped the handle of the trap door, raised it quietly, and climbed down the ladder. He let the door back down without making a sound. He wrapped himself in the towel, stepped out the door of the boat-house and made his way across the yard to the house. He dressed quickly. When he picked up his watch and put it on, it said twenty-five after two. He found a pad of memo paper on the kitchen counter. The heading on the page read "Don't forget!" He tore off a sheet, took the ball-point pen from his pocket and wrote a note. "Dearest Mary, I shall never forget this night. Thank you for everything. I'm sorry I have to go. I love you. Walter."

He stood and looked at what he had written: "I'm sorry I have to go." He thought of Mary asleep in the boathouse loft. "Oh, my dear Mary, I love you with every fiber of my being, but I have to leave." Anger welled up inside of him; he wanted to bring his fist down on the counter and scream, "Why, why do I have to leave? Why, God, why? Why do I think I have to choose between you and her? Why can't you leave me alone?"

But he didn't scream out; he listened—hoping to hear a message. There was no voice in the silence, only the sound of his own heavy breathing. "I know you won't leave me alone, God; there's no way you ever will leave me alone." He shook his head. "I can't go on like this; my heart is at war with my soul. I'm being ripped in two."

He looked out through the kitchen window. The yard light shown on his black VW perched like a paltry beetle in the turnaround next to the massive four-bay garage. He sighed and nodded his head. "This is not my world; it could never become my world. I could never belong here; I need to be where I do belong." He walked across the kitchen, let himself out the back door, and walked to his car. He got in, shut the door quietly, started the engine, turned the car around, and drove down the drive in darkness. He didn't turn on the headlights until he was at the end of the driveway.

His car headlights flashed briefly into Adele Simpson's bedroom window when he drove into the manse driveway. She raised herself up and looked at the window and then at the luminescent face of the clock on the table next to her bed. It read three-thirty. She wondered what urgent pastoral errand had kept her minister out past three in the morning. But she knew that she wouldn't ask; it would not be proper to inquire.

He shut off the car's engine and closed the door gently when he stepped out. He walked up the sidewalk and mounted the steps on to the porch. There was no note tacked to the screen door.

Just after eight o'clock Monday evening he was sitting in his study choosing hymns for the Sunday service and listening to the Yankees-Kansas City game when he saw her yellow Rambler station wagon drive into the manse driveway. He shut off the radio and walked out through the side kitchen door. He met her on the sidewalk at the bottom of the porch steps. She was carrying a brown bag. She handed it to him.

She grinned. "You forgot your bathing suit."

He reached out and took the bag. "Thanks for bringing it. You didn't have to rush. I'm not going swimming again anytime soon." He paused. He felt awkward. Finally he said, "Last night was beautiful." She smiled and nodded. "Would you like to come inside?"

She stood still. "I was disappointed when I woke up and you were gone."

"I didn't want to leave, but I realized that no one here knew where I was. I was afraid someone might need me, and not be able to reach me." He looked closely at her face; he couldn't read what she was feeling.

"I'm not coming back to Schuylerkill Falls in the fall. I met with Jerry Ward at the school this afternoon. I gave him back my contract for next year unsigned. I told him I'm not coming back. I'm going to New York City. I'm going to school; I've been accepted in a literature PhD program at Columbia. I want to teach at a college like my parents do."

He felt weak and dizzy; everything was spinning around him. He couldn't speak.

"Well?" she said, "Is that all you have to say? Nothing?"

"Ah . . . congratulations," he stammered. "I . . . I know you will do well in the program . . . you will be an excellent college professor."

"That's it? You would send me off with 'congratulations'? Last night you said you loved me. You said you never wanted anything or anyone in your life more than you want me. I believed you. You made passionate love to me. You were very convincing."

"I did say that. I do love you; I love you very much."

"Then come with me, Walter. You could go to Union Seminary. It's right across the street; they have a joint doctoral program with Columbia. You are bright and capable; I know you could get into it. You have so much to offer; if anybody can ever discover how to bridge that gully between the church and the rest of the world, you can. I have enough to keep both of us for as long as it takes—even for the rest of our lives." Her green eyes pled with him. "Just let go like you did last night. Come with me, my beautiful Walter; please come with me."

He stood and looked straight at her. She was far away—standing on the opposite side of a chasm a thousand feet deep. He could see her, but there was no bridge from him to her. He knew he could never leap across to her. If he tried, he might fly briefly, but then he would fall and perish on the rocks at the bottom of the abyss. His feet felt like lead; his heart pounded; he couldn't find his voice. Finally, he stammered, "My dearest Mary, my heart cries out inside of me; I want to be with you for the rest of my life, but I can't leave here to go with you. If I do, I will betray everything I believe in and everyone who believes in me."

He shook his head back and forth in denial of what he was saying. "I have to stay here; this is my world. Whatever I can do, I have to do it from here." He looked at the sky and then back at her. Tears ran down his face. "I love you and I want so much to go with you, Mary Kerrigan. But I can't; my world is here."

"I was afraid that's what you would say." She scrunched up her mouth and shook her head slightly. "I didn't win, did I?"

"No," he said quietly. "You didn't. But neither did I."

She walked slowly up onto the bottom step of the porch. He turned and faced her. She smiled bravely and then kissed him on the cheek. She stepped back and looked at him. "You're still beautiful." She shook her head back and forth. "What a shame, Walter. Such a loss, such a tragic loss."

He walked with her to her car. He held the door as she got in. In the open window he could see tears running down her face. She started the car and backed out into Church Street, turned toward School Street, and drove away. She didn't wave; neither did he. After her car disappeared past the front of the church he walked up the walkway to the porch and sat down on the bottom step and sobbed.

It was nearly dusk when his sobbing subsided; he raised his head and listened. He could hear the sound of a siren fading away in the distance. When he could no longer hear the siren he stood up and walked slowly down the walk and out the driveway to the street. The street was empty and quiet. He turned his head and looked up at the church steeple. A lone swallow circled around it once—and then she flew away.

Acknowledgements

I AM GRATEFUL TO many friends and colleagues who shared my journey and offered their support as I wrote this novel. A few deserve special mention. When the manuscript was in a very early form Stephanie Cotsirilos read and commented on several chapters; I took her pointed comments to heart (especially "too much John Wayne"). Pat Onion and Deb Chase reviewed and critiqued several versions of the manuscript. Their suggestions along the way helped me give clear shape to the characters. Jerry Cayer was my athletic coach as I formed Walter's character. I called upon Craig Lewis MD to serve as consulting physician when characters became ill. Nancy Lockwood served as copyeditor and saved me from multiple linguistic embarrassments. Matthew Wimer, my managing editor at Wipf and Stock shepherded the novel through its final journey from manuscript to book. Thanks, friends, for your gifts.

Most of all I am grateful to Sherry, the love of my life. She read and reread every section of every chapter. Her "you still haven't got it" pushed me again and again to rewrite. If I finally got it, she deserves the credit: every page of the novel is marked with her imprint. Thanks, my love.